THE Bitterroot Cabin

DONALD F. AVERILL

INK START MEDIA
265 Eastchester Dr Ste 133 #102
High Point NC 27262

Chapter 1

In January, a couple of weeks after Christmas, I came inside after cleaning snow from the sidewalk. It was Saturday afternoon about three o'clock. Elaine had a mug filled with hot chocolate and I was content with coffee. We were staring at each other across the dining room table.

Elaine broke the silence, "What?"

"I can't stand retirement. We should never have sold our business. I need a job. Our saving account is being depleted at an alarming rate."

"Yes. I was going to mention it. The bank statement was distressing."

We had a brief discussion but nothing came of it. The days flew by.

Elaine and I discussed taking a short road trip after her fifty-sixth birthday in February but the Butte, Montana weather was not cooperating. We decided to stay put until Spring. The vernal equinox came and went before the weather cleared. I was all in favor of getting out of Butte even if for only a day or two. I didn't want to succumb from inactivity. It boiled down to needing work. I was bored with my daily routine. At fifty-seven, I still had a few years before official retirement. Then social security might look appealing.

It was a Sunday, ten days into the new season when Elaine said, "Efren, we need to go to Suddenly to check out this small hardware business." She held up the Helena newspaper so I could see what she was referring to. "It looks like it's just what we're looking for."

After scanning the classified advertisement and agreeing with my wife, I commented, "Suddenly is only about an hour and a half away, let's make a day of it and investigate." The outside temperature was still chilly, so I grabbed a couple of blankets and pillows from the hall closet and put them in the back seat of the car. If the heater failed in the mountains, I wanted some protection from the cold. SUVs are great vehicles when everything worked properly, but I recalled a story about a family that froze to death when they ran out of gas and lacked proper clothing for cold weather. Elaine packed a sandwich lunch and a thermos of tea and enough extra food for a lite dinner if we were forced to start home late in the evening or had limited access to dining establishments.

As I slid my six foot frame into the driver's seat, I quickly surveyed the atmosphere. A few cotton-like clouds were scattered randomly across the blue sky. Far off to the west was a contrail over what experience told me was the Bitterroot Mountain range. I figured the condensation was from a military plane traveling directly south or a Canadian airliner at thirty thousand feet. There was a slight darkening of the sky near the northern horizon.

It was ten thirty when we pulled onto Route 15 headed south. We were out to enjoy a leisurely excursion to Suddenly, Montana, to investigate the little mountain town and the hardware store for sale advertised in the Helena newspaper. Both of us were enthusiastic about starting a new small business venture.

We stopped in Dillon for lunch after being on Route 15 for slightly over an hour. Elaine suggested we stop to stretch our legs and I suggested we take time to eat lunch at a park, just off the highway. There was an easy off/easy on sign as we drove south and slowed while going through the small town watching for the recreation site. Elaine laughed when she saw the population sign with the last digit written over. She snickered, "Someone had a baby, the six is changed to a seven."

Noting the sign, I remarked, "Dillon is about twice the size of Suddenly." Almost missing the turnoff to the park, Elaine called out just in time, "There it is. A couple of buildings and a grassy meadow surrounded by trees." As we approached, we saw some picnic tables, tennis and basketball courts and various parking areas. An asphalt parking spot next to one of the tables looked good and I stopped.

Two boys were playing with dogs chasing balls thrown into the grassy meadow but no one else was in the park. We enjoyed the solitude, the quiet only occasionally punctuated with barks or yells from the boys. There were subtle noises from not too distant highway traffic, resembling the sounds when camping next to a stream and hearing the movement of water. As we were finishing our picnic, the boys and dogs approached us. When they came within normal speaking distance, I asked, "Can you tell us how far we are from Suddenly?"

The slightly smaller boy replied in a soft voice, "It's only about thirty minutes from here, but the road snakes through the trees. Don't drive too fast, there are some tight curves."

"Thanks. It looks like you gave the dogs a good workout."

"Yeah, my brother and I got some exercise and had fun, too."

It abruptly struck me that I was talking to a girl, not a boy, an easy miscue from the short hair and athletic motions I observed when they threw a ball for the dogs to chase.

They continued walking and as they passed by, the young lady said, "If you see Danny Drum, tell him Lisa said hi."

I smiled and said, "Will do." We watched the siblings and their dogs disappear down a pathway into a small stand of fairly tall fir trees. Elaine tucked our refuse into a paper grocery bag, deposited it in a waste container and we climbed into the car.

We had been on the asphalt and gravel road to Suddenly for about twenty minutes when Elaine said, "Stop, Ef, I want to look at something."

I slowed and pulled over in a wide spot on the shoulder and stopped. "What is it? What did you see?"

"Please back up. No, you'd better turn the car around, it's a little ways back from here. When I first saw it, I didn't recognize it, but then I realized what it was."

"I don't understand, what did you see?"

"It's that house, the one in the picture on our dining room wall."

"I didn't notice anything. I must have been concentrating on the curvy road that needed maintenance. This is wild country and I don't want to hit any animals. If we hit a large one, like a horse, a cow, or even a deer, the car would be damaged. Then we'd have insurance details, repairs and a police report about striking an animal, maybe killing it."

Elaine grinned, "You didn't mention a moose."

"I'm not sure we're in moose country, dear, but maybe a bear or Sasquatch." Elaine shook her head and raised her eyebrows knowing Big Foot had never been reported in this area. "I'll turn around and drive back. How far do I need to go?" There was a spot wide enough to make a complete U-turn and we started back.

"I think about a quarter of a mile. We had just passed a dirt road on the right. Maybe it leads to the house."

"Okay. Should we follow the dirty brown road?" I thought for a second, picturing Dorthy following yellow bricks. I grinned at my clever query.

Elaine replied, "Why not? We're not on any time schedule. I'm thinking we might want to stay over in town for a day or so."

The last time we did something like this, Elaine got out her sketchbook and we spent two hours at the side of an old logging road. Fortunately, I had reading material while she drew with charcoal. I remember we were near a creek and we could hear water swirling and cascading over rocks. She later added acrylics and won first prize at the county fair in Butte. She is a bona fide artist and could have seriously pursued fine arts if she hadn't had to raise two children.

But she gladly agreed to set her career aside while I supported the family as a school administrator and hardware store owner. After our children reached their late teens, Elaine became the curator for the local art museum. She was able to display some of her paintings and was recognized in The Bitterroot Mountains Art World, a semi-annual magazine.

After turning the car around and retracing our path until I saw the dirt turnoff, I slowed, let a logging truck rumble by on the adjacent lane and turned quickly onto the bumpy path. About thirty yards in, we saw a crooked sign: S. M. Dugger. White paint was peeling from the nearly horizontal wooden board bridging two two-by-four posts. We continued down the rough weed infested path toward the house. I had not seen what Elaine observed, but her artist's eyes have always been better than mine.

Aside from the house and a rickety carport-like shed containing an old orange CASE tractor, there was a ramshackle windmill, an outhouse and a relatively new barn behind the living quarters. As we got closer, I noticed the tractor had a broken axle and was canted to one side. Plywood covered the front window and what appeared to be a one by six board was nailed across the front door displaying 'STAY OUT'. Obviously, the sign was painted by someone lacking artistic ability.

Elaine opened her door and got out to take a closer look at the old house. As I joined her, I looked for any neighbors, squinting to peer through openings between the surrounding trees but couldn't see any other buildings nearby. The place was isolated. I followed Elaine around the front west corner of the home. I knew she was trying to find a window to inspect the interior.

The circular window found was too high for us to peer into the residence but I discovered a wooden crate among a patch of weeds and deposited it next to the wall under the porthole. Elaine steadied herself by resting her left hand on my shoulder and stepped in the top of the crate. She glanced inside and exclaimed, "Oh!" She abruptly turned and dropped to the ground, her hand still on my shoulder. "Ef, there's someone in there, an old woman."

"I guess we should have knocked."

"But the place is all boarded up. How could we expect someone to be inside?"

"Were lights on inside?"

"Not electric ones, oil lamps, two of them."

"Maybe we should get back in the car and continue on to Suddenly."

We turned around and started to the car when we heard noises emanating from the back of the house. We had gone only a few steps when we heard a deep male voice, "What d'ya want? Why are ya lookin' inta my winda? Lookin' to steal somethin', are ya?"

"No, my wife and I thought the house looked like one in a picture in our dining room. We just stopped to take a better look. Sorry to have interrupted you. We mean no harm." That's when I noticed the old man was carrying a revolver at his side.

"Ef, we'd better go. This isn't the same house, it just looked like it from the glance I took from the road. My mistake."

The old man stood like a statue, but his eyes scanned us side to side, feet to head.

I inquired, "Are you Mr. Duggar? Do you and your wife live here?"

"Wife? Na, she died years ago. I'm Samuel Miles Duggar. I've lived here for thirty-five years. Mining is a tough life for a woman. But we had plenty of good times. Who are you people?"

"We're the Sandovals, Efren and Elaine. We're here from Butte to see about purchasing a hardware store. Do you know anything about the store?"

"That's Erickson's store. He was killed in a loggin' accident last year. Wife and son are sellin' and movin' to Butte. Only store like it in town. Used to go there lots."

"Well, we're sorry to have bothered you Mr. Duggar. We'll be on our way." I turned to follow Elaine to the car when another vehicle pulled in behind us, a police cruiser. When did Duggar call the cops?

The driver, a man about forty got out and reached back into the car. When he stood up, he had a large box the size of a pizza container but much thicker. He gave us a questioning look and said, "Just making a delivery—Meals on Wheels. Do you know Mr. Duggar?"

"No, we just met him. Are you the sheriff? He's carrying a pistol."

The officer glanced at Mr. Duggar. "That old gun hasn't been fired in at least twenty years. He doesn't have any ammunition for it; just uses it to scare off trespassers. I guess it's worked," he smiled.

The cop extended his hand and said, "I'm Scott Wilson, Suddenly's Sheriff."

We shook hands. "I'm Efren Sandoval and this is my wife Elaine." She stepped closer to me and said, "We're on our way to Suddenly to see about purchasing the hardware store. Who do we contact about that?"

"Just a moment, I need to give Samuel this package." Sheriff Wilson took about ten steps toward Samuel and gave him the cardboard box. The container was large enough to be a three-tiered cake from a bakery. They spoke for a moment, shook hands and Samuel disappeared to the back of his house.

The officer returned and commented, "If someone from town didn't come out here every few days, Duggar wouldn't be with us much longer. Suddenly feels responsible for him for all his contributions to the town. He was Sheriff for sixteen years starting about the time of the Korean War. His wife was a woman he arrested once. I don't recall the infraction. It couldn't have amounted to much."

We stood there silently, facing each other for a moment. I thought I would have to ask about the hardware store again but he volunteered, "You should see Arlene Stafford, she's our most accomplished realtor. If it's property, she knows all about it. She'll be in her office on Main Street about one o'clock tomorrow. She works half days on realty and volunteers at the grade school playground in the morning. I'm on my way to town, why don't you follow me."

"Thanks, we'll do that. We were warned about the road being a bit tricky."

The sheriff pondered my words and replied, "Logging trucks take more than their share of the road sometimes but since this is Sunday you shouldn't have any problems. Just follow me to the hardware store so you can take a look. There's a nice place to rent a room within a couple of blocks. I assume you'll be staying over."

I glanced at Elaine and she nodded her approval. The cruiser backed up, turned sharply and started toward the rough roadway. Elaine and I followed him through the trees, leaving Mr. Duggar's home in our rearview mirror.

Sheriff Wilson never exceeded twenty-five miles per hour, so the drive was relaxing. We were several car lengths behind so we couldn't be accused of tail-gating.

Chapter 2

As I followed the worn asphalt through the mature trees, some of them huge and overhanging the road, I asked Elaine, "What did you see when you looked in Mr. Duggar's window?"

"Well, as I said before, there were two oil lamps. I thought a woman was sitting at a small wooden table in the center of the room. It looked like a woman because of long scraggly hair, but because the window was kind of dirty, I didn't have a clear view. When the figure moved toward the window, I was scared and stepped down from the box. I'm glad you were there or I would have fallen."

"Hmm. What do you guess he was doing in there."

"Playing solitaire?" She grinned.

"Most likely reading the Bible. Don't you think?"

"Yes." She nodded, "You're probably right." She mulled over the vision she had and suggested, "He might have been writing something, or sketching."

"An artist?"

"Gee, Efren, I couldn't see clearly and my perception lasted but a second."

The sheriff stopped at Main and turned right. My first impression of Suddenly was that it seemed to be the interior of an old west army fort. Tall trees at the edges of the little town suggested walls to fend off invaders but perhaps my imagination had taken over my mind. I just finished a three volume set of western novels.

We followed the officer along Main Street for about three blocks when he pulled over to the curb and got out of his cruiser. I parked next to him and before I could shut off the car Elaine said, "Look Efren, the realtor's office is directly in front of us." I looked up through the windshield and saw a red neon sign in the office window: CLOSED. A black and white sign on the front door stated: Open Monday at 1:00 p.m.

The sheriff came over to my window and I lowered it to talk. I remarked, "Sheriff, is the town always this quiet? There's hardly any traffic."

"The usual hustle and bustle are absent today. As we were coming into town from Duggar's, I got late winter storm warnings over the police radio from Spokane and Missoula. We could get a foot of snow tonight. People are staying home this afternoon preparing for a storm. I think you'd better find a place to stay before the weather turns sour. The temp is already beginning to drop and the north wind is picking up."

"Ask about a motel, Ef." Elaine sounded concerned.

Sheriff Wilson heard Elaine and said, "Continue down Main one block, turn right, then left at the next street. You'll see Jean's B and B. It's a nice place to stay. It's not expensive, either. Jean likes to have guests around."

I could feel the cold air and closed my window. The sheriff got back in his car, made a U-turn and vanished from view. I backed into the street and followed his directions. The B and B was an obvious structure, an older two story home with two chimneys. Elaine suggested it was a log cabin on steroids. It was set back from the street with parking room for at least a half dozen vehicles. There were two parking spaces occupied, so I concluded there were vacancies. Elaine wanted to investigate, so I remained in the car.

I pressed the button for the radio and listened to the end of some music from the University of Montana radio station, KBGA.

Then a weather announcement came on reinforcing the sheriff's statement about the possibility of a foot of snow. It was a late polar blast coming down from Canada and large amounts of snow were expected in the Bitterroots. The music resumed with an orchestra playing *The Grand Canyon Suite.*

The car was getting colder as I waited. I slipped on a pair of gloves that I carried in my glove compartment and started the engine to run the heater. What was taking Elaine so long? I suppressed the desire to follow her into the building but I imagined going inside and inquiring about my wife. Thoughts came to mind of a counter next to a stairway where a large gentleman stood. He wore jeans, a red and black plaid shirt, and cowboy boots. He responded saying no one had been in to ask about a room since noon. That concept faded away like waking from a dream when Elaine came out of the entryway waving a keycard in her right hand. She had rented a room.

Elaine hustled to the car, got in and said, "Sorry I took so long, dear. Jean asked me some questions and I ended up telling her about our experience with Mr. Duggar. She said she thought he had passed during the Bitterroot fire two years ago. She hasn't seen or heard of him in a long time." She took a deep breath and continued, "Let's take our things in and get settled. Our room is on the second floor, number twenty one. It's nice and warm. Oh! Jean's last name is Baxter."

I told her what I had imagined when she took so long and she laughed. "You'd better stay away from that science fiction series on TV. I think it's scrambling your senses."

Except for some scraps of trash on the floor behind the front seat, we carried everything we had inside, up the stairs and into our room. After piling everything on one of the beds, we sat down on the other one to catch our breath and check out the furnishings. A small writing table with two chairs, a large cedar chest of drawers, two extremely soft beds, a bathroom with sink, toilet and shower made the room comfortably habitable. There was a floor lamp between the two beds.

I glanced at Elaine and asked, "How much for the night?"

"Not bad, just a hundred dollars. Jean said if we get snowed in, each extra day would only be fifty more. Don't you think that's a fairly good deal?"

"That's fine, but lunch and dinner are extra, right?"

"Yeah. Jean's husband, Arnold, said their meals were cheaper than dining at other places."

"How old do you think Jean and Arny Baxter are? They look to me to be about sixty."

"Yes, I believe they're a few years older than we are. They look relaxed and seem to be having a good time running the accommodations."

We took off our coats, visited the bathroom, and started downstairs to see what else the private residence offered us. Elaine wanted to see if there was any artwork from residents of Suddenly displayed on the walls. She was rewarded when we came to the landing about halfway down to the first floor. We stopped to admire a winter scene of a cabin covered with about two feet of snow. The painting was so realistic we could almost take a drink from the cold stream water. The winter scene was signed, Margret Duggar.

"I'll bet that was Mr. Duggar's wife, Ef. She was a talented artist."

"You should know, El. I'll bet you could do as well."

"Maybe. I'm glad you have confidence in my ability. Thank you. I'm gonna to ask Jean about the artist."

"I'm wondering if that picture is of a real cabin located somewhere nearby. I'd like to see the place. I bet fishing in that stream is great. I can almost smell the trout cooking over a campfire."

We continued down to the lobby where other guests were seated. A teenage girl and boy, perhaps siblings, were engrossed with a mobile phone and magazine, respectively. Two couples, fortyish, were standing near the check-in counter talking together. They stepped back to allow us access. I struck the little gong to see if Jean could answer Elaine's question with regard to the painting.

The slightly taller of the two women approached and said, "We're the Morrisons, Walter and Clair. That's our son, Chad. We drove to Suddenly on his spring break." She smiled and resumed,

"Mother nature doesn't want to cooperate offering nice weather. I sure hope it doesn't snow tonight."

Apparently, Chad was listening. He called out, "Mom . . . it's already snowing."

Elaine and I joined the other adults at one of the two picture windows to observe the white stuff. The snow was swirling down in large flakes. Visibility was decreasing so I could barely see our car only twenty yards away. I was next to Mrs. Morrison so I said, "We're the Sandovals, Elaine and Efren. We're in town to investigate purchasing the hardware store."

Elaine added, "We didn't think we would stay over, but changed our mind when we were advised about the approaching storm. The realtor isn't available today."

The other couple had drifted away to the young girl, I guessed their daughter. A second close look and I decided she must be about thirteen or fourteen, about a freshman or sophomore in high school. I heard the girl say, "I know, Mom, but I want to talk with Mrs. Wilson but she's out of town. The policeman said she'd be back from Helena tomorrow. Then we'll go back to Dillon. It's not that far and the road is usually kept clear. That's what they told me."

Jean appeared at the counter and said, "We'll serve dinner at 5:30. Please let me know if you intend to have your evening meal with us."

I nodded to Elaine and she gave me a thumbs up. I watched her beckon to Jean. Jean came out to talk with Elaine, but hesitated for a moment, "Have you all met?"

The girl's mother announced, "We've met the Morrison family but not the other couple."

I joined Elaine and extended my hand to the girl's father. We shook hands and he disclosed, "We are the Singletons, Ervin and Kate with our daughter, Tina. She wants to talk with a female forest ranger, Mrs. Wilson, the sheriff's wife, to be specific. Tina's got her mind set on becoming a forest ranger." The wife and daughter drifted away toward the window. Ervin leaned toward me and whispered as he grinned, "I think she's going through a phase."

I smiled and explained why Elaine and I were in Suddenly. When he heard Sandoval, he reacted, "Are you related to the Sandoval family in Virginia City?"

As far as I was aware, Elaine and I were the only Sandovals in the state, so I said, "No, I don't believe so but who knows where all the branches of the family tree extend." I didn't bother to mention I was aware of several Sandoval families in New Mexico and Arizona where distant relatives lived. Ervin volunteered that he was a loan officer in a small finance company and his wife taught high school choir.

I joined Elaine who was waiting to talk to Jean after she completed the count for dinner. I felt Jean was staring out the window, but her eyes seemed to be wandering. She must be doing some calculations. Then she abruptly said, "All eight plus four makes an even dozen. I'll call in Vivian for some help."

Elaine quickly spoke to Jean. "If you need some kitchen help, I'll volunteer with my husband. It will give me a chance to ask you some questions, too. Maybe you won't have to get any outside help."

Jean thought for a split second and responded, "You're on, Elaine. I hope you have some experience with restaurant style cooking."

"About four years of it when I was in college. I worked for a food service company that fed about a thousand male students three meals a day—two meals on Sundays." Elaine glanced toward me and said, "My husband can assist, too. He just needs a little direction."

Jean gave me the once over, blinked her eyes and replied, "All right, come with me."

I didn't have the slightest idea what she was thinking but I must have passed the test. We followed her into a kitchen that had been remodeled from the original to accommodate more people than a normal size family. I was amazed to see all the stainless steel appliances. The oven lights were illuminated and a countdown was proceeding. Something was already cooking.

After showing Elaine the dinner menu, Jean gave us aprons, hair nets, latex gloves and put us to work. Elaine knew I needed direction, so she gave me two heads of lettuce, a wicked looking knife, a large bowl, a few instructional words and I was put to work.

As she turned away, she said, "Watch your fingers, Ef."

During the hour that we worked preparing dinner for twelve, I listened attentively to Jean's answers to Elaine's questions about the picture by Margret Duggar.

Chapter 3

Elaine and I sat at the sides of Jean during dinner so we could help retrieve items from the kitchen. She told us what she had heard about Mr. Duggar and Gene Erickson, the owner of the hardware store. She confessed that it might be a rumor, but Duggar used to pay for hardware items with gold dust.

"Margie and Samuel used to go out prospecting after he retired from being sheriff. After about five years, Margret's artwork was their only support. Samuel spent all his savings searching for gold. I purchased that picture by Margie for eighty-five dollars nearly thirty years ago. I bought others from Samuel but over the years I've sold them to visitors and made a tidy profit. But that one is my favorite and I'm not going to sell it until I can get the right price. I want a real art lover to get it, not someone that will put it in their attic or garage when they grow weary of it."

"Do you know if it depicts a real place?"

"Uh-huh. According to Samuel, it's a real place. But I've asked him where it is and he just grins and says, 'It's Margie's and my secret place. Someday I might tell you all about it'."

As I listened, I counted heads. There were ten people at the dinner table, but Jean had said we were preparing for twelve. Where were the other two? It wasn't long before my curiosity was satisfied.

When dessert was completed and families were dispersing, I observed Jean lightly touch Elaine's wrist and say, "I have someone I'd like you to meet. Could you and Efren come with me?"

We followed Jean through the kitchen to a hallway where two doors were located. She extracted a large key from her waist apron and unlocked the most distant door. When the door was open, I could hear some familiar music playing. Elaine gave me a questioning look and grabbed my left wrist. I was unaware of anything abnormal until I noticed one bed was occupied by an elderly man, a woman of about the same age sitting beside the bed reading aloud. When the woman saw us, she stood and said, "I guess it's dinner time, Jean. And who are these nice looking people?"

Jean introduced us to her mother, Helen Adair, who had stepped away from the bed. The older woman commented, "I was just reading a story to my husband, Edwin. Ed has dementia but enjoys hearing my voice and stories like *Jack and the Bean Stalk*. I heard the wind buffet the window. Is it snowing today?"

"Yes, Mom. Mr. and Mrs. Sandoval have been helping me with dinner today. We'll bring in your dinner in just a minute. Do you have to use the bathroom? I'll sit with Dad if you do."

"No, dear, we're fine now. I think Ed is getting hungry—and so am I," she grinned.

We followed Jean to the kitchen and helped prepare two large serving trays with plates of food, desserts, napkins and utensils.

I asked, "Do your parents drink coffee?"

Jean glanced at me and said, "No, they'll have ice water with dinner."

I could see tears in Jean's eyes. Her concern for her parents was obvious. Without any hesitation, Jean swung open a large base cabinet door and removed a serving cart. She sprayed it with disinfectant and wiped it clean and dry with a paper towel. "No bugs included with my folks' dinner," she grinned. "They can't risk getting sick."

Elaine commented, "Your mother looks like she has things well at hand. She appears to be a strong woman. Is there anything else

Efren and I can assist you with? If not, we'll retire to our room and talk over plans about the hardware store. Thank you for introducing us to your parents. We enjoyed helping in the kitchen."

Jean said, "I hope you folks stay in Suddenly. You are a genuinely nice capable couple. I hope your talk with the realtor goes well. Arnold and I will see you for breakfast. Good night." Jean began guiding the cart down the hall toward her parents' room. Elaine and I went to the dining area and began transporting dirty dishes to the kitchen area. I saw Arnold in the foyer talking with a person that had just entered the building. The man's hat and shoulders were covered with snow.

"Hey, Efren, we're not finished with the dishes yet."

Elaine, she would admit, was a slave driver but I appreciated her suggestions. We had to finish our job before going to our room, no dilly-dallying allowed. When the table was cleared, we adjourned to our room. I was curious about the depth of the white stuff and took a look out our window. I could make out our car as a bump in the snow which I estimated to be about a foot deep. Much deeper drifts were at the sides of the cars. It was still snowing at ten o'clock but there was nothing we could do about it. When I turned out the light, I commented to Elaine, "You know, El, we didn't bring snowshoes or skis."

Elaine said, "Go to sleep, dear, maybe it will melt by morning."

We started laughing.

We didn't have bedclothes, so we slept in our underwear. The comforters were about four inches thick, so we didn't have any sensation of the outside cold snowy night. We awoke at seven o'clock to what sounded like a garbage truck picking up trash but I had to investigate. I wrapped one of our blankets around my body and took a look out our window.

"What is that noise, Ef?"

"It's a gigantic snowplow. The streets are being cleared and trucks are hauling off the snow. We'll probably have to dig out our cars to get on the road. I hope Jean and Arnold have shovels."

"Maybe they have a snowblower."

"There's no place to blow the snow. We'll have to draw lots to see who gets dug out first. That will create some space to pile the snow."

"Oh, I don't even want to get up but I guess we have to get dressed and go downstairs for breakfast."

I spent a minimal amount of time in the bathroom and got dressed while Elaine freshened up. At eight o'clock we went down to see what was in store for our morning meal. I had a yearning for bacon and flapjacks. I feared disappointment but was pleased to find several large stacks of pancakes surrounded by pitchers of syrup and two blocks of butter, but no bacon. There was a large container of coffee so we could serve ourselves, and two plastic pitchers of orange juice. It seemed we were the last guests to arrive at the table.

Everyone but the teens said good morning. The kids were talking animatedly and stuffing their mouths. They had on winter coats so they were prepared for the snow and low temperature. I couldn't imagine they would be shoveling snow unless encouraged by their parents. They didn't strike me as having much initiative, but since I had known them for only twelve hours, I could be surprised by any diligence.

Elaine and I had been sitting at the table eating for less than ten minutes when half a dozen teenage boys entered the B and B. They were not boisterous but exhibited a reserved demeanor and asked to see Arnold. He greeted the boys and began talking with a nice looking blond youngster nearly six feet tall. I had an impulse to ask the boy if he knew a girl named Lisa from Dillon but I held off from interrupting the conversation.

The boys exited and Arnold approached the dining table. "I have good news for you. That group of boys came by to ask if they could clean off the snow from your cars and the parking lot. They're part of the local football team and need exercise during school closure. They can't use the facilities at the high school. I told them to go ahead. I hope that's all right with you."

Everyone agreed with Arnold's decision. Tina excused herself, got up from the table and went to the front window. At least one of the boys had caught her eyes. Maybe it was Danny, the same one the Dillon girl mentioned at the park. If Elaine and I buy the hardware store and move to Suddenly, perhaps my curiosity will be rewarded.

I took two more pancakes from the serving plate, applied butter and syrup and looked forward to an eventful, even rewarding day. Elaine nudged me with an elbow, smiled and asked, "Are you close to being full yet?"

My mouth was full so I nodded and uttered, "Uh-huh." After swallowing and taking a sip of coffee, I replied, "Let's wait awhile for those boys to do their job. We can't see the realtor until one o'clock anyway. All we can do is drive around and get stuck in snow drifts. We don't have snow tires or chains."

"We'll be warm in the car, Ef, and we can take a peek at the store and find another place to eat for lunch. I'm guessing Jean would like to get us all out of her hair for a while—or permanently."

I overheard Tina ask her mother, "Is it okay if I go outside for a minute? I'd like some fresh air."

I couldn't resist smiling. I was sure that Tina wanted to venture outside to check on at least one of the boys, maybe the one called Danny. I had a sudden microburst of envy for Danny that faded as quickly as it had struck. That feeling might have been a serious thought forty years ago. I'd like to know what his last name is.

The six boys cleared the snow rapidly. The sun shining on the cars warmed the interiors, so the last traces of crystals on the vehicles were gone by nine-thirty. I couldn't see much of the roads from the building, but I imagined the snow was piled high at the sides of the asphalt. Elaine and I decided to wait for the other guests to leave so everyone wasn't rushing to leave simultaneously. Our plans were to look over the hardware store, eat lunch and meet with the realtor. If we say goodbye to Jean and Arnold by eleven thirty, we should have plenty of time for our activities.

The Morrison family was first to leave. I watched their car maneuver from the parking area to the street and disappear from view. The Singleton's took more time in exiting the B and B. The women hugged Jean and expressed their heartfelt thanks for the accommodations. I heard Tina say, "I'll come by to say hello during football season. I want to see Mrs. Wilson's son again."

Jean smiled, "Yes, Danny Drum is a nice young man. He comes by occasionally to see if we need any help."

The question about Danny had been answered without my involvement. The boy's last name is Drum but his mother is Mrs. Wilson. That generates another question. Is Danny adopted? Maybe I should keep my mind on hardware.

We started repacking the car with our things at eleven fifteen and said our goodbyes a few minutes after eleven thirty. Jean wished us good luck with the hardware business and gave us both a hug. We told Baxters how much we enjoyed our stay with them and said we would probably see them again if we purchased the hardware business. We'd need a place to stay when looking for a home. I shook hands with Arnold and we went to our car.

Arnold had given us directions to Erickson's store. It was an easy find, two blocks from the realtor's on the other side of the street, a two-story brick corner building painted light brown. It seemed to fit Suddenly's decor in timber country. I parked in front of the structure with the front bumper against the piled snow. Even though we weren't wearing heavy winter coats, we got out to look in the windows.

Elaine remarked, "I expected it to be really cold, but with the sun out, it's not too bad."

We walked about twenty feet to get around the snow and then back to the entrance. The entranceway was recessed about six feet from the sidewalk and with my hands, I shielded the reflections in the glass and peered into the unlighted interior.

"We can't see much, Elaine. We'll see if the realtor can let us in and turn on some lights. I'd like to see what stock is present."

Elaine commented, "They probably have been selling but not replenishing items since they want to rid themselves of the business."

I had the same thought. We'll find a place for lunch and visit with the realtor.

Elaine stomped her feet, grabbed onto my right arm and pulled me toward our car. "Let's go, Efren. I'm starting to get cold."

I felt the cold air as we retraced steps to the corner to get around the snow pile. The warm car seats helped lessen the chilliness as I started the engine. I backed into the street and noticed a sign for Dairy Queen. We were pointed in the right direction.

"Burgers but no ice cream, okay?" Elaine smiled.

Chapter 4

Fortunately, the restaurant was open. I was a bit worried at first but when I saw cars driving in and out, I knew the fast-food outlet was doing business. When we were inside, enjoying the warmth and odors of fried food, Elaine poked me in the ribs and said, "Look, Efren, the Singletons are here."

Ervin saw us and waved. We sat in the adjacent bench seats and said hello. Elaine asked, "Have you visited with Mrs. Wilson yet?"

Kate replied, "We have a one o'clock appointment with her at the Forest Ranger Office Building. It's just outside the town limits. The road is still being cleared."

While the women talked, I ordered some burgers, fries and two coffees. I probably should have ordered hot chocolate but I had already chosen coffee before it crossed my mind. I don't think Elaine will mind my choice; she'll be happy to drink something hot. However, a moment of doubt did occur. I might end up with two coffees and a hot chocolate. There were only a few customers inside the restaurant, so the service was excellent. I didn't have to wait for more than two minutes before returning to our table with our order.

When Elaine saw the coffee, she gave me a quick scowl and said, "I guess you didn't hear me say I wanted hot chocolate."

"Oh, I'm sorry. I'll get you some. It will only take a minute."

I returned to the counter and the girl handed me the chocolate drink. I guessed she overheard what Elaine said. When I tried to pay, the girl said, "No charge today."

Was she feeling sorry for me? I said, "Thank you! We'll come again."

As we ate, I scanned the menu items, wondering how many people would order a blizzard today.

The Singleton family left the restaurant a few minutes ahead of us driving in the opposite direction. Elaine and I pulled up to the curb in front of the realtors office as a woman was entering, undoubtedly, it was Arlene Stafford. She appeared to be a tall substantial woman, but she was wearing a well-insulated winter coat perhaps concealing her true form.

We sat there looking for a place to access the sidewalk through the piled snow but I couldn't see a pathway without going to the end of the block about thirty yards away in either direction. Just as Elaine said, "How do we get . . . ," the woman reappeared carrying a shovel and began to dig through the three foot high snow ridge. I watched for a few shovelfuls and got out to assist her.

"We're coming to see you about the hardware store. Let me dig a path through the snow."

She seemed to be a bit winded, took a deep breath and said, "I don't have another shovel, but you can certainly borrow this one." She smiled and extended the handle to me. I started removing the snow so there was a two-foot-wide passageway through the ridge. When I took a few moments to evaluate, Elaine got out of the car and stopped me from continuing.

"That's enough, Efren. You'll have a heart attack! You are sweating. Let's go inside."

I sensed the burger and coffee trying to escape my stomach in a most inconvenient manner, so I ushered Elaine through the cleared path, leaned the shovel against the glass outside the door and followed her into the realtor's office. The woman had watched from the window and commented, "Thank you for the assistance, I'm Arlene Stafford. What can I help you with? You mentioned the hardware store."

I opened my coat to help cool off and introduced ourselves. I told her we had come from Butte to see about the hardware store. She motioned for us to sit beside her desk, then opened a manila file folder. "The structure is a two story brick, 3,400 square foot corner building. The owners, Beth and Randy Erickson evaluate the stock at a quarter million dollars. They would like a down payment of fifteen percent based on the value of the stock. That amounts to thirty seven thousand five hundred dollars. The building is leased from the city of Suddenly at the rate of four hundred dollars per month."

Neither Elaine nor I exhibited any dismay with what she had related. I think she was impressed with our restraint when we heard the numbers. I glanced at Elaine and received a nod.

"Could you let us inspect the store's interior?" I asked.

"Not a problem. It's right down the street."

Elaine replied, "Yes, we were just there but couldn't see through the windows very well. The inside lighting wasn't on."

"We can walk if you can tolerate the chilly weather. Otherwise, I'll get my car and drive you."

"We'll take our car. Elaine will ride in back," I grinned.

"Well, all right. I'll lock up. I have a sign when I temporarily leave the office."

A few minutes later, Mrs. Stafford unlocked the front door of Erickson's Hardware. It was cool inside but pleasant, apparently a furnace was programmed for winter weather. The overhead lights gave us an entirely new view of the interior. What we hadn't seen before was a spacious balcony. Elaine pointed to it and I said, "Go up and take a look. See what is up there. I'll tour the aisles down here." We parted and I took out my pocket recorder to make notes of things needed in a well-stocked establishment. Elaine's memory didn't require any help from a gadget.

Mrs. Stafford followed me to answer questions. After I had toured the ground floor and Elaine returned from upstairs, I asked about the furnace and the realtor replied, "The heating and air conditioning are relatively new; updated two years ago."

Elaine volunteered, "There's not much up there, Efren, just a small office. We could live up there until we find a place to stay. We'd have to store most of our furniture though."

So, I wasn't going to have to talk Elaine into making the move to Suddenly. Since we agreed to take over the hardware business, I asked the realtor, "When do we sign the papers?"

She replied, "When can you pay the fifteen percent?"

I smiled, "Well, I can't use a credit card, but I'll write you a check. It should clear right away; I transferred money into our account last week just in case the hardware business looked favorable. We like the town, too, at least the part we've seen and the people are nice, even the police."

"Let's return to my office to sign the papers. I'd like you to meet the Ericksons, too. I'll give them a call to see if they can come downtown."

We returned to Arlene's office where she immediately made a phone call. Elaine and I waited for about a minute. She hung up the phone and said, "The Ericksons will be here in about ten minutes. I have an idea for you. It just might work out great for you and the Ericksons."

"What are you thinking?" I inquired.

"I want the Ericksons to be here so I can suggest it to both families at the same time. It will only be a few more minutes to wait."

Arlene got up and went to the front door to watch for the Ericksons. At least that's what I assumed. Elaine got my attention by touching my wrist and said, "What has she got in mind? Do you have any idea?"

"I could guess but it would be a pretty wild one."

"So, what's your guess?"

"Okay, she's gonna suggest we trade homes. No money would be involved and only a small amount of furniture would have to be moved. It would be a big surprise if it works out."

"Gosh, I would never have thought of doing that, Ef."

But do they want to move to Butte? I was curious about the square footage of their home. How did it compare to ours?

The Ericksons arrived in a large dark-blue Ford pickup. It looked new. I expected Arlene would want us to sit down for a discussion so I found two more chairs and placed them next to her oversized oak desk. Arlene introduced us to Beth and her nineteen-year-old son, Randy. He looked like he had just graduated from high school or had been in college his first year. He was relaxed but looked eager to conclude the meeting. He kept glancing outside. Maybe he wanted to go skiing with some friends. Beth, his mother, was about ten years younger than Elaine, well-groomed and nice looking. She would have no problems finding dates in Butte.

Arlene started the meeting speaking to Beth and her son, "The Sandovals are ready to purchase your business at the asking price. But I have a proposal for both families. What do you think about exchanging homes? It would save costs, time and also eliminate most paperwork. No realtors would be involved."

Beth reacted, "But wouldn't each of us want to see the other's property first?"

"Yes, I've thought of that. Sandoval's could visit your home today and you could accompany them to Butte tomorrow, or later today if you would like, to see their home. If the exchange is agreeable, I can take care of the transfers for you. I'll only charge for the hardware business purchase."

I commented, "We'd have to sign some documents, right?"

"Yes, I think you would have to sign at least twice agreeing to the transfer."

Beth whispered something to her son, who smiled and nodded. She then said, "We're in. Let's give it a try."

Elaine and I were of the same opinion. I looked at Beth and said, "Take us to your home."

Randy drove the pickup and Elaine drove our car. She wanted more experience driving through snow. I didn't mind, knowing she was a good driver and could handle our car with ease. At first, I felt a bit uncomfortable sitting in the passenger seat. I didn't really know what to do with my hands, so I interlaced my fingers on my seatbelt. Ericksons lived on the south side of town two blocks from the road leading to Mr. Duggar's home. The area was sparsely settled, only three houses were built on the entire block, plenty of room for new neighbors.

Snow was piled over four feet high on both sides of the driveway but Elaine squeezed in beside the pickup on the gravel pad leading to the two-car garage. The house looked well taken care of but what did the snow conceal? Since Elaine and I liked garden work and Elaine loved flowers, landscaping would not be a problem if the snow ever melted. How cold could it be in June? Undoubtedly, we'd have to put up fencing to keep animals out of our vegetable garden.

The house looked to be about the same size as ours in Butte, about seventeen hundred square feet. I noticed the houses in Suddenly possessed a steeper pitched roof than those in Butte. It was not difficult to know why. Deep snow was a common occurrence in the mountain location. So far, the trade idea seemed a good possibility. But what about the inside?

We followed Ericksons through the front entrance directly into their living room. Except for the colors, the furniture and arrangement was remarkably like ours. Elaine poked me and said, "We could let our furniture go and keep these, couldn't we?"

Beth inquired, "Your living area is very similar?"

I estimated the area and replied, "Very similar to ours. What is the square footage of the house?"

"Seventeen hundred fifty-two. I'll show you the bedrooms and the kitchen. There is room in the attic for storage if you need it."

"Ours is almost the same, seventeen hundred sixty. It's in a nice neighborhood, not far from a shopping center and the university."

We continued through the house, checking the layout, the plumbing and furnace. Beth showed us the tax assessments and local fees and Randy added a comment that excited Elaine. He said the high school art teacher was leaving this summer and the position would be open. He said, "Does Mrs. Sandoval have any interest in art? She probably needs a teaching certificate."

"Who should I talk to about the teaching position? I could get a provisional certificate."

Beth answered, "You need to talk with Dr. James Savage, the Principal. I'll give you his number. I sold a home to him and his wife, Mary, when they arrived three years ago."

Elaine was a bit reticent to talk about her artistic talents but I informed the Ericksons about her accomplishments in Butte.

Randy said, "Wow, I'm glad I mentioned that Mrs. Silverton was leaving. Your wife might be a good fit. Dr. Savage wouldn't even have to advertise."

While the talk about the teaching position was going on, I could tell Elaine was thinking ahead to the property exchange. I had seen that look in her eyes before when we were thinking of early retirement. I handled the logistics and Elaine took care of the company books, including taxes and our retirement investment funds.

Chapter 5

"I have an idea," Elaine said. She had been fairly quiet but I knew she was looking closely at the interior of the house. She had our attention. "Beth, you and Randy will accompany us to Butte and inspect our home. If you agree to the trade, we'll rent a U-Haul truck and return to Suddenly with the things we want to keep. The men will drive the truck back to Suddenly and Beth and I will drive the car. When we've unloaded our things, you can load your items and drive back to Butte with the two trucks."

I asked, "Randy, you can drive, right?"

"Yes sir. I like to drive our pickup but I haven't driven a truck before, but Mom has. I think she can drive anything; well, maybe not a tank," he grinned.

So, Beth and Randy liked the idea. We returned to Stafford's Realty and sat down with Arlene and signed some papers. I agreed to wire the down payment Tuesday morning. Arlene noticed Erickson's pickup wasn't parked outside and asked about it. Beth explained what we were planning.

Arlene raised her eyebrows when we mentioned the U-Haul truck, but I told her, "If things don't work out with the trade, we'll figure out an alternative plan, don't worry."

Beth backed me up, "I think it will work—according to plan. It's a good idea. Efren said their house is close to the university, and I can commute to work. It should be fine." She nodded as she smiled.

I wanted to get rolling on the road to Butte. I knew Elaine had the same idea; we had been away for longer than we originally planned. I asked Beth if she and Randy needed to get anything from their house but they said no, they had all they needed. We thanked Arlene for her assistance, said goodbye and climbed into our car. Randy rode with me up front and the ladies got in back. I didn't need directions to get on the road to Dillon, it was an obvious route traveled before.

Randy and I didn't have much to say until we drove past the Duggar turn off. I was curious to see if he had ever been to see Mr. Duggar and his house.

"I've been out here several times, usually to deliver something from our store. I came out once with David Drum to deliver for Meals on Wheels."

"David? Don't you mean Danny?"

"Not Danny, David is my age. I don't think Danny can drive, legally that is. I think he's about fifteen. The brothers are four years apart."

"How does Mr. Drum earn a living?"

"Oh, he died in a fire about ten years ago. Three or four years ago Mrs. Drum married Scott Wilson. He was here when he worked for the FBI on a kidnapping. He flew a fancy helicopter back then."

"Now I'm beginning to see the picture."

"Yeah. It's kinda complicated when you're new to Suddenly. I'm sure you'll adjust—having the business will help. Some people are here only in the summer. Right before the snow is three feet deep, they disappear." He snickered, "Mom and I are here all the time. I'll be glad to go to school in Butte."

"Well, Randy, it will still get cold in Butte but not so much of the white stuff. Do many people have snowmobiles in Suddenly?"

"Not very many. There's only one place that works on them and they own a bike shop."

"Motorcycles?"

"Nope. Bicycles but they also fix motorcycles. John and Dexter Young, father and son. Their shop is Dex's Bikes."

"Tell me more about Mr. Duggar. He seems a bit odd. Is he mentally fit?"

"Oh, yeah. He's real smart. He just enjoys the solitude. Ever since his wife died he's been kind of a hermit."

"Do you know how his front window got broken?"

I glanced at Randy. He was thinking about something, maybe he knew more than he wanted to tell me. But perhaps he was reliving an old event.

"Sure, some kids went out there last Halloween. I think they might have been drunk and they started yelling about rumors of him having gold hidden in his house. He tried to run them off but they started throwing rocks and broke his window. Then they ran off. There was a notice in the paper about it, but nothin' ever happened that I know of."

"You weren't involved?" I didn't think he would lie since he was moving to Butte.

"No sir, but I know one of the guys that was out there. He told me he didn't throw any rocks."

I pulled off the highway in Dillon at a Texaco gas station at four fifteen. I asked the ladies, "Do you need to use the facilities?" I didn't hear a definite yes from either one. "It's another hour to Butte. I'm gonna stretch my legs and fill the gas tank. The dash thermometer indicates the temperature here is in the low fifties. Not too bad."

I followed orange cones to the only pump that was operating. An attendant came to my window and I asked him for eight gallons of regular. The concrete around the station was wet with water in a few shallow puddles. I guessed not much snow had fallen in Dillon. The ladies got out and went into the station. A few seconds later,

Randy went inside. Maybe the sound of gasoline rushing into the tank triggered their need to use the bathroom. I felt no impulse and figured I could last another hour.

I watched the accumulating charge on the pump. The numbers stopped turning over slightly past twenty-eight dollars. I remembered my father filling up his pickup for about ten percent of that total. I paid with my credit card. The attendant cleaned the windows and thanked me for stopping. I moved the car away from the pump so another vehicle could get service.

Randy exited the station chewing on something, most likely a candy bar. He was still a growing boy, always hungry. When I was his age, I loved Baby Ruth bars but I haven't had one in years. When I was a teen, they were ten cents, now they're probably about two dollars. The ladies emerged a moment later clutching their coats tightly around their necks. It must have been warm inside. Elaine had a small bag of pretzels in her hand and after getting back in the car, gave the container to Beth. She offered some to me, but I declined with "No thanks." The salty taste would have to be washed down, increasing the pressure below my belt.

The trip from Dillon to Butte took just over an hour. Randy was quiet. I glanced to the right and saw that he was asleep with his head against the window. Elaine and Beth talked about the activities in Suddenly and some of the town's notable characters, including more anecdotes about Mr. Duggar. It seems that he also is somewhat of an artist but not as accomplished as his wife was. His drawing was with charcoal or pencil but never in color. Beth had never seen any of his work with color added.

He never exhibited anything but occasional visitors to his house commented about his artistry.

I pulled into our driveway at ten 'til six and shut off the engine. The sudden quiet, lack of car vibrations or hunger pangs aroused my three passengers.

"We're home! Thank heavens there's no snow." Elaine exclaimed. "Let's get inside and have something to eat. We have a casserole that has an appointment with the microwave."

Elaine and Beth couldn't get in the house fast enough, Elaine to get to the refrigerator and Beth to begin examining our house. Randy stayed beside the car and asked if he could help with anything.

"You sure can. I'll put the car in the garage and you can help carry in the blankets and leftovers from Elaine's and my picnic in Dillon. That food will go into the garbage, there's not much remaining anyway—but it's been too warm to be safely eaten. We don't need any barfing."

Randy laughed and grabbed an armload of blankets. I picked up the picnic basket, shut the car doors and locked the garage up tight. Elaine told us where to deposit our armloads. Then we went into the living room and stood beside our comfortable sofa. I had seen Randy eyeing our sixty-five inch TV, so I flipped it on and handed him the remote. I headed for the bathroom. I was afraid if I heard any running water, I'd suffer an immediate wet reaction.

Randy said, "Please leave the light on, Mr. Sandoval."

I did as Randy requested, used a puff of air freshener and went to the kitchen to talk with the ladies. As I arrived, the microwave sounded with its four beeps and the ladies laughed, associating my arrival with the readiness of the casserole.

Elaine pointed to the dining room table and said, "Sit, Efren. We're almost ready. Where's Randy?"

Randy must have heard Elaine. "I just washed my hands, Mrs. Sandoval." He entered the dining room rubbing his hands together and wiping them on his shirt. He sat opposite me at the oak table capable of comfortably seating six. Elaine carried in the main dish and Beth brought in a salad. I noticed there wasn't any dressing, so I got up and retrieved the French, Thousand Island and Blue Cheese sauces from the refrigerator.

"Thank you, Efren. I was so worried about overheating the main dish, I forgot a few items."

After dinner, we toured the house with Beth and Randy. Beth commented favorably, especially about the kitchen and the master bath. She loved the master bedroom with its accompanying bath and Randy remarked that he liked the arrangement of the rooms and the large two-car garage.

When we returned to the dining room, I glanced at the picture on the wall and wondered what Elaine was thinking when we stopped to look at Mr. Duggar's house in the woods. I couldn't see much resemblance between the two buildings. If we take our print to Suddenly, I'm sure she'll have an explanation. Maybe it has to do with the light and shadows.

Our guests wanted to know more about Butte, so we talked about the city and the university for nearly half an hour. Randy was interested in architecture or perhaps city planning. Elaine and I were not of much help. Elaine knew about the art department and finance and I knew about mechanical engineering and school administration.

Beth volunteered to help Elaine with the dishes and they headed for the kitchen. Randy and I talked about football. We found a TV show about the Western Athletic Conference football programs. We were ten minutes into the presentation when Beth motioned to Randy to join her in the kitchen. I assumed she wanted to ask him if he needed a snack before going to bed.

Elaine joined me and asked, "What are you watching?"

I didn't bother answering right away, the program didn't interest me, so I turned it off. I told her what it was and she said, "Oh, I shouldn't have asked. Wasn't there something better on?" She grinned and said, "They're talking about the trade of homes. I hope they like our house."

"Me, too. It would save the Ericksons and us time and money."

Beth and Randy reappeared, both smiling. Beth announced, "We're going for it. You've got a deal. What's next?"

I said, "Congratulations! Elaine and I like your house and hoped you'd like ours. If we had some booze, I'd offer you a drink . . . but not for Randy. He could have a Pepsi or a root beer, our only choices for soft drinks."

Beth replied, "Let's shake hands and go to bed. It's been a long day."

We all shook hands and I said, "Tomorrow, we'll pile everything we want to take to Suddenly on the garage floor. That will give us an idea how big a U-Haul truck to rent."

Elaine commented, "Beth, you can sleep in our extra bedroom. Everything is ready for a visitor. Randy, can you take the couch? We'll get you some blankets and a pillow."

"I can sleep anywhere, even on the floor. I'm used to camping out on the hard bumpy ground without an air mattress. There aren't many places around Suddenly where the ground is level. We always take a shovel when camping."

Chapter 6

Elaine and Beth must have prearranged their get up times. I was up and dressed by seven forty-five and could smell coffee. Randy exited the bathroom as I entered. "Good morning," was said simultaneously, both smiling and trying to avoid banging into each other. I pictured a mug of dark roast as I brushed my teeth.

The women were sitting at the dining room table making some sort of list. I stood there for a few seconds before Elaine looked up and said, "You and Randy will have to cook eggs and make some toast for yourselves. Beth and I are making lists of things we want to take with us. We'll start moving things to the garage while you go to the bank to arrange payment to Arlene, okay?"

"Elaine, the bank doesn't open till ten o'clock. Randy and I will take care of the heavy stuff. Are we going to take any big items, besides the beds?"

"Uh-huh. I want the dining room table and chairs. That's about all. Everything else will be clothes and blankets—soft stuff. Do we have enough boxes to pack it all?"

"I'll get some boxes from U-Haul after I get an estimate of quantity needed. I want to take some of my tools but I'll leave most of them and get new ones in Suddenly."

"Oh, I want this painting." She twisted and pointed at the framed scene of the house she was reminded of when she saw Mr. Duggar's place in the woods.

I made a mental note to put the picture on top of other items so it would make the trip undamaged. Randy was in the kitchen and I joined him to take over preparations of breakfast. I probably should have let him manage, but it was my last breakfast in my Butte kitchen. I was still in charge. There wasn't much evidence of the ladies' having eaten. I think they had some cereal and coffee and sat down to plan. As Randy and I ate breakfast the women toured the house looking for items to haul to Suddenly. Elaine carried out the search and Beth took notes.

Randy and I just finished eating when Elaine called to us, "You men have to carry out the mattresses and take the bed frames apart. Put them in the garage with the dining table and chairs . . . please."

That was our call to arms. I went into the garage and with Randy's assistance spread a tarp on the concrete. Then we went to the master bedroom, dismantled the bed and started relocating heavy or awkward to carry objects from the house to the garage.

Elaine and I had moved before, many times over the years, I've lost count. Maybe because of my age but the prospect of moving again was beginning to grate on my nerves. I guess I hadn't thought of the energy it required when planning. The physical labor was already getting me down and the day was still young. I had to make an important trip to the bank to wire money to Arlene Stafford.

But first, before the mood completely escaped me, Randy and I had to move the dining table and chairs. Elaine and Beth piled bedding and clothes on the sofa while the heavy table was being relocated. Then, the ladies could pile it as high as they desired. Randy and I took some deep breaths after exertions and drank some water. He was getting tuckered, too, and he was an athlete, thirty plus years younger than me.

I needed a break, so I suggested to Beth and Elaine, "Let's go to the bank so I can arrange for the transfer of funds and Beth can get information on setting up accounts. She might not like our bank."

"Recess!" Elaine announced with some laughter. "I'm practicing my teacher's language."

"Mrs. Sandoval, that's for grade school," grinned Randy.

I was the first to get my coat on and eye the possessions heaped in the garage. I stood there estimating the volume and quickly decided we would need a fifteen foot truck. We might not fill it up, but Beth and Randy might, depending on the amount of furniture they want to bring back to Butte. After our trip to the bank, we'd drop by the U-Haul office and rent a truck for a round trip. I figured to pay the entire cost, unless Beth volunteered half—kind of like treating the Erickson's to dinner. I imagined Beth was going to be helping Randy with college expenses, so they could use all the money they could lay their hands on. I'm sure they still owe money on former business obligations. A university education is two to three times more expensive now than when Elaine and I were going to school.

I wired the payment to the bank in Suddenly in care of Arlene Stafford Realty. I'd verify the payment with Arlene when we returned to our new mountain home. Beth told me the bank president is Mr. Bruce Isaacs. His wife's name is Sarah and the Isaacs have a daughter, Megan, the same age as Randy.

After being at the bank for thirty minutes, we left to rent a truck. Randy rode with me as I drove the truck through residential neighborhoods. Curious eyes watched, especially from our nearest neighbors as I backed into our driveway. It had been a significant time since I backed a truck and it took some jostling around to get the beast lined up with the garage door so loading would be easily accomplished. Fortunately, the U-Haul people gave us instructions for loading.

When Randy and I were beginning to load the mattresses and dining table, Beth suggested something I would never have thought of, a fire extinguisher for the truck.

Elaine beckoned to me to say something, "Be careful and don't pull any muscles. You'll have to unload and help Beth and Randy load their things. Beth and I are going to buy an extinguisher—just to be on the safe side."

The ladies took the car and left Randy and me to slave away packing the heavy items. We decided to work together and move one thing at a time even though some articles were not heavy, just awkward. Randy grinned and observed, "That's to conserve our strength." I gave him a thumbs up.

By the time the ladies returned from shopping, the truck was loaded. I decided to take our sixty-five inch TV. There was plenty of space and the last thing I loaded was the dining room picture Elaine was fond of. I wrapped it in a blanket and put it on top of containers of clothes. When I saw the extinguisher, I commented to Elaine, "Was that the biggest you could find?" I thought a smaller model would be adequate.

She gave me a heavy sigh and a killer stare. "No, Efren. We stopped at a fire station and got some advice. The gentlemen suggested this one, so I bought it. Beth said they have one in Suddenly. They'll bring theirs to Butte."

That was good thinking, I couldn't criticize the women for doing a smart thing. "Good job, ladies, very smart. Should we have some lunch before hitting the road?"

Beth volunteered, "Elaine and I bought some burgers and fries. We didn't want to leave any dirty dishes. We'll have coffee or soft drinks. Elaine said you have enough for all of us, coffee and pop."

A half-hour later, we had used the bathroom, locked the house and were headed south on Route 15, the ladies in the car, Randy and I following in the truck. Randy had the fire extinguisher stored at his feet for easy access.

Elaine never exceeded fifty-five miles per hour. It seemed like every car and truck on the road passed us but I liked the comfortable pace and enjoyed talking with Randy as we followed the women for slightly over an hour. Elaine and Beth didn't stop in Dillon, took the turnoff to Suddenly and slowed to thirty miles per hour.

Randy commented, "I think your wife is being over-cautious, Mr. Sandoval. The place most people back off the gas is about ten miles from town where the road narrows and curves through the big trees."

"That's roughly where the road to Mr. Duggar's place is, isn't it?"

"Yeah, that's about right. I remember one time when a bunch of us rode our bikes out there to check on the old guy." Randy laughed, "He ran us off. Said he didn't need any help. It was a good ride though; a couple of girls came with us and we stopped and tossed rocks into a creek. We kidded the girls and told them to look in the water for gold nuggets. They waded in and we splashed them. They got mad but it was hot that day and eventually everyone got wet to cool off. We sat down in the water."

"Did you blame them for getting mad?"

"Naw, we just wanted to get their shirts wet. Kind of stupid I guess. That was a couple of years ago during the summer."

"Let me know when we get close to Duggar's turn off. I'm curious to see how his house looks from the road when we're going slow."

I glanced at Randy as he watched the trees. A few minutes passed and he said, "It's about five miles from here."

I figured in six to seven minutes and we'd see Duggar's buildings in the woods. I'd slow so I could get a good look. I wanted to see what Elaine saw when we came here before. I could tell it was cooler as we made our way slightly uphill along the forest road. Patches of snow remained in the shade of trees. Shielded from the sun's rays the frozen water would undoubtedly last for days before completely melting, soaking in or evaporating.

Elaine and Beth had moved ahead and I lost sight of the car on a straight section of the road. I'll bet they wanted to get to the house and make room for the U-Haul truck. Beth would have to move their pickup away from the garage.

Randy broke the silence, "Mr. Duggar's turnoff is coming up; better slow some more if you want to take a good look."

I was watching for the turn out to the dirt access road, so backed off on the gas. The truck was moving so slowly, I could probably walk and keep up.

Randy was watching more closely than I and remarked, "It looks like Mr. Duggar is burning some trash; there's lots of smoke."

I stopped the truck to get a better look where the road flared out to the dirt lane. It appeared to me that the gray haze was coming from the house, so I told Randy to grab the extinguisher and get ready to fight a fire. I stepped on the gas and the truck lurched ahead toward the cloud of fumes. In ten seconds, I stopped the truck and yelled, "Go, Randy, shoot at the base of the flames."

"I know, Mr. Sandoval. See if you can find Mr. Duggar!" He jumped to the ground and started running toward the house carrying the red extinguisher in both hands.

I had stopped a safe distance from the house, stuck the keys in my pocket and ran after Randy.

The smoke looked as if its origin was the living room area because it was escaping from around the plywood that covered the broken window. I put both hands on the one by six that said KEEP OUT and ripped it away. Randy rammed into the door with his shoulder and broke through into the smoke filled room. I had been trained to hold my breath for up to three minutes when I was in Special Forces. I dropped to my hands and knees, took a deep breath and yelled, "Mr. Duggar! Where are you?" I heard a groan and crawled to Duggar lying on the floor under a small table. He was clutching a wad of papers. He coughed and as Randy sprayed with the extinguisher, I dragged Mr. Duggar out the front door to fresh air.

Randy appeared from the house with the extinguisher and called out, "I got the flames but the whole house is full of smoke." He coughed a couple of times, walked to the truck and leaned against the grill. I had Mr. Duggar sitting on the ground leaning against the left front tire. His eyes were bloodshot. He was wheezing and coughing but still holding onto a bunch of papers clasped tightly to his chest. I couldn't imagine why they were so important to him. After the fire got out of control he must have gone into the smoke filled room to get what looked like sheets of copier paper.

Duggar wiped his eyes with his free hand and said, "I know you. You were here a few days back with a nosy woman."

I grinned, "That's right. The sheriff brought you a box from Meals on Wheels that day."

He coughed again and inquired, "Why'd you come today with this truck?" He grimaced, grinned and said, "Delivering more meals?"

"No, sir. Randy and I are moving some furniture from Butte to Suddenly. I bought the hardware store. My wife and I are going to run the store."

"How did the fire start, Mr. Duggar?" Randy asked.

Duggar rubbed his eyes and blinked, "I knocked over one of my oil lamps like a damned fool, pure carelessness. I guess I'll have to sleep outside tonight. The smoke will be gone by tomorrow. I can build a fire in the pit out back. That'll keep me warm enough."

Chapter 7

I glanced at Randy and shook my head. Randy frowned and Duggar coughed again, more violently. Duggar's eyes closed and I mouthed 'hospital' to my travel buddy. He nodded.

"We're taking you into Suddenly so a doctor can check your lungs, Mr. Duggar. You'd better cooperate or we'll hogtie you. Are you going to come with us quietly?"

He eyed both of us and said, "Well, I guess I'd better do what you say. You're both bigger than me." He looked back at his house and remarked, "I guess there's no sense in locking up. There's not much in there I'd be afraid to lose. I got to keep these papers, though. I spent lots of time on 'em."

"Okay. You hang onto the papers and we'll get you in the truck sitting between us."

I got in the cab and slid over to the passenger side. With me pulling and Randy pushing, we sandwiched Duggar between us. I backed the truck to the road and drove to Suddenly at twenty-five miles per hour. All three of us coughed at some point before reaching the hospital. Randy gave me directions since I had never been there before.

I parked the truck far enough away from the hospital entrance so it didn't interfere with passenger vehicle traffic and made sure I wasn't blocking the emergency room entrance. I asked Randy to run ahead and get a wheelchair for Mr. Duggar. Randy and I could carry him but the mobile chair seemed a better approach, a lot safer for all.

Mr. Duggar and I waited for a short time when Randy and a nurse came rushing toward the truck pushing a wheelchair. Randy looked like he was a charging lineman shoving a heavy sled at football practice. I figured he was having some trouble getting his breath after inhalation of smoke. I felt fine, but I didn't get but a whiff of fine gray particles from the fire. Randy had gotten his lungs full and was now feeling the results of the exposure. That's when I thought we should all be checked by a doctor.

The nurse took over when the chair reached the truck. She said, "I'm nurse Berg. You all need to come to the emergency room for a checkup. I want to listen to your lungs." I recalled a drill sergeant from army training camp, same style and just as insistent.

Randy and I wrestled Mr. Duggar into the wheelchair and nurse Berg started pushing it with Randy and me trailing behind. The automatic door opened and we followed the nurse to the ER. She didn't bother to get her patient on an examination table or gurney before she had a stethoscope listening to sounds from Duggar's chest. He sat seemingly drained of normal color taking shallow breaths. Nurse Berg didn't look away from her patient but directed Randy and me to take a seat.

A male nurse appeared from the main hallway and surveyed the situation. I read the monogramed name from his light-blue hospital jacket. He wasn't a nurse, he was Dr. Rennick.

"What have we got here, Mrs. Berg?"

"Smoke from a fire at Duggar's. All of them inhaled fumes but Samuel got the worst of it. I don't know what burned."

Duggar croaked, "An oil lamp broke and set the fire. I did it—by accident."

Another nurse entered the small room and asked, "Mr. Duggar, can you tell me your birthdate?"

I watched as he tried to breathe more deeply, coughed and said, "Five, nine, thirty four."

That made Mr. Duggar almost ninety. It was just a month until his birthday. Does he even realize his birth date is four weeks away? Since he lives ten miles from Suddenly with no electrical power or ways to communicate with residents of the town, he probably isn't aware of calendar dates. Dr. Rennick took over from nurse Berg and ordered oxygen for Mr. Duggar. He then came over to talk with me.

"I'm Doctor Rennick. You are new to Suddenly, aren't you?"

I stood and shook hands with the doctor and introduced myself. "My wife and I just purchased Erickson's hardware store. We were living in Butte but wanted to run a small business enterprise for a few years before we retired permanently."

He nodded and said, "I know Randy. I gave him his physical so he could play football. He's a good kid."

I continued, "Randy and I were driving a U-Haul truck past Duggar's and Randy was the first to notice the smoke. He attacked the fire and I pulled the old guy from the smoky inside of his house. Duggar was on the floor clutching a bunch of papers. They seemed to be of great importance to him."

"Well, Samuel is a tough old bird. He seems to avoid contact with others but I've never seen him openly hostile. I'll keep him overnight and release him in the morning after breakfast. We'll give him a good meal. Do you want to pick him up and take him home?"

I didn't hesitate, "Sure, I'd like to see the damage to his house. Elaine and I can help clean up and fix a few things. What time should I come by?"

"We'll have him ready to go by nine o'clock. Would that work for you?"

"Sure, that's fine. How is Randy doing?"

"Oh, he's fine. I had a nurse take him to another room for some oxygen therapy. Let me listen to your heart and lungs. If you're okay, you and Randy can leave."

Ten minutes later, Randy and I were headed for the front door when I heard, "Mr. Sandoval, your wife is on the phone."

It was the admissions desk and a woman was pointing at me with a phone. I had forgotten about Elaine and Beth because of the excitement of Mr. Duggar's problems. I should have had the hospital call Erickson's number to inform the women of our delay. I put the phone to my ear and said, "Hi, Elaine."

"Efren, what happened? Were you or Randy injured?"

"Elaine, we had a slight delay. We'll be there in about ten minutes and tell you all about it."

"I called the police and they said you might be at the hospital, so I called the main number. What happened?"

"I don't want to be on the hospital phone, Elaine. Someone might need to call for an emergency. Randy and I will see you in ten minutes. We'll tell you what happened. Bye."

"Randy, can you drive the truck?"

"Sure, let's go."

I figured if Randy drove we would shave at least a minute off our travel time, so I tossed him the keys and we jogged to the truck. I checked my watch when we arrived at the Ericksons'. It took us only eight minutes to travel from the hospital. Randy backed the truck to within ten feet of the garage and shut off the engine. Elaine met us and said, "I'm so glad you guys are all right. What in the devil happened?"

"It was Randy's fault," I laughed as he joined us. "No, I'm kidding. When we slowed down for me to look at Mr. Duggar's place, Randy saw smoke. At first we thought Duggar was burning trash but it wasn't trash, his house was on fire. We broke in through the front door, put out the fire and dragged Mr. Duggar out of the house." I coughed slightly and took a deep breath. "And then we took Mr. Duggar to the hospital. He's staying overnight."

"They put him on oxygen. He got a snoot full of smoke," said Randy.

I added, "Dr. Rennick checked us out at the hospital. I guess they didn't charge us anything. They didn't ask for any insurance info or bill us."

Elaine hugged me and said, "I'm glad you are all right. You need to change your shirt; I can smell smoke. Then you can start unloading. Beth and I made plenty of room in the garage."

I watched as Beth sniffed Randy's jacket and shirt and ruffled his hair, she said, "I might start calling you smoky. Oh, after you finish unloading, we'll have dinner. You should have a good appetite."

Randy grinned, "I'm hungry now, Mom."

"That's not unusual. You're hungry all the time." Beth returned to the house. Randy and I began unloading the truck with some of Elaine's assistance. She wanted to take care of the bedding and clothes to make sure heavy objects weren't piled on top of them. In slightly less than a half hour, the truck was empty.

I looked at my watch. It was a few minutes past five thirty. I was ready for a break and needed dinner to recharge. What could Beth have for us to eat? I doubted if it would be anything special since Randy and his mother would be leaving in the morning. Surely Beth would be taking certain foodstuffs that were mainstays to the Ericksons. But then I imagined Elaine and Beth must have discussed ingredients they would be leaving in each other's cabinets and refrigerators. I couldn't remember Elaine packing anything from our kitchen but she might have placed a few items in boxes and loaded them without any help. I kind of hoped we would have something like pizza delivered. Suddenly must have a pizza place, a Pizza Hut or similar establishment.

It didn't take long for me to find out about an Italian style baked pie. Beth must have had at least one frozen pizza in her freezer. My nose led me into the kitchen where I was shooed away by both women. I had to wash and change my clothes before I was allowed to sit at the dinner table. I couldn't smell anything, but with Beth and Elaine insisting, I found some clothes in the garage boxes and changed in the bathroom, washed my hands and combed my hair. My hair probably had some smoke residue but I had to stop removing smoke odor from my system at some point. I'll take care of my hair in the shower after we've loaded the truck for the return trip to Butte.

We completed dinner by seven and with the garage lights illuminating the truck's cargo area, Randy and I loaded all the heavy stuff and most of Beth's boxes. Randy packed his clothes in two large boxes. A hunting bow, a dozen arrows, a twenty-two rifle and a fielder's baseball glove completed his possessions and were all loaded. He helped his mom with last minute items and locked the truck for the night.

We weren't finished yet. We had to set up beds, bring in the dining table and chairs and other items so sleeping accommodations for four were available. Nine o'clock arrived and passed and we were all noticeably slowing down. We took opportunities to sit and catch our breath whenever possible. Loading and unloading, reloading and fighting a fire had robbed Randy and me of the spark we had when the day started. I was pooped and so was Randy, although he was much younger and in better shape than me.

As I sat on the sofa taking some deep breaths, I realized the young man would be by himself when unloading the heavy items in Butte. I'll have Elaine give him our former neighbors' numbers so he can request some helping hands. Without any warning, Elaine appeared behind me and put her hands around my neck. A well-deserved neck and shoulders massage ensued. Beth noticed our activity and motioned for Randy to sit in one of our dining chairs. As soon as she began a message, Randy leaned forward and placed his head on his arms resting on the table.

"That feels so good, Mom. When I get married, my wife has to learn how to give massages."

I smiled and Elaine bopped me on the head, she knew exactly what I was thinking.

With Ericksons' belongings loaded and most of our things close to their destination or minimally scattered throughout various rooms, we prepared for a full night of restful sleep. All of our bones and muscles needed slumber to regenerate. Beth and son would be leaving us for Butte in the morning. I hoped Beth could spell Randy so he wouldn't have to drive the truck the entire distance. Randy might get tired after working so hard today and fall asleep while on the hourlong drive. I'll mention my thoughts to Beth in the morning.

There was another important task, I had to remember to visit the hospital and give Mr. Duggar a ride home. The medical facility was only about ten minutes away, so I could leave our new home at eight-fifty. I wrote on a small notepad Elaine kept in her purse and put the message in my shirt pocket so half of it was sticking out. That would be enough to get my attention as I dressed before eating breakfast.

When ten o'clock arrived, we were all in bed.

Chapter 8

Beth was up and in the kitchen by seven o'clock. Elaine and I heard the muted noises and hurried to help with the Ericksons' last breakfast in their Suddenly home. I made coffee while the women cooked sausage and eggs. Randy reached his long youthful arms past his mother, made toast and then disappeared from the kitchen. I followed him outside and we checked the truck tires. No problems were found so we returned inside to eat.

By eight thirty, we said goodbye to Ericksons. Beth planned on driving their pickup to Dillon and the U-Haul chugged out into the street with Randy behind the steering wheel. Elaine looked concerned at the sounds and asked, "Is there something wrong with the engine?"

I nodded, "Yes, it has a Suddenly cold. It'll be fine when he gets on the road." We watched as the truck stopped at the corner, turned left and disappeared from sight behind trees and houses.

Elaine reflected, "I'm kind of sorry to see them go, Efren. They are so nice."

"We'll see them again. We know where they live in Butte. Next time we go to the city we'll stop and say hello. Beth might contact us about something she forgot to pack. We can deliver . . . like UPS."

Elaine had a death grip on my left arm and started pulling. "Let's go inside and move a few things around before you have to transport Mr. Duggar."

I had momentarily forgotten about Mr. Duggar and checked my watch; it was eight forty. I had ten minutes before taxi service began. Elaine had begun to transfer clothing from haphazard piles to organized closets in the master bedroom. She handed me a few items to hang at my end of the narrow walk-in along the wall to the outside.

Conscious of the time, I said, "I've got to pick up Mr. Duggar and take him home. I should be back in about an hour . . . about ten o'clock. We'll see Mrs. Stafford about document signing this afternoon."

"Won't Beth have to sign too?"

"Don't worry about Beth, dear. Arlene will undoubtedly send her some things to sign. See you later."

I felt a slight bit of guilt as I drove away, leaving Elaine to do all the sorting and organizing, but she was much better at the task than I could ever be. I pulled into the hospital parking area at exactly nine o'clock. When I entered the building, a nurse I had never seen before approached.

"By any chance are you Mr. Sandoval?"

"Yes. I've come to give Mr. Duggar a ride home. Is he ready to go?"

"She smiled and replied, "He's already gone. We couldn't keep him against his will. Dr. Rennick said we had to release him."

"Who gave him a ride?"

"I don't know. He just walked out. I guess he's walking home."

"Okay. Thank you. I'll see if I can find him. He lives ten miles from here. When did he leave?"

Nurse Cooper glanced at her watch, "About an hour ago, sir."

"Thank you, I'll see if I can find him."

A quick calculation meant Samuel could have walked nearly three miles unless someone gave him a ride or he developed a cramp of some sort which would have slowed him down. I'll start down the road toward Dillon. Maybe I'll get lucky and find him.

Twenty five miles per hour on the highway was too slow for cars going to Dillon. Horns blared and dirty looks didn't deter me, vehicles passed as soon as it was advantageous. I watched both road shoulders for Mr. Duggar for two miles and was getting disappointed. He might have gotten a ride and already be home. Just as I decided to speed up to thirty, I saw him sitting on the trunk of a downed tree about ten yards off the left shoulder.

I pulled off on the right and stopped. The road was devoid of traffic, so I walked across the blacktop and called out, "Mr. Duggar, can I offer you a ride?"

He looked up from the ground and answered, "I don't know. You gonna rob me?"

I had to laugh. "No, Mr. Duggar. Don't you remember me? Randy Erickson and I took you to the hospital in a U-Haul truck. My name is Efren Sandoval. We met a couple of days ago when Sheriff Wilson delivered a container of food to you. My wife had looked in your window and you scared her."

He stood up holding a plastic hospital hand bag containing jumbled papers. He was wearing a different coat than before, something he obviously had been given by the hospital staff. It looked fairly new and more substantial than his previous garment. When he stepped forward, he nearly fell, so I rushed over to give him support.

"I stepped on a rock and turned my damn ankle. There aren't any sidewalks out here."

"Come on, lean on me. I'll give you a ride in my car. I want to see the damage to your house caused by the fire. Maybe I can help you repair things. I'm good at those activities. My wife and I bought the hardware store in Suddenly. I think there are some things I can donate to you."

He gave a shallow cough, "Like coordination or brains?"

I chuckled, "I'm afraid I can't help you there, those are better served by the hospital. Come on, Mr. Duggar, show me your house."

I helped Samuel into the front passenger seat and we were off at thirty miles per hour. No one passed us but there was no traffic, either coming or going. It took us about fifteen minutes to reach his turnoff. He surveyed his home with eagle eyes as we approached. I assumed he was looking for damage caused by riffraff or sightseers.

I parked a few feet from the front door where Randy and I entered during the fire. The door wouldn't require much to fix it, some clamps, a little glue and some longer screws for the hinges. I could smell the odor of burned wood when we entered the main room where the small table remained on its side but remarkably unburned. His chair had suffered; one leg was broken off and the paint scorched. The floor was blackened and strewn with small chunks of broken glass from the oil lamp disaster. I watched as Samuel hung his papers on a nail protruding from the closest wall. I hadn't asked him about his papers, thinking he would eventually tell me what they dealt with. Perhaps he was writing a book or keeping a log of his activities, he certainly had a long rich life to record for posterity.

"You have some time to invest in clean up, Mr. Sandoval?"

"Sure, do you have a broom and dustpan?"

"I do. Wait one moment." He went into a back room and reappeared with another chair, a broom and dustpan. He sat in the chair and held out a well-used broom and shiny metal scoop. I assumed I was being put to work while he rested. But that was not the case. As I began to sweep and collect refuse, Samuel limped to retrieve his papers and returned to his little table.

He must have been observing my progress, for a minute later he commented, "There's a barrel out back, just toss that stuff in with the garbage. I'll burn it later when the barrel is full."

With the broken glass and wood splinters processed, I noticed the ceiling and walls were soot-covered. A broom was not the correct implement for removing soot. Soap, water and rags were needed and maybe some air freshener.

I told Elaine I would be back in an hour or so, and I was going to be at least fifteen minutes overdue. I had to leave Samuel to his own resources until after lunch. I asked, "Have you got something to eat for lunch, Samuel?"

He looked up from his papers and frowned, "Lunch? No, I don't eat lunch. They fed me plenty at the hospital. I'll warm up some soup and have peanut butter and crackers this evening. You have to be goin'?"

"That's right, I told my wife I'd be back at ten. It's after ten now."

"You'd better get a move on then. You don't want your wife unhappy with you."

"Right. I'll be back this afternoon with some more cleaning supplies."

He flipped his hand at me as if to brush away a fly. I leaned the broom against the wall and exited through the front door.

Since I was used to the road to town, I stepped on the gas and except for one tight curve, I kept my speed at forty until entering the city limits. Driving at twenty-five miles per hour almost felt like walking.

Elaine was sitting on the front steps waiting for me. I was twenty minutes late. I explained my tardiness telling her what I had done to find Samuel and clean up the mess on the floor of his home. I told her I wanted to go back after lunch with cleaning supplies to scrub soot from the walls and ceiling.

Elaine listened intently and said, "Good for you, but I got a call from Arlene. She has some papers for us to sign and keys for the hardware building. We're to meet with her at one o'clock. Cleaning at Duggar's will have to wait until later."

"That's okay, Samuel seems devoted to his papers. I've wondered why they are so important. He didn't express much interest in cleanup from the fire and he didn't have any desire for lunch, just plans for dinner."

"Don't you think he's suffering from dementia . . . a little bit? I mean, the way he acts."

"I don't think that's his problem, he's just got a one-track mind—thinking about his papers. He doesn't want to be bothered with mundane things. I'm wondering if he has a project in mind and he wants to finish it before he passes."

I took Elaine's hand and entered our new house. "Let's do more unpacking, have lunch, see Arlene and go to our store. I want to take another look at our inventory. Oh, I want to get some soap and rags to clean soot deposited on the interior of Duggar's house."

Elaine answered, "I'll put cleanup stuff in the car."

We signed two more documents, received keys to the store and were out of the realty office by one-thirty. Arlene was going to correspond with Beth to complete Erickson's part of the transaction. As soon as we stepped out of her office, we exhaled simultaneously and laughed at our coordinated breathing. Only a few people were on foot coming and going to various stores. We didn't see anyone we recognized, but that wasn't unusual, having spent little time in Suddenly's downtown area.

I held out the keys and said, "Would you like to ride to your luxury purchase, madame?"

"No, Ef, let's walk and save gas. You'll need it when you drive to see Samuel." Elaine began walking, "I have an idea for you."

"What's that?" I hurriedly caught up.

"Something I saw when we investigated the store the other day. You'll see."

Elaine had me buffaloed. I couldn't fathom what she was thinking about without any overt clues.

We walked to the store in silence until I unlocked the big entrance door and closed it behind us.

Elaine said, "Follow me upstairs."

Aha, her idea involved something she had seen on the balcony, a part of the store I hadn't yet visited. No wonder I couldn't conjure up anything useful. I have never possessed any psychic ability.

Is there is a men's intuition like women are purported to possess? I followed Elaine to the rear of the balcony and she pointed at a large cardboard and wood framed container.

She looked at me and asked, "Is that thing what I think it is or is it an empty shipping container?"

I tried to lift one end and found the box wasn't empty. I didn't recognize the product name so I said, "I need a hammer. I'll be right back."

"Hurry, Efren. I'm dying to see if my hunch is correct."

I held onto the railing and took two steps at a time to the ground floor. I remembered where the hammers were, grabbed a clawhammer and rushed back upstairs. I pried apart the crate and cut open the cardboard box with my pocketknife. Inside was a gas powered electric generator.

Elaine exclaimed, "I thought so. It's not new though, is it?"

"No. It must be a demo model. It has some scratches and a small dent. Maybe it was damaged in shipping and someone refused the purchase. I'll bet the supplier didn't want it back either—it's a freebie.

Elaine stepped closer to see the unit. "Do you think Mr. Duggar could use it? He could retire his oil lamps."

"God, what a great idea, Elaine." I gave her a big kiss and hug. "Mr. Duggar will be intoxicated having electric lights!"

"We can toss in a hotplate, too," she said. "He can have some warm food without setting himself on fire."

I grinned, "He might find a way."

Chapter 9

Stuffed inside the crate was a thick, sealed Manila envelope labeled in large red letters: INSTRUCTIONS. I sat on the balcony steps and scanned through the ten pages. Most of the information was not new to me, having helped install a similar unit before in the Colorado mountains. All I needed to get the generator operating was some fuel line hoses, a propane tank and the appropriate tools. Fortunately, Elaine was tool conscious and began gathering them as I wrestled the AC power source to the ground floor. An elevator would have been handy.

"We have two barbeque propane tanks, Ef. Do you want both of them?"

"Can you tell if they are full or empty . . . or partly full?"

"How can I tell? There's no gauge."

"Let's consult with an expert, Mr. Internet. There's a computer in the office. See if you can get online."

As Elaine sought an answer to my question, I retrieved our car from in front of the realtor's office. I loaded the generator into our SUV and tossed in a canvas bag of tools. I found three and six foot gas hoses and added one of each length to the cargo area.

Elaine had carried the tanks to the bathroom and came back a couple minutes later exhibiting a big smile.

"They're both full!"

"Great! I'll load them. Where are they?"

"In the shower stall in the bathroom. They're a little wet."

"You washed them in the shower? They were that dirty?"

"They weren't dirty, Efren. I just followed some directions from the NET. Let's dry the tanks and put them in the car. I'm going with you to see Mr. Duggar."

I chuckled, "I don't think he's very fond of you because you looked through his window."

"Oh, phooey. He won't even remember."

I looked over the supplies in the car and started to lower the rear door. Shoot! I had forgotten some key items, two electrical boxes for outlets, a spool of twelve gauge wire, a battery operated hand drill and drill bits. I tossed everything in the cargo area, shut the cargo door and locked the building. We were off to see Mr. Duggar. I hoped he wouldn't object to having electricity. It might change his life.

On the way out of town I voiced some thoughts to Elaine. She sat silently while we drove about a mile before responding.

"Do you think Mr. Duggar will protest? I guess he might say we are meddling in his affairs," Elaine remarked. "When I found the generator, I didn't consider he might object. He's been without modern conveniences for so long."

"I think we can talk him into making a change, especially after he nearly burned his house down with him inside."

"Well, I certainly hope so."

I glanced at her and speculated, she's got something else on her mind. She was staring out the windshield and biting her lower lip. I couldn't imagine what's brewing in her pretty head.

Ten minutes later, we pulled up in front of Samuel's home. It looked just as barren as the first time we were there, when we made our first trip to Suddenly, except the sign from the door was leaning against the outside wall under the boarded up window.

As we exited our car, Samuel limped from the front door and greeted us with a big wave. He actually seemed to be pleased that we had come to see him. What's he going to say or do when he realizes our intentions. I hope the sheriff is right, his gun doesn't work.

We shook hands and I said, "You remember my wife, Elaine, don't you?"

"Yeah, the nosy one, looking in windows." He grinned, "But that's okay, she's with you. I trust you."

"You can use our first names, Samuel. Elaine and Efren."

He gave a hearty laugh. "Which one are you?" We joined in the laughter and I said, "We brought you something. I want you to take a look. It will change your life."

He cocked his head to the right and frowned. "You brought me something? What is it?"

"It's a gas powered electric generator. It will give you electric lights so you can work on your papers without them getting ignited from burning oil."

"You'll have to show me. Let me take a look. I might not want it."

I opened the rear door on the cargo compartment and pointed at the gray and black generator encased in heavy cardboard. Samuel limped over and took a long look.

"How does it work?" There was no doubt he was skeptical.

"Well, it runs off propane. It's like a steam engine that makes electricity."

"I've been told about them propane tanks exploding. Is it gonna be in my house? I won't have it in my house."

"It won't be in your house, it runs outside. You won't even hear it running. I'll put it far enough from your house so there's no risk of an explosion. Do you have any sacks of concrete, Samuel?"

He shook his head and said, "Nope. How about some bricks, like ones used in chimneys?"

"That will work. We just need to mount the unit on a solid flat surface."

Mr. Duggar seemed satisfied with the location I picked. I flattened the ground and he helped lay out a three by four foot rectangular footprint of bricks taken from a jumbled pile behind his house. I backed the car to the site and manhandled the heavy cardboard container onto the flat surface. After cutting away the packaging, I attached one of the gas hoses and Elaine handed me a wrench to tighten the connection. After attaching one propane tank to the other end of the hose, I said, "Let's take a break and then figure out where you want lights inside your house."

Samuel was pleased to assist inside. I was going to mark locations on the walls and ceiling but he prevented my actions. He sat at his table in the middle of the room and used a sheet of paper to sketch the interior of the house marking preferred locations for lights and switches. We discussed positions I chose from my experience with electrical wiring. Samuel acquiesced and nodded in agreement after I explained.

While we talked, Elaine retrieved the wire and tools from the car. She remembered her acquaintance with hardware from our previous business. She dropped the material in a pile by the front door and wiped the adjacent wall with her fingers.

"There must be soot everywhere, Efren. I don't think anybody should be getting it in their system. It can't be good for a person's health."

"If you could start cleaning, I'll start wiring with assistance from Samuel. I know you didn't want to be put to work."

Elaine grinned, "Whatever made you think that? A woman's work is never finished. I'll get the cleaning materials."

Samuel and I discussed where to bring in the lines from the generator. It was either from a pole to the attic or burying the lines in the ground and bringing them in from the floor. Samuel took only a second to say, "From the ground, Efren. Snow and ice might cause a problem with elevated wires."

"Okay, then, we'll have to dig a trench eighteen inches deep. I'll bring some more materials tomorrow so we can finish the job. We'll help Elaine with the soot cleanup this afternoon, electricity will be installed when we have more tools."

Samuel stood there like a totem pole with his eyes fixed on me in a hard stare. "How much is this gonna cost me, Efren?"

"Not one cent, Samuel. This unit is a gift from us. It was abandoned property because it had some cosmetic imperfections. Elaine and I want to get it out of our store and we thought you could use the upgrade to your house."

"I can pay for the installation materials, I'm not a poor man like everyone thinks. I had a deal with Mr. Erickson and when he passed, Mr. Isaacs at the bank took over the agreement."

"I don't think the total cost will exceed about a hundred dollars for supplies. Let's not worry about the expenses. Perhaps you can do something for us sometime." I thought for a moment and had a sudden idea, "How about supplying Elaine and me with firewood for next winter?"

He nodded vigorously, "Say, now that's a good idea. There's a couple of downed trees on my property but I need some muscle to cut them into firewood."

"Let's not bother with it now, bad weather is six months away."

"Six months?" He reflected for a moment, "That's about right, but bad elements hit with a fury when it's their time. No one is spared in these mountains."

We ignored the wiring and tools for over an hour as we set about the job of scrubbing every surface that might have a layer of soot, no matter how thin, blanketing it. Samuel was the first to utter, "My arms are tired, I have to take a break and get something to drink."

Elaine and I stepped back from the wall we were scrubbing and nodded to each other. It was time to relax for a few minutes. We had water in the car, but Samuel came from his bedroom carrying a bottle and three medium sized glasses.

"Here. Take a nip. It'll take the soreness out'a your muscles."

Elaine balked, "May I see that bottle, Mr. Duggar?"

"Why, sure. I guess so. It's just a bottle of whisky I got at New Years Eve two years ago. I'm not much of a drinker myself, use it for medicinal purposes—usually," he grinned.

Elaine inspected the half-full bottle, uncorked it and took a whiff. She looked at me and commented, "It's whisky all right and I don't see any worms."

"I know it will burn going down, but I don't mind a small amount. It's been a long time since those army days."

We watched Samuel clear the table of his papers and pour about an ounce of booze into each glass.

"I poked Elaine, grinned and said, "Get ready for a shock to your system." I was sure she had never consumed any whisky or actually knew how it smelled. But she had heard somewhere about worms in an alcoholic drink. I'll ask her later. I raised my glass, said, "Bottoms up," and downed the whisky in one daring gulp, trying to preserve some sense of machismo.

Samuel downed his drink without blinking an eye and said, "Now that'll tie your shoestrings in a knot."

Elaine had watched us, took a tiny sip, just enough to wet her lips and gave it to me. "I can't drink that, Efren. That's paint thinner."

I had to agree with her evaluation, but I hadn't wanted to disappoint Samuel. It obviously wasn't a big deal for him and he seemed to understand Elaine's negativity.

I poured Elaine's portion back in the bottle and handed it to Samuel. "Thank you. Let's install some wiring. Do you have any heavy staples, tacks, or roofing nails?"

He stroked his scraggly beard and went into a back room. He returned with a small wooden box and a large glass jar, both full of assorted nails and fasteners. "Can you find what you need in these?"

I asked, "Have you got an old newspaper?"

He looked at me as if I were crazy, then said, "Jest pour 'em out on the table and pick out what you can use."

I inverted the box and found what I needed to get started. Elaine opened the coil of wiring and I moved a chair so I could reach the ceiling. I tacked the wire overhead from the center of the room to the wall in line with the generator and ran the conductor down the wall to the floor. That was all I could do for today. I had to drill through the floor and make the connection to the generator tomorrow. I now knew what other tools I needed and also at least twenty-five feet of conduit.

"Will you be warm enough staying here tonight?" I asked Samuel. I was going to offer him a bed in our house but he seemed prepared for a cold night without a furnace.

"You bet. I'll start fires in my potbellied stove and in the fire-place. I've got plenty of wood out back. Come with me, I'll show yah."

Elaine said, "I'll wait in the car."

I followed Samuel through the house to the backyard. I saw a mechanical log splitter and about two cords of dried wood stacked against the back wall and covered with tarps. I could readily see he was prepared to stay warm for tough times during the winter months. But what did he do for food?

Elaine and I said goodbye after telling Samuel we would return tomorrow with supplies to complete the installation. He waved, limped into the house and closed the front door as we drove away.

Chapter 10

"What do you think he is doing with those papers, Efren? I haven't had a chance to see what's on them. Do you think he's writing his memoirs?"

"I really don't know, Elaine. But Samuel isn't a very learned man, he grew up in the nineteen thirties and forties, during the depression and the second world war. He probably had to work and didn't have much time or opportunities for much education."

"But he was Sheriff of Suddenly for a long time."

"Yes, about fifteen years. Then he went prospecting and married Margret, the artist that painted the picture we admired at the B and B. She was somebody he arrested once. I bet it was for smoking weed."

"You're probably right. It wasn't as well received back then."

"I have to go to the bank and talk with Mr. Isaacs. Maybe he will provide more details about Duggar. The old man told me he wasn't destitute like rumor has it."

Elaine sat there quietly as we rolled into our driveway. I started to get out of the car and she suggested, "Maybe he found gold. He might have a mine and pays for everything in gold."

"I don't think so. He lives like a hermit, or a monk. If he had money, don't you believe he would have a few modern things? I don't think he even owns a flashlight. He's using oil lamps for light.

Those were given up eighty years ago, well, maybe not out here in the mountains."

"When did electricity come to Suddenly?"

"You got me there. Come on, let's go inside, relax, eat dinner and go to our store to work for a couple of hours. We need to have an opening before too long so we have funds coming in, not going out all the time. I don't have much appreciation for red ink."

It was seven thirty when we entered the front door of the store. We closed and locked the door and stood there surveying the organization of stock and locating spots that needed systemization.

I exhaled, "Where do we start?"

Elaine answered, "I'm going in the office to see what I have to work with."

"Okay, I'll pick a spot and get started. No telling what I'll encounter." I chose nails and discovered little organization. Just as I started separating common nails from galvanized, a loud knock from the entryway startled me. I turned toward the door and saw Sheriff Wilson shining a bright light into our storefront windows and flashing blue lights reflecting in the windows.

I waved to him and opened the door. "Hello. What can I do for you?"

"I was driving down Main and noticed your lights. No other stores are open in the evening, so I thought I'd better investigate. I was worried about a break in. Why are you working after normal hours?"

"Elaine and I spent the day out at Duggar's. On the way home, we decided to start getting a few things organized at the store so before long we can open for business. We would like to get some money coming in soon." I laughed, "I just started organizing nails, they're in complete disarray. I believe the Ericksons were overwhelmed and unable to keep up with demand."

"I believe your analysis is right on. Beth and Randy started losing interest in the store after Stan died. It became an anchor around their necks. If you need help during the summer, my stepson, David, will be home from college in a couple of months. I'm sure he'll be looking for part-time employment and he knows the area almost as well as his forest ranger mother. He operates a lawn service and is acquainted with nearly everyone in Suddenly."

"Thanks for the tip. David could be very useful—a big help."

"Well, I'll let you get back to work. Good night."

"Thanks for stopping by. Good night."

I watched Scott return to his car and extinguish the flashing blue lights. I stood there for a moment contemplating what he said and returned to sorting nails. Bulk nails were in bins and small boxes were organized according to size. There were numerous odds and ends, so I put them on a shelf labeled: Miscellaneous."

An hour later, Elaine reported that the office was in pretty good shape and asked, "Are you going to take conduit to Duggar's in the morning?"

I had almost forgotten, so I grabbed a staple gun, staples and a package of seventy-five feet of conduit. I put the materials in the car and locked the store front door. We were finished downtown for the evening and went home.

As Elaine loaded the dishwasher and I reheated a cup of coffee, she stated, "I think I'm going to have dreams about Mr. Duggar's papers. I keep wondering what he is concentrating on. Aren't you curious, too?"

"No, I'm too tired to think about Mr. Duggar's papers. I just don't care. I'll bet he's just doodling to pass time. It's not important. As soon as I drink this coffee, I'm going to bed. We can talk about it in the morning, okay?"

"Oh, all right, but I still think he's hiding something."

I slept so soundly, dynamite exploding outside our windows wouldn't have awakened me. I didn't stir until I smelled coffee brewing. It was eight o'clock, an hour later than my normal wakeup time. Before dressing, I started for the bathroom, but it wasn't where my instincts directed my movements. I opened the door to a bedroom. The bathroom was in the other direction. "Jesus!" I exclaimed. Talk about creature of habit! I laughed, spun around and found the toilet. I must reprogram for the new house.

After dressing, I reported to the kitchen where Elaine made some toast and gave me a mug of coffee. She remembered grape jelly, my favorite spread for morning toast. She usually had oatmeal or Total cereal and tea, but this morning she had a bowl of Wheaties.

"I'm coming with you to Duggar's, Efren. Do you mind?"

"Nope, the more the merrier. I know why, you want to find out what's on those papers."

"Well, that's only a wish but not the only thing. I want to make sure Samuel understands how to use that hotplate. I think we need to tell him how many things he can have on the system at one time."

"I was planning on telling him what the limits are. But, one thing, he trusts us, so I don't want you to do anything concerning his papers that would cause him to distrust us."

"Don't worry, I won't embarrass you." She gave me an impish grin.

I knew she had some sneaky plan in mind, but I have faith in her. I'm going to stay clear of anything tricky.

By nine o'clock we were on the road, dressed in heavy sweaters and wearing lightweight jackets that wouldn't hinder arm motion. The car thermometer indicated thirty-eight degrees, so mornings were still chilly but all traces of snow were gone. Elaine made enough sandwiches for three hungry men, so we were prepared for several hours of labor. I couldn't remember if I told her Samuel didn't eat lunch. But maybe he will join us for a bite—something to accompany an ounce of whisky. Who knows, we might start a new routine for him.

When we arrived at Duggar's, Samuel was leaning against the front door holding a steaming mug. Was it a drink or was he warming his hands with hot water? He wasn't dressed in warm clothes but the cold didn't seem to bother him. He took a drink and motioned for us to come in the house.

Surprisingly, the interior of the house was warm. I noticed a few dying embers in the fireplace.

He remarked, "I've been up since five. I hoped you would come a little sooner but now that you're here, good morning."

"Good morning. We worked at the store last evening and got a slow start today. We brought the materials to finish the job." Since Elaine had come to investigate Samuel's papers, I thought I'd prime the pump. "You know, Samuel, my wife is a talented artist. While we work, she wants to investigate the surroundings to locate a subject for a painting. Can you suggest a location?"

Elaine stepped forward and stated, "When we first arrived in Suddenly, we stayed at Jean's B and B. We saw a beautiful painting by Margret Duggar. We were told she was your wife."

"You mean Jean still has that painting? I thought it would have been sold long ago. Yeah, Margie and I got married and were out prospecting when she sketched that cabin. It was during the summer, but she wanted to make it a winter scene. I've been trying to remember just how it looked but I don't have it right yet. I'll show you my drawings. Maybe you can give me some advice about shadows and perspective."

Bingo! Samuel's papers were not secrets, he was guarding them as references as he tried to recreate the look of that cabin in the picture, only in the summer. Elaine's wish was coming true. Before Samuel and Elaine got entangled in his artwork, I asked, "I need to make a one inch hole in your floor. Do you have a drill or a chisel I can use?"

"You betcha! Just one minute." He disappeared into the back and we heard a door slam. Samuel returned holding a brace and bit, something I should have expected since he didn't seem to own any electrically operated tools.

He held them out and said, "Can you use these or do I need to help?"

I laughed, "I can use hand tools, Samuel. You and Elaine discuss your drawings."

Elaine was in artistry heaven and trying to control her excitement as Samuel displayed his sketches on the table and the floor. The table was covered with about eight sheets of paper and several more were laid on the floor as I began drilling through to the crawl space.

After I completed the hole, I went outside to the trench and extended it under the rock and cement foundation. Back inside, I fed about two feet of the conduit through the hole. I reached under the footing and grabbed the end from outside and pulled a couple of feet of tubing into the trench. I could have used a helper, but my only candidates were busy discussing cabin sketches.

Back in the house, I shoved conduit through the hole about four feet at a time, pulled from the other end, went back inside and repeated the maneuver until I reached the far end of the generator. That gave me some excess to work with. Pulling the wire through the tubing was not difficult with the addition of some bear grease, Samuel's contribution. After another thirty minutes, Samuel had his living room illuminated with two LED electric lights.

He sat on the floor in the midst of his drawings gazing at the light on the ceiling. He must have spent a least a minute fixated on the new addition to his home before he smiled and got up to shake my hand.

"Efren, you did a wonderful thing for me. How do I turn the light off?"

I handed him the remote control and pointed to the on and off buttons. "Here you go. Try it out."

He frowned, accepted the remote and stared at it. "So, all I do is press the off button?"

"Just point the remote at the generator and press off."

He started outside but I stopped him. I explained, "Just point it in the general direction, you don't have to see the generator. Radio waves penetrate the walls."

Samuel pressed the off button and the lights went off. He laughed heartily and pressed the on button. It took a few seconds and the lights came on. It was a pleasure to see the smile on his face. He reacted like a kid with a new toy at Christmas.

I explained the remote required a battery that would need to be replaced at some point, depending on use.

"So, if the battery fails how do I turn the lights on and off."

"You have to unscrew the bulbs, but there is a manual switch on the generator. You'll have to go outside. I'll get you a replacement battery. The one in the remote should last a couple of years before you need another one. Keep the new one in a handy place."

"Okay, that seems easy enough. What about the gas that runs the unit?"

"I'll order you a large tank, say a hundred gallons. It will take a few days to get one in. I'll schedule a truck to come in and fill the tank. Should I have Mr. Isaacs arrange for payment?"

Samuel nodded.

That was the first time I noticed how frail he looked. For his height, he must be twenty to thirty pounds underweight. Two meals a day were not enough for him in the cold weather, especially when I suspected the quality of the food was under suspicion.

Chapter 11

I guessed that Samuel hadn't shaved in at least two weeks. I imagined him leaning over quiet water in a stream trimming his hair and beard with a Bowie knife. Bits of whatever he ate didn't appear in his beard so he must be aware of that possibility. Perhaps he owned a mirror and comb.

The next job was to install an electrical box for plug-ins. It was easy to locate a stud behind the unfinished drywall. I cut a rectangular hole, nailed the box in place and continued the wires from the lights to the box. I didn't like to have the wiring exposed but I had no choice. I was careful to eliminate bare wire.

Elaine was watching me and asked, "Is it about time for the hotplate demo, dear?"

She rarely calls me dear when we aren't alone. She must be very comfortable in the presence of Samuel. Maybe she thinks he doesn't hear well. I assumed they were finished with their art discussion and said, "I'm ready, have at it."

I listened to her explanation of the capacity of the generator and the warning she gave Samuel. She mentioned that he should keep track of the wattage of the appliances he used so not to exceed two thousand watts. I wasn't sure of the capacity of the generator but Elaine must have read the manual and noticed the specs. I went along with her explanation.

Samuel nodded, apparently understanding. What appliances might he want to buy in town? Maybe he would invest in something from our store. Nah, I'll bet he will buy an electric shaver and give up using a Bowie knife. I couldn't imagine him buying a food processor, but I could picture him purchasing a table lamp or an electric blanket. Perhaps he would buy an electric fan for use on hot summer days.

Samuel limped over to me slowly and asked, "Can a radio operate off the generator?"

"Sure. That would give you something to listen to, news, music and sports broadcasts. That would be a very good item to buy."

"You people sell them?"

"No, but I can order you one. You could find one in town at the drug store or at the furniture store. You could get one that plays CDs, too."

He looked a bit dazzled with all the information we had fed him in the last hour. I had a feeling he didn't know about CDs but didn't want to show his ignorance. But that wasn't Samuel's problem, he started swaying and began to lose his balance. I grabbed his arm and helped him to a chair.

Elaine said, "I don't think he has eaten since yesterday, Efren. I'll get our lunch from the car."

"Have you eaten today, Samuel?"

He thought for several seconds and replied, "I had some rabbit stew yesterday night. I was gonna make some this morning and cook some biscuits."

"But we came and interrupted your normal activities. Elaine made a bunch of sandwiches for us. We've got enough for a small army. She's bringing them in from the car. We'll all have something to eat. Do you like hot coffee?"

His eyes sparkled, "Sure do, can we make some on that hotplate?"

"We have some in a Thermos but it's just warm by now. We can warm it up or make some new on your hotplate. What would you like to do?"

"If it's not too much trouble, I'd like to make some fresh. I've got a can of coffee in back, I'll get it." He turned around and hobbled out of sight into a rear room, returning with a one gallon plastic jug of water and a quart size ceramic container marked coffee. Coffee was written with an artistic flair, undoubtedly done by his wife long ago.

Elaine returned carrying our picnic basket, set it on the table and began to unpack the wicker container. She saw the water and coffee containers and asked, "What are you men planning?"

"Samuel wants to make some fresh brew using the hotplate," I answered.

"Does he have a metal can or pan to boil water?" She queried.

We heard a rattling coming from a back room. We looked toward the sound and Samuel appeared with a small metal pan having a diameter of about six inches. He held it for us to see.

"This'll work for boiling the water, won't it?"

"That will do. It should hold about three cups, maybe four," observed Elaine. "That's about the right size for the hotplate." Elaine spread out a small tablecloth on the floor and knelt beside it. Paper plates magically appeared and each was soon loaded with three sandwiches. Adjacent to each plate was a colorful paper napkin.

I dropped to my knees and stated, "I don't think Samuel can get on the floor. Why don't we move to the table?"

"No, he wants it for his drawings. I'll get his chair. He can sit with us."

Samuel was watching the water begin to boil and he poured coffee into the boiling water. I could imagine the grit getting stuck between my teeth after drinking some of Samuel's coffee. The aroma filled the small home, almost like visiting a coffee shop. Samuel presented Elaine with a ceramic mug of the brew. He and I drank from metal cups made from empty cans. The coffee was surprisingly good with hardly any solid particles.

Samuel sat and agreed to eat two of the sandwiches. "How's the coffee?" he inquired.

Elaine and I both said, "Fine." I thought for a moment and added, "Damn fine. How did you know how much coffee to add to the water?"

"Well, Efren, I got eyeballs and ears that still work," he chuckled. "My Margret showed me how to make good coffee. I never forgot."

We discussed the Bitterroot weather, especially during the winter. Samuel related several stories of hunters, prospectors, and sightseers getting caught unaware of the sudden onset of snow and cold. He once took part in a search and rescue party that saved a family of four from freezing after their car stalled near one of the lookout towers north of Suddenly. We listened attentively for half an hour.

Elaine poked me and whispered, "I have to pee. Is there a bathroom?"

Samuel laughed, "My ears are just fine, Elaine," said Samuel. "My bathroom is in that modern shed out back. There's a Sears catalog out there," he chuckled. "Go through the house and straight out to the shed. It's got running water—saved from the rain. But it's not heated."

While Elaine was gone, Samuel explained he had originally constructed an outhouse but when he got married to Margret, he had a septic tank installed. "Sewage travels downhill to the tank. It's on the other side of that little hill where the shed is built. I think it's a good bathroom, except for lack of hot water."

When Elaine returned, she asked, "Samuel, that painting in your bathroom is the same one that's at Jean's B and B, except it's a summer picture, isn't it?"

"Ah, you do have the eyes of an artist. You are correct, Elaine. That one was the first, the winter scene was done later. I kept the summer one."

"Is the cabin nearby?"

"It's not too far off, maybe fifteen miles or so. It's a two day hike out. It takes a good set of legs—the hills you know. With a car on those logging roads, it would be faster."

Elaine's eagerness to be an artist was flaring up as she glanced at me. I could feel her desire to visit the cabin in the pictures. She wants to sketch the cabin from different angles to study the feelings the shadows evoke in the viewer. She's mentioned investigating shadows before but never in the Bitterroot mountains. I think the environment has caused her artistic expressions to sprout again. If she can help run a business, teach art at the high school and create her own portrayals, she is going to be a very busy but happy woman. I will have to assume the life of a bachelor again. To keep busy, I can operate the store, perhaps do a little prospecting and keep in touch with Samuel. I believe I can learn much about the Bitterroot mountains from him. The new experiences in Suddenly should be very satisfying for both Elaine and me.

After downing Samuel's coffee and an additional cup from our Thermos, I was next to visit the bathroom. The picture of the summer cabin was nearly as beautiful as the one in the winter scene. Margret was certainly a skilled artist. Had she produced other works before settling with Samuel in Suddenly? Maybe I'll ask Samuel after we have been acquainted for a longer time. I don't want to invade any more of his cherished memories.

We gathered our tools and extra supplies and left the remaining sandwiches with Samuel. As we packed our things into the car, Samuel attempted to give the extra ham sandwiches to Elaine.

"You have given me enough already. I have plenty of food available. I don't want to deprive you of your normal fare."

I said, "Samuel, you don't want to argue with my wife. You will lose every time."

He stood by his front door contemplating and then said, "You know Efren, she reminds me of my Margret; stubborn to the core."

I gave him a thumbs up and started to get in the driver's seat. Elaine said, "Efren, the window. Remember?"

"Oh, geez, I almost forgot." I went back to the boarded up window and measured the dimensions with my pocket tape measure.

The size was easy to remember, three feet high by four feet wide. I'd order a replacement for him.

On the way into town, Elaine mentioned something about Samuel's pictures. "The cabin in his pictures is the same, all seventeen of them. The same door, the same window, although sometimes open, sometimes closed, the same sagging roof and one chimney on the left."

"That's the same as the cabin in the paintings?" I asked.

"Uh-huh. They're almost all the same. I can't understand why the cabins are all nearly identical."

"Did you ask Samuel?"

"No. I didn't think about it until we started back home. Something was bothering me and it came to me as we were on the road."

"What about the surroundings of the cabins? Are they all the same?"

Elaine was quietly reviewing her memory. After about ten seconds, she said, "The trees are different and sometimes the sky has clouds." She paused for a moment, "And the streams differ from the water in the painting; but it's about the same in all his pictures."

As we pulled into our driveway, we decided to call our discussion the cabin mystery and let it drop. It was a few minutes after two. Inside, we sat on the sofa to relax. We talked about the needs of the hardware store. I jotted down the dimensions of the window to order for Samuel and included the large propane tank. I'd check with the local gas stations before I ordered one from Dillon or Butte. There was no use having to pay an excessive shipping charge.

Elaine suddenly hopped to her feet and went to the phone. "I'm calling the high school—about the teaching position."

She was slightly confused. It was Saturday, school was closed. "Elaine, this is Saturday."

"Oh, I've lost track of the days." She frowned and returned to the sofa. "I'll call the school on Monday. I'd really like to work with kids on art projects."

Elaine and I spent the rest of the weekend relaxing and planning our activities for the store. We figured we would have a grand opening in about three weeks if we could get things ordered, priced and put in place. We made lists of items we had to order. Most everything could be shipped from Butte. I'd have to wait until Monday to check on ordering the large propane tank. Before I outsourced a tank, I'd call the local service stations. But I didn't think that option held much promise.

Chapter 12

We were at our store by eight o'clock Monday. As I worked on organizing tools, I thought maybe we should rename the store as Sandoval's General Store. Elaine was working on seeds and gardening equipment. We had such a variety of items not identified as hardware; we concluded the name change was necessary.

When Elaine began working on our stock of sinks and toilets, she commented, "You know, Efren, the only hardware in this part of the store is faucets, bolts, nails and metal pipe. Maybe we should come up with another name, but not general store. That's too much like a term from the eighteen hundreds. We don't sell yard goods or medicinals. I've been thinking, how about Sandoval's Emporium?"

"What about The Bitterroot Emporium?"

"I don't like it. It's too encompassing and it sounds like the title of a novel."

"Okay then, it's Sandoval's Emporium. I hope we don't have to trade for chickens, eggs, or pelts. Let's stick with gold or money." We had a good laugh.

"I'll design the lettering for the store windows. I found some silver paint upstairs. It will look nice on the front windows. I'll outline it with white."

I started straightening out bolts and nuts and had spent half an hour on the project before Elaine joined me with two mugs of coffee.

"Where did you get the coffee? I didn't hear you leave the building."

"I found a Mr. Coffee unit in the back corner of the office. It was concealed behind some reams of paper and a printer. It was really dusty so I cleaned it. There was a can of coffee and filters in one of the file cabinets, bottom drawer."

I had been thinking of a phone for the store and wondered who to call. "What should we do about the phone? We have to have a business phone."

Elaine responded, "Let's wait for a bill and then we can change it to our name, same with the home phone."

I took a sip of coffee and nodded, "Sounds like a good idea."

Elaine sat there quietly holding the mug with both hands, staring off into space. Something important was coming up.

"What do you think, should I call the school about the art teaching position?"

That took me by surprise. When had she decided to follow up on the high school teaching position? We hadn't talked about it since Saturday. I was happy she was serious about teaching; she's always been good with all ages of kids but she hadn't expressed interest in teaching art before moving to Suddenly. Something had ignited a change, perhaps her experience with Samuel and his cabin pictures. Whatever the cause, it had to be recent. Hmm, maybe it was that picture in the B and B.

"Come with me to the office." She grabbed my right arm and pulled, forcing me to get up from sitting on the floor. I followed her to the phone and watched her punch in digits. But what number was it? Then I realized she must have looked up the school contact and memorized it when we were at home on Saturday. She had to have mulled over teaching for a couple of days.

"I'd like to talk to Principal Savage. Is he available?" Elaine put the phone on speaker.

"Who is calling?"

"This is Elaine Sandoval. It's about the art teaching position."

"One moment please."

Elaine lowered the phone to her side and gave me a disgusted look shaking her head. She returned the phone to her ear, blinked and smiled.

"This is Dr. Savage. How may I help you?"

"I'm inquiring about the art teaching position. I was told the position was open for next year. I would like to apply."

"When would you be available for an interview?"

"Tomorrow at any time that is convenient for you."

"Well, classes end at a quarter to four. I will see you tomorrow at four o'clock. My secretary mentioned you are Mrs. Sandoval. Is that correct?"

"Yes. My husband and I just purchased the hardware store. We're new to Suddenly."

"Good for you. We need that store. I will see you tomorrow. Thank you for calling. Goodbye."

"Goodbye."

She hung up the phone, turned to me and said, "Whew! That was easier than I thought. What should I wear?"

"Something that shows lots of cleavage."

"Efren! I'm serious."

"Okay, wear that dark blue suit and take your portfolio from the Butte Art Museum and that art magazine stuff. Those things should impress Dr. Savage."

"We can work until three, then we'll go home and I'll get ready. You'll need to clean up too. You're going with me."

"I don't know anything about teaching art. Can't you go alone?"

"No. I want you along so he won't think I'm a defenseless woman begging for a job and I'll feel better with moral support."

"I was thinking of going with you anyway. I'd like to see what the school looks like and check out the secretary." I grinned and she stuck her tongue out.

"Oh, go back to your bolts and nuts." She flipped her hand at me, "Shoo!"

I had just returned to my position on the floor when a rap at the entrance got my attention. I scrambled to my feet and went to the door where an elderly gentleman was holding a dirty furnace filter. I unlocked the door and let him in.

"I need a filter. Do you carry these?"

"Ah, we sure do. What is the size?"

"I didn't measure it. Aren't they all the same?"

I shook my head and said, "No. There's about half a dozen common sizes. The dimensions are written on the filter. Let me take a look."

I was careful not to shake the air filter, preventing dust from being deposited on our floors and in my nostrils. The filter was common: 16x25. I knew we had about ten in stock, so I took his filter, put it in the trash and presented him with a new one.

"Here you go."

"How much is it?"

"It's free. You are our first customer Mr. . . ."

"I'm Henry Jantz. I'm a local barber. This filter, it's free?"

"That's right. We're not open for business yet. We don't have sales records set up and are not able to print receipts. We'll have an official opening before long."

"What happened to the Ericksons?"

"They moved to Butte. My wife and I bought their business. Don't tell anyone that we are giving away free things. This is a one-time transaction, okay?"

"And what is your name, sir?"

"Efren Sandoval. My wife's name is Elaine. We're from Butte."

Mr. Jantz and I shook hands and he left the store whistling.

I relocked the door and finished organizing bolts and nuts. I now know someone that might give Samuel a shave and haircut, maybe free of charge. The next customer that knocks on the door or windows will be charged for their selections from the store. I don't want the idea of free merchandise to get out of hand. Mr. Jantz might be a talker and let something slip, after all he is a barber. I tinkered with various items until Elaine called me for lunch. We ate in the office and ignored a couple of knocks at the entrance. Each time we heard tapping at the door, I glanced down from the balcony. The young people briefly peered in the windows, realized we weren't open yet and continued down the sidewalk, apparently looking for something insignificant. At this time, Samuel Duggar was the only person I would have allowed in the store.

When Samuel came to mind, I remembered I had to order a large tank for propane. Fortunately, the Ericksons had kept good records of source materials in Suddenly and Dillon. I called Gas Distribution in Dillon and ordered a one hundred twenty gallon tank. When I was told the price, delivered, installed and filled at Duggar's, I balked. Previously when talking with Samuel, I had imagined the cost would be about four hundred dollars, not over a thousand. I would have to talk with Mr. Isaacs at the bank before spending that much of Duggar's money without his approval. I put the order on hold. I'll call back in a day or two.

It was close to two o'clock when I went to the bank. It was a short walk, only a couple of blocks. It was not evident how to get the attention of the president of the bank, so I asked one of the tellers about getting a commercial loan. I figured a teller wouldn't be able to handle a business loan and would have to refer me to the management.

I was right. I was instructed to wait a few minutes in a small alcove where I could serve myself coffee from a machine and take a seat. After a short wait, only a minute or two, Mr. Isaacs appeared and requested that I come to his office. We had never officially met but recognized each other's names. Arlene Stafford, the realtor, had established an account for our store when Elaine and I made the purchase. So, I knew of Mr. Isaacs and he recognized my name.

After shaking hands, he seemed a bit puzzled about my request to establish a commercial loan. I confessed that it was a ruse to see him about Samuel Duggar's finances. I explained my concern about the expenses of the propane installation system and he nodded in agreement about the dollar amount involved. He hadn't talked with Mr. Duggar for several weeks and didn't realize I had installed a generator. After I informed him that Elaine and I had done the work at no cost, he was impressed.

"I have an idea, Mr. Sandoval. Although Samuel has enough money in his account to handle the cost in a lump sum, I think it would be better to pay the bill in monthly installments. Will the gas company agree to such a plan?"

"No. They want the entire payment, no installments." I thought for a few seconds and developed an alternative strategy. "How about paying the gas company from my business account and have Mr. Duggar pay my account in monthly installments? Would that work?"

"That is a good plan. Samuel usually makes a large deposit at the end of summer." Mr. Isaacs smiled and shook my hand again. "That's an ideal solution. I'll arrange payments as soon as the bank receives the Gas Distribution charge to your account."

We talked about the hardware store finances for a few minutes before he remarked about another appointment. I excused myself and returned to the store. Elaine wanted to know all the details of my discussion with Mr. Isaacs, including a description of him. I told her he looked like a banker. I laughed when she scowled and I mentioned he was about five years younger than us, a bit chubby, about five-nine, wore glasses and had a full head of light brown but graying hair.

I tinkered with organizing pipe fittings and gave up after realizing the project was going to take another hour. My fingers were tired and dirty, so I said, "Let's go home, Elaine. I'll get a fresh start in the morning." Without any more prompting, the balcony lights went out and I heard footsteps coming down the stairs as I started toward the bathroom. Elaine was waiting for me at the entranceway when I finished washing my hands.

Tuesday morning was sunny but cool. We worked at the store until twelve o'clock, closed up and returned home for a lite lunch. Elaine didn't want a full stomach when she had her interview with Dr. Savage at the high school. After eating, she had me listen to her pitch for the teaching position. She presented a promising case for being hired, even though she didn't possess teaching credentials. I was pleased she didn't sound like she was begging for the job. I considered her application to be highly professional and I told her so.

I asked her, "What should I wear?"

She thought for a second and replied, "Your brown sports jacket, yellow shirt and brown slacks."

I was picturing myself in what she said and a second later, she added, "And wear that thin light-brown tie, oh, and wear your brown shoes, not the black ones."

That meant I would have to put on those shoes that pinched my big toe on my right foot. I think those shoes are a half size too small, but I could stand the pain for an hour, at most two. I'd wear slippers in the evening and the next day.

Elaine looked like a teacher when she asked me to evaluate her casual outfit. She was dressed in Goldilocks' attire, not too fancy and not too drab, just right. We had a lengthy discussion about the store while having coffee and before long it was approaching time for final preparations. I knew the high school location, so we decided to leave at a quarter to four. We thought we would arrive five minutes early. Showing up late was not an option.

Only four vehicles were in the parking lot when we arrived near the main entrance to the school.

I didn't think much of it since the students had departed. The principal and the janitor came to mind and maybe a teacher or two finishing up the day's work. The pickup looked familiar but I couldn't place it. It had Arizona plates, a visitor far from home. I hoped someone was not going to be competing with Elaine for the teaching position. I mentioned it to Elaine and she said, "Don't cast a spell, Efren." I laughed and we tried the door. It was locked.

I knocked twice and stepped back from the double doors. We didn't have to wait for long before a nice looking woman appeared and unlocked the entrance.

She smiled and declared, "You must be the Sandovals. Please come in. We have to keep the doors locked after hours to prevent unwanted visitors. I'm Mary Savage, the principal's secretary."

Chapter 13

I was slightly surprised when we entered the principal's office. Dr. Savage greeted us with warm handshakes and asked, "Would you like some coffee? My wife just made some fresh." Apparently, the woman that met us at the door was Mrs. Savage, in addition to being the principal's secretary. I had initially thought the Savage name was coincidental, or she was the principal's daughter. She looked too young to be the wife of a school administrator. We declined the coffee.

But Dr. Savage could only be about thirty years old, fairly young to be in charge of a school. The administrators with whom I had been acquainted were usually in their forties or fifties or close to retirement. Dr. Savage must have taken the job in Suddenly right after graduation. I'll bet his wife was a cheerleader, she certainly looked the part. I was curious about what her major had been in college.

I'm sure Elaine was sightly unsettled when we entered the office. We expected to be interviewed by Dr. Savage, but there were two female students sitting beside the principal's desk, both extremely good looking. Dr. Savage introduced the two young ladies.

"Mr. and Mrs. Sandoval, I'd like you to meet two of our former students, Jennifer Kincaid and Spring Wisdom. They have just returned from spending the winter at the Navaho Nation in Arizona."

We shook hands with the Suddenly High graduates and had a short conversation about their trip from Arizona. Elaine and I expressed our surprise that the young ladies had driven over eight hundred miles, especially since some of the roads were being repaired. Fortunately, they took their time and made the trip in two eight-driving hour days. The girls were excited to hear Elaine's presentation and afterwards, Jennifer remarked that she had seen some of Elaine's artwork in the Bitterroot Art magazine.

"Your work is truly impressive, Mrs. Sandoval," Jennifer commented.

"Thank you. I'd like to see your portrayals of life on the reservation."

"I'm mostly interested in fashion and have been designing clothes incorporating Navajo art."

Spring interjected, "The reservation landscape where we were has lots of rocks and shadows, not much else. Our environment in Arizona is quite different than the Bitterroot mountains. I'm glad we've returned to Montana; I missed the trees. I experienced one winter in Suddenly and am looking forward to more."

I was listening intently to what the women were saying but from the depths of my brain, I dredged up an idea. I had to ask about the pickup, but not while Elaine was the center of attention. There was a pause in the conversation and Principal Savage stood and stated, "Thank you for coming in today, Mrs. Sandoval. Your experience in the art world is certainly impressive. However, I must say since you do not have any teaching credentials, we cannot hire you at this time. If we do not receive any other applicants, you can be hired provisionally with the understanding you would enroll in teacher education studies following your first year of employment. How does that sound?"

"Well, I had hoped to at least be competitive as a result of the interview. So, what you are telling me is that I have a chance but slim." Elaine smiled, "I'll pray no one with credentials applies for the job. I'll give you my contact numbers for home and at the store if the position remains vacant. Thank you for the interview. It was nice meeting all of you."

The girls and Mrs. Savage walked with us to the entrance. As we walked to our car, I jogged ahead to the two girls as they were getting into their pickup.

They heard me coming toward them and Jennifer said, "Can we help you, Mr. Sandoval?"

I took a deep breath and said, "I have a request." The stares were a bit unsettling but I continued, "By any chance, could I borrow your pickup for an afternoon?"

I guess they thought I was going to say something academic. The girls looked at each other and laughed. Their reaction forced me to explain.

"Elaine and I have been helping an elderly man install an electric generator that runs on propane. The barbeque tanks we have are too small for extended use, so I've ordered a large tank from Dillon. The delivery cost is rather high, so I thought I could transport the tank to Mr. Duggar and lessen the expense. But I don't have a truck. If I could borrow your pickup, I can deliver the large tank. I'd pay for the gasoline. Would that be possible?"

I was about six feet away from them and couldn't hear what they said to each other in whispers. I couldn't read lips either, but Jennifer turned back toward me and said, "We can do that. When would you like to borrow the truck? Give us a day to get settled in our house. It has been closed up for the last six months. We'll have to buy some things in town and will need wheels. Would Thursday be all right with you?"

"That would be great. How about one o'clock? I'll leave my car in case you need transportation while I'm gone. I expect it will take me a couple of hours."

Spring wrote something on a small tablet and handed me the note. It was their address at the edge of town. "If you have trouble finding us, ask anyone where the old Kincaid house is, they'll know. It's kind of a landmark." The girls grinned.

"Okay, I'll see you at one o'clock in Thursday."

Spring replied, "It's a date." They laughed, got into the truck and waved goodbye.

Elaine waited patiently for me in the car. When I got in, she asked, "What did you talk about with those girls? Did you ask their opinion about the cabin pictures Samuel has?"

I shook my head, "No, I wanted to borrow their pickup to transport the propane tank from Dillon to Samuel's place. It will save about a hundred dollars. I told them I would pay for the gas, a couple of gallons. They said I could borrow the truck on Thursday; they need it tomorrow."

"Let's go home, Efren. I want to change these clothes and get into something more comfortable."

As we left the school, I asked, "Do you want to go to the store this afternoon? There are still two hours for working."

She didn't respond immediately. After we drove a block she sighed, "No. I'm burned out from the interview. I've never sweated so much." She fanned her face with her right hand. "I'd like to relax. We'll work all day tomorrow, okay?"

I smiled as I reflected about the work idea, "Sounds like a book title, Wednesday at the Emporium."

Just as planned, we spent all Wednesday at the store. By lunchtime, Elaine commented, "We're making such good progress, let's open the store this coming Monday. I think we'll be ready. I'll work on the window lettering tomorrow while you deliver the fuel container."

After eating, I called Dillon about the propane tank and arranged to pick it up at one forty-five Thursday afternoon. With that business out of the way, I finished organizing garden equipment and chainsaws. Carpentry levels, hand saws, chop saws, and tile saws were priced and displayed beneath the stairway to the balcony. Plumbing items were the last remaining items put in order before we quit for the day.

Elaine purchased all our office materials from Butte Office Warehouse. The supplier promised to deliver everything on Saturday afternoon. We will be finishing final touches two days before our grand opening on Monday. Expecting to be working late in the evening Saturday, Sunday will be our final day of freedom before the intense summer months. Ericksons warned us that the summer in Suddenly would be a hectic time at the hardware store.

Elaine spent Thursday morning designing our storefront window sign. I assisted by steadying her when she climbed on the third rung of the step ladder. Tracing with a felt-tip marker went rapidly for a couple of letters before she told me I could work on something else. She had gained confidence climbing the ladder and keeping her balance as she outlined the new sign. I did janitorial work while she drew on the windows. When the lettering was complete, we went outside to evaluate the primitive uppercase message.

A few onlookers passed by and asked when we would be open. Elaine answered politely and they continued down the street. I was pleased with Elaine's design and commented, "You're sure you can do that in an afternoon?"

"No problem. I'll keep the door locked. I'm going to make a sign for our front door saying we will be open on Monday. Do we have a large sheet of cardboard?"

"Sure. How big?"

She indicated the size with her hands and I retrieved a large shipping box from our trash area. I cut it to size and she drew the message with a black marker. She gave me the sign, smiled and pointed, "Tape it to our front entrance. Use that good tape so it doesn't fall off while I'm painting. I don't want to smear my work if startled."

"Yes, Sir!" I saluted and she started laughing.

I left the store at eleven thirty and returned with burgers and fries. I could smell a faint odor of paint thinner. Elaine prepared the silver paint while I was gone. It was too thick, so she added thinner and strained it to remove particles present from a previous user not adequately sealing the can. She used a small artist's brush to test the paint on a glass bottle to make sure it adhered properly to a smooth surface.

After turning on the ventilation fans, we ate and listened to radio broadcasts from the college station in Butte. At a quarter to one, I left for the Kincaid residence. Elaine had found a city street map in Ericksons' files, so it was an easy drive. I recognized the black pickup parked at the side of the house and drove to the front and parked. I was close to the porch where the girls were sitting, talking to a young man. A dark blue bicycle with a small trailer was leaning against the pickup's front bumper.

The girls waved as I got out of my car. I returned the greeting.

"Mr. Sandoval, you are right on time," said Jennifer. When I was within a few feet of the young people, Spring said, "I'd like you to meet a friend of ours, Dexter Young. We graduated together last year. Dex and his father have a bike repair shop."

Jennifer said, "Dex, Mr. Sandoval and his wife just bought the hardware store from the Erickson family. He's here to borrow my pickup." Dexter had a firm handshake and a charming smile. Which of the girls was in his sights?

"Is that your bike?" I asked and pointed.

"Yes sir. My dog is in the trailer. You should meet him."

The friendly little furball called Skimmer sniffed my pant leg as his tail wiggled. I bent over to pet him and he licked my hand then ran to the girls who picked him up.

Dexter commented, "Spring, I think he wants a drink."

"Okay, we'll take him inside to his water bowl while you men get acquainted."

As I watched the girls enter the house, I had an idea. Dexter looked to be a strong young man and not busy today, so I asked, "I know we just met, but I'd like to ask a favor."

Dexter smiled and quickly replied, "I don't kill people."

So, this kid has a sense of humor. I chuckled, "I don't have any enemies to get rid of—yet. No, I am going to Dillon to pick up a large propane tank and need some muscle. Could you spare an hour or two?"

He answered, "Sure, I guess I can do that. The girls can watch Skimmer for me."

I watched Dexter hop on the porch and knock. I didn't hear what was said through the screen door but he returned and pointed at the pickup, "It's all set, let's go."

He parked his bike against the porch and slid into the passenger seat.

I drove through town as directly as possible to the road to Dillon. A few miles from town Dexter commented, "I had an accident near here on my way to Suddenly two years ago. A truck ran me off the road."

"Did you get your car repaired?"

"No, I was on my bike. The handlebars got bent but I was able to fix the damage."

"You came from Dillon on a bicycle?"

"Well, yeah. I started from St. Louis."

"Jesus, Dexter, isn't that over fifteen hundred miles?"

"Uh-huh, but I had help. Some nice people gave me rides and meals. It took over a week. At a rest stop, two guys tried to steal my bike. That was a memorable trip."

Chapter 14

I was attempting to process what he was telling me when we passed the turnout to Sam Duggar's place. I pointed and remarked, "That's where we're to deliver the propane tank."

"Mr. Duggar still lives there? He lacks running water and electricity, doesn't he?"

"I helped him install electricity. That's what the propane tank is for—an electric generator. Have you met the gentleman?"

Dexter nodded, "Yeah. About a year ago, David Drum and I rode out here to deliver some mail to Mr. Duggar. It was a notice from the Forest Service about preventing forest fires. We spent an afternoon helping him clear brush from around his house. He was living like someone from the eighteen hundreds and didn't want any modern conveniences."

"That sounds like Samuel, all right."

"How did you get the old man to accept electricity."

"He seems to be dedicated to drawing pictures of an old cabin. Do you know anything about his devotion?"

"David and I talked about it but never figured out what he had in mind. He had about eight or ten pictures of a cabin in the woods. He was kind of secretive about his artwork. I think his wife was a really good artist, though."

"My wife and I noticed a beautiful winter scene picture at Jean's B and B. It was painted by Duggar's wife, Margret. We think Samuel's sketches somehow relate to that picture. He's added more sketches since you visited him. He's actually a reasonably good artist himself. He only draws with a pencil; no color at all. We wonder what else he does with his time."

"He didn't have much to say to David and me, just watched what we were doing and followed what we did. He offered us dinner but we had other plans with Jenny and Spring."

I looked at him and smiled, "Hot dates?"

"We double dated. Took them to a movie and soft ice cream."

Our conversation on the road to Dillon ended when we entered town. I had driven past the town a few times but hadn't stopped except for gas, so I didn't know the streets. Fortunately, Dillon is only about twice the size of Suddenly and Dexter knew the location of the company where the propane tank was being held for me. It was a short drive to the eastern edge of the county seat.

A half hour after arriving in town, we started back to Suddenly with an empty hundred twenty gallon tank secured to the truck bed. Dexter asked if he could drive, so I was sitting in the passenger seat. After fifteen minutes, I began to watch for the turnout to Duggar's property. I wasn't sure Dexter was going to recognize the dirt road that abruptly veered to the right.

"I'll warn you when we approach the turn to Duggar's."

He slowed the pickup to about twenty miles per hour after a gray pickup honked several times and sped by. Dexter waved and sounded the horn.

"Who was that? You recognized them?"

"I think so. I believe David Drum was in the passenger seat."

"I thought he was still at the university. Are classes over for the summer?"

"I don't think so. Jenny said David would be home next week. I'm wondering why he just passed us."

"We're coming to Duggar's lane, better get ready to turn."

Dexter nodded, he saw the turnout and slowed the truck to a crawl, made the turn and continued to the house. Samuel appeared from around the side of his home carrying a hoe. He looked like he was going to use the garden implement as a weapon. A dirty dog with muddy, matted fur was beside him.

I got out of the pickup, approached Samuel and announced, "I'm Efren Sandoval, remember me?"

"Sure, I remember you. Who's the young fella with you?"

We shook hands and I replied, "This is Dexter Young. He told me he met you some time ago when he came from Suddenly with David Drum."

"Oh, yeah. I recollect them helping clean up some brush to keep my house from burning down in a forest fire. How are you, young man?"

They shook hands and Dexter said, "Mr. Duggar, you have a dog. What's his name?"

"Don't know. Showed up about a week ago, so I've been feedin' him. Needs a bath; really smells. Been lettin' him sleep in the bathroom out back. He's smart though."

"What about Stinky for a name?"

Samuel shook his head, "No, the smell will wash off. I think I'll call him Alone—Al for short."

I interrupted, "Samuel, we've brought a large propane tank to install for you, to replace the small barbeque ones. The gas supplier from Dillon will arrive once a month to fill the tank. Mr. Isaacs at the bank will take care of the payments for you. You will probably have to sign for each fill-up."

"Okay, I can do that. When will they come to deliver?"

"The last Saturday of each month. That's when they bring propane to Suddenly."

Samuel nodded and looked down at the dog, "You really smell bad, Al. Let's go to the stream and give you a bath." Duggar turned around and disappeared behind the house with the dog following him.

I glanced at Dexter, "Can you back the truck up to those two small containers? Let's get this tank situated and hooked up."

Dexter backed the pickup to the site Samuel and I had previously prepared. I signaled for him to stop when the pickup was within about ten feet of the brick pad. He cut the engine and started to join me when we heard the sounds of an approaching vehicle, a newer model gray pickup. Was it the same truck that honked at us about ten minutes earlier?

Dexter yelled at the two occupants as they exited the pickup, "Hey, David, it's good to see you. Who's that with you?"

"I'd like you to meet Artie Mayfield, one of my classmates. Artie, this is Dexter Young. I don't know this other gentleman."

I stepped forward and extended my hand. "I'm Efren Sandoval, the new owner of the hardware store in Suddenly."

David responded, "Oh, that's right. I heard that Ericsons wanted to sell their business. Randy wanted to go to college in Butte." David glanced at the black truck and asked, "Isn't this Jennifer Kincaid's pickup?"

I answered, "Yes, Dexter and I borrowed it to transport the propane tank. How would you like to give us a hand?"

The empty two hundred pound tank would have been awkward for Dexter and me to handle but with the added help of two college men, the container was easily placed in position.

"Thanks, guys. Your good deed has been done for today. I assume you're going into Suddenly to see Jenny and Spring. We'll be along after I talk to Samuel."

"Happy to help, Mr. Sandoval. It was nice meeting you."

Dexter and I waved to David and Artie as they backed out to the highway. They beeped once when back on the main road. I could tell Dexter was anxious to get back to see the girls. I figured he was wary of what would happen when Artie met Spring. I told him to wait in the truck while I talked with Samuel, I would make it quick. He nodded and slid into the driver's seat.

I hustled around the house and found Samuel drying off his new companion on the stream bank. I could see the dog was fairly young, only about two, maybe three years old. After the grimy dog's bath, I recognized the animal was a collie, obviously someone's pet. It must have been scared and run away or lost from its owners on a trip into the mountains. It might have an identification chip.

"Samuel, your new friend looks much better."

"Smells lots better, too. I'll get him to a vet in Suddenly to see if he has a chip. Might need some shots, too."

"We have the tank in position. When the propane is delivered, they'll give you some instructions. You'll have to sign some papers. I'll be out to check on everything after fuel is delivered. We're heading back to town now. See you next week."

"Thanks, Efren." He smiled as he continued to dry Al with a large light-green bath towel. "We'll see ya."

As Dexter and I drove back to town, I wondered what Samuel was feeding his new friend. I was sure Samuel hadn't been to town to buy dog food. Maybe he had something on hand or caught squirrels, a racoon, or trout. I wouldn't be surprised if Al was eating dry breakfast cereal and drinking coffee.

As we drove, Dexter asked, "What does that old guy do out there alone? I assume he hasn't had electricity for years."

"When my wife and I met him, he was sketching cabins with pencils, all in black and white. He's a good artist, but his lighting was from oil lamps and when he knocked a lamp over a fire started. After that, we donated an electric generator. The factory didn't want it returned because of blemishes and we couldn't sell it because of discoloration and slight rust damage."

"So how does he earn a living? Does he have a pension?"

I chuckled, "Some say he pays for things with gold. But that's just a rumor."

When I saw the Shell gas station at the entrance to Suddenly, I had Dexter pull up to a pump and fill the tank. It only took twenty bucks, a small amount to pay for the loan of the pickup. Borrowing the truck from Jenny had saved me from paying a delivery and installation fee to the gas company.

In his haste to get to the Kincaid residence, Dexter exceeded the speed limit, but only by a few miles per hour. Due to a small police force, there wasn't much of a chance of being pulled over. I kept quiet about the slightly excessive speed, knowing his concern for one of the girls, namely Spring. I was fairly sure David and Jenny were dating. I expected to see the gray pickup at Kincaid's but when we arrived, only my car was present, just as I had left it. There was no sign of the gray truck. Perhaps the girls had taken off with David and Artie.

Dexter stopped the truck, dropped to the ground leaving the door open and started toward the porch. Spring appeared at the door and Dexter stopped in his tracks, just before he was about to leap onto the porch. He wavered and rocked back on his heels.

"Are you all right?" She asked, giving him a concerned look.

"Ah . . . yeah. I was worried."

"Worried? What about?"

"You. I thought you might have gone for a ride with David and his friend."

"Is David back home?"

"Yeah, he stopped at Duggar's and helped us unload a big propane tank. I assumed he would be coming here with his buddy to see you and Jenny. I thought Artie might have intentions."

She grinned and said, "I'm happy you thought of me, Dex."

"I think about you all the time. When I was out here this winter checking on the house, I thought about you living in Arizona. We should have written."

Jenny, carrying Skimmer, joined Spring on the porch and asked, "I heard you mention David. Is he back from school already? I thought he was coming home next week."

"He'll be here to see you, Jen. I think he went home first to say hi to Danny, Gwen and his mom. He's with a classmate named Artie in a gray pickup. They were in Dillon earlier today. He didn't say why." Jennifer opened her mouth to say something but tilted her head toward the screen door and said, "I hear the phone. Just a minute, it might be David." She put Skimmer down and ran in the house. The screen door banged as she disappeared inside.

Spring giggled, "I think she's excited about seeing David again."

Dexter commented, "At least he didn't come home with another girl."

It was almost three o'clock and I wanted to get back to the store. Elaine would be wondering where I was if I didn't return from Duggar's as planned.

I spoke to Spring, "Please thank Jennifer for the use of her truck. Dexter and I filled the tank. He has the keys."

"Okay, Mr. Sandoval. I'll tell her. Bye."

"Bye, Spring."

As I drove to the downtown area and the store, I thought about the young people I recently met. When I was their age, I knew little of what others were doing. I lived on my own little island but responded to the wishes of my elders. When the government called, I jumped at the chance to serve. I remember being naive but learned quickly when in the service. I had few options back then, nothing like the opportunities present in the world these young people are inheriting. I had to have a long conversation with Elaine; she knows more about young adults than I do. I want her point of view.

Maybe we'll have a discussion over a beer.

I beeped the horn as I pulled into the parking space reserved for the hardware store owner. I hoped Elaine was in good spirits. We only had a few things to do to get ready for the grand opening on Monday. We should be able to enjoy a nice weekend of relaxation.

Chapter 15

"Spring!" Jenny called from inside the house. "David and a friend are coming over. Help me get things cleaned up. They'll be here in about ten minutes."

I glanced at Spring, "I guess I'd better go. I should take Skimmer home anyway. He'll be more comfortable at my place. Dad likes having him around. He's teaching the little guy tricks."

"How's your father adjusting to freedom?"

"He still has some problems, but he's doing well, thanks. How about your mom?"

"She's taking care of Grandma and wants to come back to Suddenly to be with your dad. She still wants to get married. You don't have to leave, Dex. I doubt if David and his friend will stay very long. I think they still have to drive back to Butte."

"Thanks, but I'd better get going. Tell David hi for me. We should all get together and plan a camping trip now that the weather is warming up."

"That sounds like fun. I'll tell Jenny and David what you said. I'm glad you came over. Bye."

"Bye, Spring. I'll come by again next week. I'll call ahead."

Spring mounted the steps to the porch and went in the house. I called, "Come, Skimmer. Let's go home to Granddad."

Skimmer got to my bike before I did. The word granddad excited him. My dad had formed a close relationship with my traveling buddy. I helped him into his trailer, swung my leg over the seat and shoved off. The dirt and gravel path to the city street was uneven and bumpy but we made the distance to the road without incident. I shifted gears when the tires came in contact with the asphalt and by avoiding the downtown streets, I kept my speed at about twenty miles per hour. I encountered one stop sign, could see no traffic so didn't bother to stop. I should have stopped, but I had Spring on my mind. I hoped she didn't think much of Artie, I didn't want any competition.

When I got home, a renovated barn, Dad met me with an announcement, "Hey Son, two orders for bikes came in while you were gone."

"Great! Did they leave a downpayment?"

Before Dad could answer, Skimmer began to bark, so I let him out of his riding home and watched him scamper to Dad.

Dad crouched down, snapped his fingers and asked, "Skimmer, do you want a snack?"

Skimmer stood on his hind legs and danced around in a circle, something I had never seen him do before. A new trick courtesy of my dad.

I chuckled, "Geez, Dad, you'll have him performing in a circus before long.

Dad confessed, "I have to get him a snack or he won't perform for me anymore. He's very smart and doesn't appreciate trickery from humans. Have you noticed?"

"Yeah. I threw a ball several times for him to fetch and then pretended to throw it another time. He didn't like trickery and wouldn't play any longer. He just sat and looked at me."

Dad snapped his fingers to get Skimmer's attention and went in the house with the fuzzball bounding after him.

I went in the side office and glanced at the bike order. The customers had made a payment of fifty percent for the bikes; one men's and one women's. We'd have to place an order to Butte. If they didn't have them to ship, we'd have to wait ten days to two weeks to get them from Denver. I was looking at the map of the United States and St. Louis caught my eye. I could have my old friend ship the bikes if everything else failed. He might even come out to visit if he could take some time off. It had been over two years since I rode from St. Louis to Suddenly. Much had taken place in the intervening time.

I sat there daydreaming for a moment and then remembered wanting to talk to David. He should be at Jenny's. When we were setting up our business, we had little money for basic equipment but I found a rotary dial phone in a box of free items at a garage sale. I dialed Jenny's number and she answered, *"Hello?"*

"Hi Jen, this is Dexter. If he's still there, could I please speak with David?"

"Sure, just a sec."

I could hear her call David to the phone. Music was playing in the background, probably from a radio.

"Hi Dex. What's up?"

"When are you off from the university for the summer? I have an idea, but I if you're going to depend on your yard care business for summer work, you might not have time for what I'm proposing."

"I'm finished with classes tomorrow. I have two finals on Monday and I'm done. I'll be home for the summer on Tuesday or Wednesday. What do you thinking of?"

"I'll talk to you about some things when you get home. I don't want to mention particulars over the phone."

"Damn, Dex. Now you've got me involved. I'll see you next week when I return home. I'll come by your place and we can talk privately, okay?"

"Sounds good. Find out what Jenny and Spring have planned for the summer. They might be included in my project."

"All right. I'll ask them, but they're gonna want to know why."

"I think they'll like my idea. Tell them it has to do with art—but not Artie." I laughed.

I listened to silence for about five seconds and then David said, *"Jen is calling me, Dex. I've gotta go. See you next week at your shop. I have something to tell you."*

David didn't mention Spring or Artie. I hoped Artie was making an ass of himself. I sat there daydreaming for about a minute before getting busy preparing bikes for summer riding. Two more had come in for a total of seven. Most of them just needed a little oil, tightening and wheel adjustments. Dad and I just charged for time involved. I did most of the work on bicycles while Dad worked on motorcycles and ATVs. The forest service had us do repairs to their all-terrain vehicles. They needed lubrication and cleaning; filters were always exceptionally dirty. We spent the entire weekend preparing vehicles for owner's active summer months.

Summer days in Suddenly began with a cool breeze until nine o'clock when the sun rose above the surrounding forest. Elaine and I got up at seven, finished with breakfast and were at the Emporium by 8:00 a.m. We had chosen the time to open on purpose, blue sky and sunlight are great motivators. I got our two coffee makers percolating with regular and decaf while Elaine arranged two large plates with doughnuts and cookies.

We were ready five minutes before nine o'clock when Sandoval's Emporium was to open for business. Wearing our light-gray personalized aprons, we greeted customers and gave directions to the first dozen or so visitors. I believe we surprised some of our customers, Elaine assisted the males and I helped the females. Elaine was getting overworked, so I helped the men, too. After the first rush, things calmed a bit. We met at the coffee table and grabbed a cookie.

"Any problems, Ef?"

"Not so far. How about you?"

"No, but I think we should have roped off the balcony. Some wanderers went up there without supervision. I didn't notice any evidence of pilfering though."

I noted the doughnut plate was nearly empty and asked, "Are more doughnuts in the office?"

Elaine nodded and started up the stairs, "I'll get another dozen. The chocolate ones really go fast. Next time we should sell them," she grinned.

My watch indicated eleven twenty-five, approaching lunchtime but customers kept coming. Fortunately, some of our visitors didn't need any assistance. They were only satisfying their curiosity and didn't stay long. I concluded some people wanted to see what alterations had been made in the store since the change in ownership.

I gave up the thoughts of lunch and grabbed a second gooey chocolate doughnut. I didn't need any more caffeine, so poured a cup of decaf to wash down the high-calorie adorned pastry. I kept my eyes scanning for individuals that appeared to be out of their element in our predominantly hardware store. I hadn't recognized any visitors but one, Mr. Isaacs, president of the bank. He entered the store as I finished off my doughnut.

Standing just inside the entrance, he seemed to be searching the customers. When he saw me, he waved and started picking his way through the meandering crowd.

"Mr. Sandoval, it looks like you are quite busy today. That's good to see. How are things going?"

"Hi. The masses are keeping Elaine and me pretty busy. What can I do for you?"

He raised his left hand and scratched his hairline. "I received a call from Dillon about the propane that was delivered Saturday. The supervisor at the gas depot said no one was at home to sign for the delivery. Samuel was nowhere to be found. Our guys said the house was locked up tight, no notices of any kind were found."

"That's strange. I told Samuel the delivery was to be each month on the last Saturday and he would be expected to sign for it. Maybe he forgot. Where did he go?"

"I've known him to be a bit forgetful. He often forgets his savings record book when he brings in his deposits. I doubt if he has a calendar. I provide him a duplicate record. I've given him half a dozen of those little booklets over the last few years."

"Do you think he's out prospecting?"

"I don't know . . . he's all alone and might do some crazy things. Old people get some crazy ideas. They even hallucinate."

I grinned, "Samuel seems in mental control and he's not alone anymore. He's got a companion."

"You mean he's found someone?"

"Not with two-legs; this one has four legs."

"A mule or horse? He could use one as a taxi."

"Nope, a dog. A dog wandered onto his property and he adopted it. It's a collie he named Alone, Al for short. He said he'll bring it into town to be checked by the vet—to find out if it has a chip. He thinks some Bitterroot visitors lost their pet."

"I doubt that's the case. We haven't had any visitors near Suddenly since last November. It must be a runaway from Dillon or from someone passing by on highway fifteen."

"Yeah, but route fifteen is twenty miles from Duggar's. You could be right. That dog was filthy and smelled bad, but I don't know why it would have been on the way to Suddenly. Samuel was giving it a bath when I was there last week. Maybe the dog took off and Samuel went after it. He seemed truly attached to the animal."

"Well, if I didn't have the bank to run, I'd drive out there to check on him. I worry that he might get lost in the forest; he's not as spry as he used to be. He could turn an ankle or get lost. I know he doesn't have a cell phone."

"I'll go out to Duggar's tomorrow morning. We don't open till nine. That will give me an hour to check on him."

"Good idea. I kind of hoped you would do that. That old man is kind of like family to me. I was happy that you got him convinced to use propane and have electricity."

"I'll come by the bank and let you know what I find out. If I don't find anything at Duggar's should we report it to the Forest Service?"

"I suppose it wouldn't hurt. The sheriff's wife might know something. She's encountered Samuel out in the woods before. He's known to hike on those old logging roads."

"You keep in touch with the Forest Service?"

"Only Indirectly. Sheriff Wilson, his wife and boys are my next-door neighbors. David used to date my daughter."

Several more people entered the Emporium and Bruce seemed to be finished with our conversation, so I said, "I'd better help Elaine. I'll let you know if I find out about Samuel."

"Okay. Thanks Efren."

I watched Bruce leave the store and turn towards the bank. Then I worked my way past several customers and found Elaine. She looked at me and inquired, "What did Mr. Isaacs want?"

"He told me Duggar wasn't home on Saturday to sign for the propane. Bruce is worried that Samuel could have gone out in the woods and might get injured. He didn't know Samuel has a dog."

Chapter 16

"Ef, why don't you go to the office and get a sandwich. I can handle this for a few minutes."

"I don't need any lunch, dear. I had two doughnuts, probably over five hundred calories. I'll have some coffee and take over. You get a sandwich. I've been talking while you've been working with the hordes."

She looked at me and laughed. There were only four or five customers in the store.

"Okay, I have to go to the bathroom first. Don't get in trouble while I'm gone."

When six o'clock became our event horizon, except for the two of us, the store was empty of people.

Elaine locked the entrance and we sat in the office to enjoy a few minutes of solitude.

"How do you think we did today?" I asked.

"Not too bad, we ran out of doughnuts and cookies," Elaine giggled. "I think at least half our visitors bought items so I'm guessing we cleared two or three thousand. I'm too tired to check total sales. Let's pull the plugs on the coffee makers and head for home."

"I'm thinking we should get some takeout pizza. We can put our feet up and relax, maybe fall asleep."

"I need a shower and change of clothes. Take-out sounds good though. You mentioned wanting to go out to Duggar's in the morning to check on him. I want to go with you and see his dog. I think we should get a pet. Maybe a small dog."

"We'd have to get two dogs. One animal would get bored with no one around during the day. It would have to be outdoors so it wouldn't tear up the house when alone. I'll build a doghouse and put up a fence."

"All right, we'll get two puppies."

What could I say? Then I had a thought, "If you get that teaching job, I would be stuck with the Emporium and taking care of two dogs. I don't like the idea; it would almost be like having another child."

"But we could hire someone to help out at the store."

"That's true, another expense in addition to the vet bills and dog food. Elaine, let's postpone getting pets for a while and let things settle down before we add to our responsibilities."

Elaine was quiet for what seemed an extended time, perhaps ten to fifteen seconds, before she said, "Okay, but I still want to go with you tomorrow to see Samuel."

"*That* I will readily agree to. I'd enjoy the company."

We rushed to finish breakfast and started on the road towards Dillon to see Mr. Duggar. It took us about fifteen minutes to drive to the turnoff. Two cars and one logging truck created little traffic this early in the morning. We arrived at Samuel's home at 8:10.

I sounded the car horn twice. We waited in the car for a couple of minutes, giving Samuel plenty of time to react. Elaine became impatient, swung her door open and exited. The sudden chill in the forest caused her to reach back into the car for her jacket. As she donned her light coat, I joined her and said, "Let's go in back and see if the door is unlocked. Samuel might be inside."

We stepped through the wet weeds and overgrown grass taking the short trek to the rear of the small house. The back door was hanging from one hinge. Obviously, someone had broken in. With caution, I entered. Elaine was close behind and whispered, "Be careful, Efren. Somebody might be waiting for you with a weapon." I took a couple of steps. I could feel Elaine's hand on my left shoulder, her grip tightening.

I took another step and heard a growl. No lights were on and the backrooms were in near darkness but the living room was dimly lit, apparently from outdoor light penetrating through the small curtainless side window.

"Al, is that you? Are you in there, Samuel? It's Elaine and Efren."

"It's all right, boy. They're friends."

I heard the dog's nails on the hardwood floor as he approached. My eyes adjusted to the low illumination in the house and I could now see the collie slowly coming toward us.

"Are you all right, Samuel?"

"Yeah. A might pissed off is all. Come on in. I'll get the lights."

Elaine and I entered into a room of shambles. When the lights came on, I saw Samuel's table inverted, missing a leg; his chair was destroyed and his drawings were torn, crumpled and scattered. Samuel looked defeated and sat down beside another dog, a small black puppy.

"Someone broke in while Al and I were gone. After I got Al all cleaned up and fed, he barked at me until I followed him to the puppy. We found the little one about a mile from here in a ditch beside a dirt road. I think he got hit by a car; he can't walk."

"So, you carried him back here?"

"Sure. I wasn't gonna leave him out there by himself to die. He can still eat and pee. I think his legs are broke. Can you take him to a vet in Suddenly? If he can't be fixed up, the vet will know what to do."

Elaine knelt beside the puppy and scratched his head. "Oh, Efren, this is a Labrador. He is beautiful. We have to do something."

"Get a blanket from the car Elaine." I looked at Samuel and asked, "Do you have a flat surface we can put him on—like a cookie sheet? I don't want to pick him up and inflict any pain."

"I carried him and he didn't whimper. I think you can pick him up."

"That might mean there is a spinal injury. I'd still like to be careful."

"Just a minute. I'll get you a piece of wood from my kitchen." Samuel hobbled to a backroom and returned with a wide board about two feet long. He chuckled, "It was a shelf I don't need."

Using all four hands, Elaine and I scooped up the pup, carefully wrapped him in the blanket and placed him on the board.

Elaine said, "We'd better get back to Suddenly, Ef. We have to open the store in about twenty-five minutes."

"Right. Why don't you sit in back and I'll hand you the puppy." I looked at Samuel, "We have to go now but I'll be back in the morning to help you fix things. I'll bring some tools. Have you got things to eat?"

"No problem. Whoever broke in didn't know about my cellar out in back. Al and I will get along all right. Let me know about the little guy. I think he'd be a good companion for Al. Al could show him the ropes."

"Okay. I'll see you tomorrow. Bye Samuel."

"Bye Efren."

I tried to avoid bumps in the dirt path to the highway for fear of causing further damage to the puppy. Elaine told me to drop her off at the store and take the dog to the vet. I didn't know the location of the animal clinic. Elaine gave me instructions. How did she know where the clinic was located?

"The animal clinic is on the way to the forest ranger station at the edge of town. It's a new building close to the bicycle shop—across the street. You can't miss it, Efren. It has a neon sign that alternates with a dog and cat wagging their tails."

My curiosity was about to explode. "How do you know all about the site of the veterinarian?"

"I was talking to Mrs. Hadley yesterday. She told me about the bicycle shop and the vet clinic. Hadleys' house is in that area, a little farther out.

I dropped Elaine off at the store and continued on to the animal clinic. There were three vehicles in the parking lot, one of which had a government license plate, a Forest Service truck. I figured someone had brought in an injured animal recovered from the backwoods.

I slid the board from the back seat, trying not to upset the puppy and carried him into the waiting room. I was greeted with a surprised look from David Drum, who I had met a few days earlier at Duggar's.

"Hello, David. I've brought a patient to you."

"Not for me, Mr. Sandoval. I'm just here for the summer to learn. I get two hours of college credit for helping out and learning the practical side of veterinary medicine. Dr. Onishi is the veterinarian. He's operating right now but will be finished in a few minutes. Tell me about your pet."

"He's not mine, David. He's apparently a stray that Samuel Duggar rescued. Duggar thinks the dog was hit by a car and can't walk. The puppy's back legs appear to be broken, maybe his spine too. The little guy doesn't seem to be in pain though. My wife fell in love with his big eyes."

"The doctor will probably want to take some x-rays. Depending on the results, Dr. Onishi might want to operate to fix the breaks. I can't speculate about the spine damage."

"If there is surgery, how much would it cost? Samuel will want to know. I don't know if he'll want to pay for an operation if it's too expensive."

"I'm sorry but I can't venture a guess. The doctor will have to decide on specific treatment. But be aware if the damage is too severe, the dog might have to be euthanized."

"Yeah, that's what I'm afraid of. Elaine will be heartbroken. She wants us to get a dog. Actually two puppies but I'm not too excited about doing that. We just started a business with new responsibilities and Elaine applied for a teaching job at the high school."

"What does she teach?"

"Nothing yet but she thinks she could do a good job as an art teacher. She's a very good artist. She also likes working with teens." I grinned, "We had two of them."

"My girlfriend is an artist. So is her friend. I think you met them last week when you borrowed Jenny's pickup."

"Oh, that's right. Dexter mentioned that you and Jenny are going together. I'm sure Dexter likes Spring. He's sure jealous. He's worried your friend might get involved with her."

"That won't happen. Artie is engaged to a girl in Helena. I'll have to clue Dex in. I got back in town last night and haven't had a chance to talk to him. I started working here this morning. I'll talk to Dex as soon as I get off today."

Our conversation was interrupted when a rear door opened and a middle aged man dressed in a blue hospital gown appeared drying his hands with paper towels.

"Next patient, David." His eyes were focused on Duggar's little friend. "What have we here?"

David introduced us and I explained the situation.

Dr. Onishi said, "Bring your youngster in back. Let's get some x-rays and see if we can come up with a diagnosis."

I carried the Labrador through the doorway into a sparkling clean area that resembled a hospital emergency room. I could hear the barking of several dogs. The sounds were coming from another room accessible through a side door labeled KENNEL. The doctor helped me carry the puppy to an x-ray table. He slid the wooden plank from under the blanket and positioned the pup for a side view.

He swung the x-ray source from the wall and motioned for David and me to step back to the doorway. As we watched, Dr.

Onishi pressed a button on the wall and joined us. He looked at me and smiled, "There is a ten second delay."

We heard a short buzzing sound and the vet moved to a monitor on the counter below the x-ray source. He clicked on a file and a view of the puppy's bone structure filled the screen. He motioned for us to join him and said, "Well, your little friend has two broken legs." Using the mouse, he pointed out the breaks. "I don't see any involvement of the spine though. I think his spine is bruised and pressure from fluids is causing the loss of feeling of his hind legs. He should recover in a few days from that.

"What about the breaks, Doctor?"

Dr. Onishi was about half a foot shorter than David and me and he glanced up and smiled, "David and I will align his bones and use splints to keep them straight. I'll sedate him so there won't be any pain while we perform procedures. We'll wrap them and keep him overnight. He's so young, the bones will start to heal immediately. After he wakes up, and we know his vitals are fine, we'll fit him for a couple of wheels so he can move around freely. We can't do that until he is completely awake. So, call us before you come to get him."

"All right, but I don't think Mr. Duggar can take care of him in his home. It's too rough an area for a small dog to have a successful recuperation."

David grinned and spoke up, "I have an idea."

Chapter 17

"My girlfriend, Jenny, might like to foster this puppy. I'll talk to her after work today to find if she would be interested. Her housemate, Spring, might also enjoy being a nurse to a small Labrador. I don't think she has ever fostered an animal or even had a pet before. If the girls aren't interested, my friend, Dexter might be. He has a small dog that might like a companion."

Dr. Onishi commented, "It sounds like David has some friends that could volunteer to take care of Mr. Duggar's dog while his little boy mends. Whatever the case, we'll know more tomorrow. Does Mr. Duggar have a telephone?"

"I'm afraid not. But I bet he would enjoy talking to those girls. They would probably be interested in looking at his sketches; maybe give him some suggestions—if they're careful. He's sensitive about his drawings. I should talk with them before they venture out to see him. They should know about his peculiarities."

"Yeah. I'll clue them in tonight when I see Jenny. I think Dexter should tag along. I can fill everyone in on the care that Mr. Duggar's new dog is receiving."

"That's a good idea, David. Mr. Sandoval has a business to run and you can take some time away from the clinic to talk to our patient's owner." He smiled, "It could be good public relations for the animal clinic."

There wasn't any more I could contribute. I said goodbye to Dr. Onishi and David and left to join Elaine at the Emporium.

After Mr. Sandoval departed, the doctor and I worked on the puppy for nearly an hour. First, the vet gave him an injection to anesthetize him. Then we set the bones, attached splints and wrapped both legs. Dr. Onishi had taken a blood sample to check for disease and malnourishment. The tests were negative.

The clinic stayed open later than normal. Only one patient arrived during the long afternoon. A little girl and her mother brought in a cat that wasn't able to eat and seemed to be frothing at the mouth. We took the feline in the operating area for investigation and discovered the cat had a burr stuck to its tongue. Dr. Onishi used a pair of forceps and extracted the burr and returned the animal to the little girl. I was surprised when he said, "No charge," to the mother.

We closed the clinic promptly at six o'clock. Dr. Onishi slid into his white Nisson and took the highway toward downtown businesses. I usually took our family car to work, but Mom wanted the SUV to take Gwen, almost three years old, to her first dental appointment. I got stuck driving Mom's Forest Service truck illegally. Mom allowed it one time. It wasn't equipped with a booster seat for a child.

The truck was always in need of service after negotiating ever present backroads of dirt, rocks, ruts, and tree limbs. I fired up the engine, swung the beast around and drove to Dex's bike shop about a hundred yards from the clinic. Since the shop was part of his remodeled barn, I figured he must be home. I knew I wouldn't scare him, so I beeped the truck horn three times. I was sure he hadn't heard that horn in some time and would come out to investigate.

I was right. Dex and his father came out of the bike shop. When his dad saw me, he waved and went back inside. I shut down the engine and stuck my head out the window. "Hey, Dex, how'd you like to come with me after dinner to see Jenny and Spring?"

Dex jogged over to the truck and said, "What's up, Doc?"

"Funny, Dex. Can you join me to see the girls tonight?"

"I don't know what they're doing. Have you called ahead?"

"Not yet. I wanted to know your plans before I call Jenny. You want to go?"

"I wasn't planning on anything. I'd like to see Spring though."

"All right! Hop in and have dinner at my place. I'll call Jenny and ask if they want some company. I have a question for the girls about fostering a dog."

I watched Dex hustle back inside the house. A minute later, he came out and joined me in the pickup. As I started the engine, he commented, "This old crate needs to be replaced. Maybe your mom should get an all-terrain vehicle or a motorcycle." He smiled and leaned back to enjoy the ride.

I grinned, "You'll have to give a pitch to my mom about an ATV or a bike. Don't be surprised if she starts laughing."

"I'm not serious but I'll ask her just to see the expression on her face."

In about ten minutes we parked on the driveway beside my stepfather's cruiser. I didn't want to block his car from backing out to the street if an emergency arose. Danny calls our stepdad's official car his battle wagon. He carries a shotgun behind the front seat and wears a holstered revolver at his waist. Dad hasn't fired either gun in three years except for scheduled target practice.

Dex followed me into the house and I asked if Dex could have dinner with us.

Mom answered, "That's fine David, we're having waffles tonight." She grinned, "Can Dexter tolerate waffles?"

"You bet, Mrs. Wilson. Anything you cook will be better than a meal Dad or I can prepare."

"Well, you men had better wash up. Food will be ready when you are."

I commented, "I'm going to call Jenny before I forget. Dex and I want to make a visit to Kincaid's tonight. Something came up today at the clinic."

"Oh? Something important?"

"Yeah, I need to find someone to foster a Labrador puppy. It was run over and both hind legs were broken."

"Whose puppy is it?"

"Mr. Duggar's. His collie, Al, took him to it and he carried it home. Mr. Sandoval brought it to the clinic."

Mom frowned, "How did Mr. Sandoval get involved? You're home one day and you already have me confused."

"I'll explain when we're eating dinner. I have to call Jen, okay?" I smiled and grabbed the phone.

I left Dexter in the living room talking to Dad. As I dialed Jenny's number, I watched Danny come in from outside tossing a football from one hand to the other. He dropped the ball on the floor, made a funny face and I started to laugh.

"*Hello.*"

"Hi Jen. Are you guys busy tonight? If not, could Dexter and I come over? I have a proposal for you."

"*David Drum, does this involve a ring?*"

She sounded really serious. I knew she was pulling my chain, so I decided to follow with something grave.

"It's very important, Jen. A life depends on your answer."

"*Your life?*"

I didn't respond but from the tone of her voice, I couldn't tell whether she was grinning or not. Spring was undoubtedly listening. I decided to quit fooling around. "I want to see you and Dex wants to see Spring. Is it all right for us to come over? It shouldn't take very long if you are planning on going to bed early."

There were a couple of seconds of silence before Jen said, "*Come on over, we're not doing anything important. We'd like to present you guys with an idea we have. We've been thinking about a project but weren't sure when you would be home for the summer."*

"Okay. We'll be coming over in about half an hour. We're just starting dinner."

"All right. We'll get dressed."

I could hear both girls laughing. I said, "Bye, Jen."

"Bye, David."

I had to wash to remove any animal residue from my hands. Dad and Dex were both seated at the table and waiting for me. I cleaned up in a flash and hurried to the table. Dad was prying open the waffle iron with a table knife as I sat down. Gwen was waving a fork around and I almost asked Mom if she had goggles for us to wear for eye protection. I didn't know if Mom had a good day, so I refrained.

As we waited for the waffles, Mom asked, "How was your first day at the clinic?"

"Dr. Onishi is calm and professional. I wasn't sure how we would get along, but he's a nice guy. We had two severe cases today, one with a dog and one with a cat."

"Earlier, I asked you about Mr. Sandoval."

"Oh, yeah. He brought in a Labrador puppy with broken hind legs. We think the dog was hit by a car. He got the dog from Mr. Duggar."

"I'm guessing; you want to ask Jenny and Spring to foster the puppy until the legs heal."

"That's right, Mom. Do you think it's a good idea?"

Dad placed a quarter waffle on my plate. I smeared butter on it and added Maple syrup. I took a big bite as Mom replied. "Jenny and Spring are very loving girls. They will take care of a puppy no matter what the case. However, they might have some plans that would not include taking care of a small dependent animal. Don't be disappointed if they refuse."

"I thought of that possibility. That's why I'm taking Dex with me." I looked at him and chuckled.

He swallowed and said, "Yeah, sure. I'm going as his backup because I have experience with a small dog."

"Skimmer is half the size of this puppy, Dex. I'll bet Skimmer would enjoy teasing a dog twice his size and not worry about being chased."

"Yeah, that's right. How's the pup supposed to get around without his rear legs?"

"I'm not sure but I'll bet Onishi has that figured out."

As Dad served more waffles, he commented, "I've seen injured animals fitted with wheels until they can get their legs functioning again. They might also require physical therapy. Sometimes they are fitted with a more permanent prosthesis."

I was amazed that Dad knew about the rehabilitation of injured animals. He must have seen a TV production or read a book about veterinary work. I didn't have enough time to ask him about it; Dex and I had to get going to see the girls. I took a look at Dex to see if he had finished eating and he motioned toward the back door with his head. It was time to hit the road.

We thanked Mom and Dad for dinner and I kissed Gwen on the top of her head.

Danny asked, "Aren't you gonna to give me a kiss?"

I walked toward him and he began to shy away. I grabbed his head and roughed up his hair with my knuckles. "That's the only kiss you'll get from me, bub." Mom and Dad laughed and Gwen squealed, "Don't hurt Danny!"

"I didn't hurt him, Gwen. I was just playing."

Dex and I took the SUV for a more comfortable and dependable ride to Jenny's. The girls were sitting on the porch steps when we arrived. Even though it was summer, the evening air was cool. Both girls wore sweatshirts and jeans and had their hair in ponytails. They looked like high schoolers. Dex and I wore light jackets I obtained from my bedroom closet. We wore jeans and T-shirts when we ate.

Both girls were grinning and waved when we pulled up next to the porch. As we exited the car, we were greeted with hugs and in my case, a big kiss, just as expected. I didn't see what happened on the other side of the car but Dex and Spring were holding hands as they walked to the front door.

I held Jenny at arm's length and said, "You look great." We held hands and looked at each other as if we had been separated for years rather than a couple of months since spring break.

"Let's go inside and you can tell me about the clinic. Spring made some fresh coffee and I baked some cookies."

I was happy to be alone with Jenny but she latched onto my left hand and nearly dragged me up the porch steps. When we stepped inside, Dex and Spring were sitting together on the sofa looking at a magazine. Dex glanced up at me and said, "Are you going to ask them?"

Jenny pushed me down beside Dexter saying, "Do you guys want some coffee?"

"And a cookie?" added Spring.

"Hold it a minute. Before we have any refreshments, I have to ask you something. It's important."

Jenny sat on the arm of the sofa, "Okay. Shoot."

I asked the girls, "Could you find it in your hearts to foster a Labrador puppy? It's hind legs are broken."

Jenny glanced at Spring and they both shrugged their shoulders. Spring frowned, "Tell us more about this puppy. Is it potty trained and how big is it?"

She looked at Dexter and he replied, "Don't ask me. I haven't seen it."

Chapter 18

"I think you know Mr. Sandoval. Right?" The girls nodded. I continued, "He brought a puppy to the clinic today and Dr. Onishi took some x-rays. Both hind legs are broken so the little guy will need to be cared for. I'm not sure how long but he'll have to wear a diaper in the house."

Jenny asked, "Did Mr. Sandoval hit the dog with his car?"

"No, he got the dog from Mr. Duggar. Samuel found the dog near a little used road and carried it home. His dog, Al, took him to the injured puppy."

Spring started laughing, "Mr. Duggar has a dog named Al?"

I chuckled, "Yeah, a dirty collie showed up at his house. Duggar didn't know what kind of dog it was until he gave it a bath. Since the dog was alone, he named it Alone, Al for short. It makes sense, don't you think?"

Jenny and Dexter were now laughing. Jenny asked, "So what did Mr. Duggar name the puppy?"

"I don't know. Mr. Sandoval didn't say. Maybe you guys can give the dog a name if you want to take care of it for a few weeks—until the bones heal. Then it will be returned to Mr. Duggar."

Jenny inquired, "Describe the little dog for us."

"It's about twice the size of Skimmer, completely black and looks discouraged. He appears sad, probably because of the inability to use his hind legs. When he looks at you, it seems he's asking for help."

Jen and Spring faced each other and talked quietly for a minute, almost whispering. Then Spring said, "We want to see the puppy before we decide. Is that okay?"

"Sure. Come to the clinic tomorrow and I'll introduce you."

Dexter commented, "Okay, how about some coffee and cookies?"

Jenny stood up and started toward the kitchen but abruptly stopped and turned around. "We have a request for you guys." Spring sat on the sofa eagerly waiting to hear Jenny's appeal.

"We want you guys to take us on a mission into the forest to find a cabin."

I looked at Dex and we both grinned. We knew of half a dozen cabins in the woods. That was an easy request to satisfy. We could ride on bicycles to several cabins. We'll take a picnic lunch and make a day of it.

"We know where several cabins are located, Jen. When do you want to go?"

"We don't want to go to just any old cabin, David. We want to go to the site of the cabin in the picture at the B and B. We want to take our canvases and oils."

I glanced at Dex, "Have you seen that picture?"

"I've never been in a B and B, so no. I'd like to see the painting though. It sounds interesting. Let's stop at the B and B and take a look on the way home tonight."

Jenny chuckled, "Spring and I have pictures of it on our phones. You don't have to go to the B and B. I'll get the coffee and then we'll show you the picture. It was painted by Margret Duggar. Was that Duggar's wife or daughter?"

"That was his wife, Jen, but she passed away about thirty years ago. She was only about sixty. That cabin might be in ruins or overgrown with vegetation. The forest might have completely changed by now. Three decades might have totally erased an isolated cabin that hasn't been cared for."

Dex added, "Yeah, we might find a pile of logs with vermin living there."

Spring reacted, "So, you guys think it's a dumb idea?"

Jen's frown was replaced with a broad smile. She remarked, "What if someone has taken care of the cabin—like Mr. Duggar? Remember, he had a bunch of drawings of cabins. What if he's been there recently?"

"Yeah, that's right! I think all of us should pay him a visit. Maybe we can get some directions so we can locate that cabin. He might even have it marked on a map." A thought instantly struck me, "But if the log house has special meaning to him, he might not want us to go there."

Spring offered, "What if we foster his puppy and when it's walking again, we can visit Mr. Duggar. Do you think he might agree to show us the cabin then?"

I scanned the girls and Dex. Everyone nodded in agreement. "Okay. Let's follow Spring's idea." I clapped my hands and said, "Now that's settled. What about coffee and cookies?"

We talked until nine thirty about activities we each had experienced in the last nine months. The girls spent the late fall and winter months in Arizona fighting heat on the Navaho Nation. Dex was in Suddenly working with his father on their bike shop and caring for the Kincaid residence while the girls were away. I was in Butte in vet school but made it home for visits during the holidays and spring break.

Dex swallowed the last cookie and I started yawning around 9:45. It was time to say goodnight.

Jen followed me out to the car, gave me a big kiss and ran back in the house. My attention was devoted to Jenny so I didn't see if Dex was having any success in the romance department. I'd notice if he had a smile on his face when he got into the car. He did.

"Spring said you should expect them at the clinic after lunch. They really want to see the puppy. She told me you should warn them if the puppy is in distress."

That wasn't a problem. One of the topics drilled into me in class was the recognition of the feelings of pet owners. Their pet was a member of the family and both pet and owner should be treated with the utmost respect. I backed the SUV to the street and took the short route to Dex's place.

Dex was abnormally quiet on the way home. As I turned into his lane, he commented, "You know, I was worried that Spring didn't think much of me. I'm not worried anymore. I guess because she's a year older than me doesn't make any difference. That's been on my mind."

"I didn't think that was a problem, Dex. Jen didn't think so either. We have confidence in you."

"Thanks, David. Good night."

"See you tomorrow. Tell your dad hello for me." Dex popped the door open, slid out of the front seat and jogged to his front door. I turned the car around and headed for home.

When I woke up Wednesday morning, my first thoughts were to get to the veterinary clinic as soon as possible to check on the puppy. Dr. Onishi had given me a key so I could monitor animals' well-being, especially if they had been anesthetized. The doctor had to take care of his own animals before arriving at the clinic, usually about nine o'clock. I was assigned the task to check things an hour earlier.

It took me about ten minutes to visit the bathroom and put on my clinic uniform. I glanced in the mirror and thought I looked like a service station attendant. Danny was still in bed, probably happy not to have a summer job. I'll have to clue him in about starting a college fund; he's only two years from attending a university.

Mom and Dad were sitting at the breakfast table drinking coffee when I moseyed into the kitchen. I noticed Gwen's absence. She was still in bed getting ten hours of deep sleep which gave Mom and Dad an opportunity to be together without interruption. I caught the gist of their conversation and listened attentively. They were talking about the veterinary clinic and Dr. Onishi. Jacob Onishi had moved into Walters' three acre farm at the southern edge of town and barely outside the city limits. He was married, had two children, a horse, several sheep and a dog. They knew more than I did; I had only worked one day with the doctor.

Mom and Dad said, "Good morning," simultaneously.

I yawned and replied, "Morning." I sat down and put two pieces of bread in the toaster. Mom got up, poured me a cup of coffee and got a jar of strawberry jam from the refrigerator.

Dad coughed and when I glanced at him, he asked, "What are you going to do with your yard care business?"

I had prepared an answer when I realized I was going to work at the veterinary clinic. "I was hoping Danny would take over. He needs to start earning money for college instead of playing around with his buddies all the time. I haven't talked to him about it yet. I might need some adult influence. I don't think he has much of a work ethic. I'll talk it over with him tonight."

Dad offered another option. "Maybe you guys can share the workload. There are several hours of daylight after dinner. You could have him do afternoon jobs and you could do evening ones. He would learn from you at the same time. Try to work something out for your mutual benefit, okay?"

"Good idea. Thanks, Dad. See you tonight."

Dad rose hurriedly, gave Mom a big hug and kiss and was out the door. I was a bit slower but gave Mom a kiss on the cheek. I stood beside the kitchen door and said, "I've got to check on the puppy at the clinic this morning. Onishi doesn't get in for another hour. Please tell Danny I want to talk to him when I get home for dinner. I'll see you later. Bye, Mom."

"Don't get bitten by an animal, David. Bye."

When I arrived at the clinic, the first thing I checked was the air conditioning unit. Summer days were going to be uncomfortable for animals without AC. The overnight temp was set for sixty-eight degrees. A quick glance at the inside thermometer indicated the system was working perfectly. Then I adjusted the window blinds to block most of the morning sun. Next was to check on the puppy.

The little Lab was curled up in the back left corner of his cage and looked up at me when I approached. His eyes seemed to have more life in them today; he wagged his tail but didn't try to move. He had probably tried moving at night and realized the casts prevented him from standing on his own. His water was running low so I opened his cage and filled his bowl. He watched me closely but didn't shy away, growl or bark. I believed he understood I was trying to help.

I talked to him so he would get accustomed to my voice. "How are you doing this morning, little guy? We fixed your legs so they will be straight and strong but it is going to take some time before you can run and play again. The doctor hasn't told me how long it takes your bones to mend. In the meantime I will try to find you a family to take care of you. Two pretty young ladies will visit you today. I think you will like them."

It was obvious that the puppy's urinary tract was working fine. His yellow stained bedding needed to be changed. I'll have the doctor assist me. There has to be a simple method. The pup must not have eaten much recently. There was no sign of any colorful fecal deposits. Could his spinal injury cause other problems? That was another thing to ask the doctor about. I didn't know if I should give him any food.

I stood there searching the kennel for anything that needed attention but everything was in order. I decided to go back to the front reception area. I left the door to the kennels open in case the puppy needed care. I booted the computer to play a game of solitaire before Onishi arrived. But I didn't have the password, so after three guesses and no success, I turned it off. I picked up a brochure about immunizations for cats and dogs and began to read.

A few minutes passed with the pamphlet and I heard a car arrive. Dr. Onishi was right on time. I placed the reading material back in the display rack and waited.

"How's our patient this morning, David?"

"He seems to be fine. He's a little wet, but no poop."

Onishi nodded and entered the kennel. I followed him into the back room. We cleaned the puppy's cage and the young dog whimpered when we put a diaper on him.

"Let's see if we can get him moving with some wheels." The doctor opened a cabinet and pulled out what appeared to be a large shoebox. He tossed the box to me and said, "Open this and let's see if we can fit the apparatus on our patient. But before we try the device, I want to check his spine."

That's when I offered, "When I came in to check on him, he wagged his tail."

"That's a good sign, but I think he's experiencing some pain when we move him. Let's see if he can tolerate our handling. It might be too soon for us to fit him with the prosthetic device."

Chapter 19

I stepped back from the cage to give the doctor access. Dr. Onishi crouched and attempted to pick up the puppy but was surprised when the pup snapped and growled at him. Onishi looked at me and commented, "He didn't try to bite you when we put on the diaper. Maybe you should try to pick him up."

I reached into the cage and slid my right hand underneath his rear end. He watched me intently but didn't growl, so I slid my left hand under his right front shoulder and lifted. Success! No snapping or growling.

"I guess he likes you, David. You have a new friend. I think we should wait on the prosthesis; maybe give it a week or so. I've been too optimistic."

I put the puppy back in his cage and asked, "What are we going to feed him? I have no idea when he ate last; probably several days ago."

The doctor responded, "Get a two pound bag of Balanced High-Diet for puppies from the admissions room and follow the package instructions. We'll see how he does on that."

I read the directions on the package and estimated the puppy's weight to be about ten pounds. That meant I should give him four half cup meals per day with plenty of water. I jotted the time and the quantity of food on the record slip at the exterior of the cage. I added the solid rations to a saucer-like feeding dish and slid it toward the puppy. He immediately began to eat, apparently famished. I refilled his water bowl and shut the enclosure door.

Dr. Onishi called me to admissions and asked, "Have you been able to find anyone to foster our latest visitor? I realize you haven't had much time."

"I visited with my girlfriend and her housemate last night and we talked about fostering. They're coming to see the puppy at one o'clock. Once they see him, I think they'll do it. But there might be one problem. When we tell them it will take eight weeks for the bones to heal, they might change their minds."

"Any other leads?"

"Well, my best friend, Dexter Young. He has a small dog that might enjoy a companion. And then there is Mr. Duggar, but he doesn't like following routines and the environment is primitive."

"If the puppy belongs to Mr. Duggar, don't you think he would want to take care of it?"

"He would probably have good intentions but he's in his nineties and might be forgetful. He's possessed with sketching pictures of a cabin; I'm not sure why but I suspect it has something to do with his late wife. She was an accomplished artist."

"You think he is suffering from Alzheimer's?"

"No, he's mentally sharp but sometimes gets sidetracked. He lives alone and seems to enjoy solitude. He doesn't have many visitors and is a bit surly with the unannounced."

"Do you think he can pay for the medical expenses incurred for the puppy's care?"

"I don't know anything about his finances, Dr. Onishi. I'm sure Mr. Duggar doesn't have a telephone, so we can't call him. Maybe you should ask Mr. Sandoval."

"Let's keep track of the puppy's expenses, I can't run the clinic free of charge, even for a forgetful elderly gentleman."

I reached into the top drawer beneath the desk computer and extracted a sales record book. I started a tally for things we had done for the puppy and stuck the pad back in the drawer. I heard the front door open and looked to see who had entered.

"Hi, David. I went over to your house to see Gwen. Your mother told me you were working here this summer. How have you been?"

I was surprised and a bit jolted by Megan Isaac's appearance. I hadn't seen my former girlfriend in almost two years. She left home to go to California to attend Stanford and we hadn't talked except for a phone call at Christmas a year and a half ago. That was nothing more than a few words to say Merry Christmas.

I swallowed quickly to prevent croaking and replied, "Hi, Meg, you've shortened your hair." She was as pretty as ever and exuded self-confidence. I guess moving to a large west coast city had agreed with her. I replied, "I've been great. I finished my second year of pre-veterinary medicine two days ago. Are you on a break from Stanford?"

"Uh-huh. I have a week off before I start working with a research group for the summer. I wanted to check my financial situation with my father. Stanford is expensive but everyone is really smart. I've had to study a lot, especially math and physics."

"Not much socializing?"

"No time for it. I have to maintain a high GPA, or I'll never get into the graduate program; there's a great deal of competition. Could we go out tonight? Get some ice cream at Dairy Queen?"

"Sorry, Megan, but Jenny and Spring are double dating with Dex and me. We have some plans for the summer. It was nice seeing you again though. Good luck with your summer research."

"Oh, I forgot about Jenny. How is she doing?"

"She's doing great. Spring and Jenny spent the last six months on the Navaho Nation in Arizona. They came back with lots of enthusiasm to investigate some cabins in the forest. The four of us are going on an expedition later this summer."

"Ugh, a camping trip—and bugs. Well, have fun. I'll be in sunny California enjoying the weather."

"Well, I'd better get back to work. Say hi to your parents for me."

"I'll do that. Bye, David."

"See you, Megan."

I watched her go out the door and climb into her dad's jeep, the same old army car I had used to teach Meg how to drive a stick shift. Geez, that seems like it was a long time ago. I guess it was, it had been four years. Had Megan gone out to Hadley's to see Rick? He learned to walk almost normally after nearly losing both legs in that logging accident. I didn't mention that Jenny and Spring were coming to the clinic to see about fostering the Labrador puppy. I was slightly apprehensive that Megan might show up when Jenny was here causing an uncomfortable situation.

"Who was that young lady, David?"

"An old girlfriend, Megan Isaacs. She's the banker's daughter."

"That seems strange. I've seen her mother and father. Where did her beauty come from? She's a strikingly beautiful young woman."

Unsure of whether I should tell Onishi that my stepfather, Scott Wilson, was Megan's biological father, not Mr. Isaacs, I decided to keep my mouth shut. According to my mom, and I agree, the sheriff is a very handsome man.

I went back in the kennel area and picked up the box containing the prosthesis or what I thought it was called. I decided to investigate, to picture how it would fit to a small dog. I cut the tape holding the box closed and dumped the contents on the counter near the x-ray station. There were two wheels with metal supports attached to a vest-like girdle with Velcro fasteners. The diagram with the apparatus on a small dog described it as a wheelchair for small dogs with deformed or damaged hind legs.

I pretended fingers of my left hand were injured and installed the wheelchair on my left forearm. My arm was too small for the girdle to fit properly but I could imagine how the apparatus would aid a dog to move around using its front legs to pull his body and damaged legs about. I toyed around with the doggie wheelchair until I heard from Doctor Onishi, "David, as soon as you are through with the wheelchair, I'd like you to take an inventory of all cat and dog balanced diet products. I want to send off an order this afternoon."

I hadn't heard anyone enter the clinic but when I went to the front, Dr. Onishi was talking to an older Asian woman who had brought in her cat for a checkup and shots. I had never seen her before. Her English wasn't very good. She was probably someone that had come to Suddenly while I was at the university. The doctor said something I didn't understand when he took the cat into his arms. I heard the lady and the doctor mumbling, so I listened closely. I soon figured out they were talking in Japanese, so I tuned them out.

I imagined Danny in this situation and what he might be thinking. This woman is probably a covert agent posing as an old lady. I grinned at the thought and continued the inventory. Dr. Onishi took the cat in back accompanied by the owner and I was left to continue to review the stock. In spite of the lack of patients, we were running low on several items.

As I completed my survey, Dexter walked in with Skimmer. "Hey, David, I decided to get Skimmer deballed."

I laughed and said, "Neutered or castrated, Dex."

"Whatever. You know what I mean. I think he needs some shots, too. Give him the works; kind of like a ten thousand mile checkup. Make sure you change the oil. Check the battery and antifreeze." He gave me a goofy smile and we both laughed.

"Okay, Dex, but it's going to cost you."

"That's all right. Anything for my best buddy. Dad will share expenses."

"Oh, guess who came in this morning."

"Danny?"

"No, come on Dex. Think, someone unexpected."

He frowned and shook his head. "I don't know. Who was it?"

"Megan. She wanted me to get ice cream with her."

"No shit? She knows you're going with Jenny. What's she trying to do?"

"I don't know. I told her that you and I were doubling with Jen and Spring so I had other plans. She'll be going back to Stanford in a week—a summer research project."

"How'd she look?"

"Gorgeous, short hair and nice tan. She seems to be content in sunny California but no social life. Onishi said he was surprised she was the daughter of Mr. and Mrs. Isaacs, since she is so good looking."

"Did you tell him about the sperm donor thing?"

"No, I didn't. Maybe someday the topic will come up and I'll explain. Let's put Skimmer in a kennel enclosure. We'll get to him this afternoon. He'll be anesthetized and stay overnight."

We took Skimmer in the backroom and placed him in the cage adjacent to the Labrador puppy. Dr. Onishi escorted the elderly woman to her car and returned to talk to Dexter about caring for Skimmer.

After introductions, we went to the kennels and the doctor carried out a quick exam of Skimmer.

While Onishi examined the tiny dog, Dexter related how Skimmer got his name.

"So, you don't know the actual age of your pet. I would guess that he's about four years old. How long have you had him?"

Dex thought for a couple of seconds, "About three years. Is he in good shape?"

Onishi nodded, "You have taken good care of Skimmer. His heart is strong and he has good muscle tone. The only thing he needs is a little dental work. We can take care of that. After the castration, it will take about forty eight hours for the anesthesia to completely wear off. He will have to wear a collar for a couple of days so he doesn't lick at the stitches."

"Okay. Can you give me an estimate of the cost?"

"It will run about two hundred dollars. That includes an overnight stay at the clinic."

Dex smiled and said, "How about a deduction for being a good friend of David?"

Onishi grinned and glanced at me. I nodded. "All right, we'll do that. Ten percent off for a close friend of a clinic employee."

We closed the clinic from noon 'til one o'clock. The doctor went home for lunch and I went across the street with Dexter. His father joined us for sandwiches, coffee and conversation. It was disturbing to hear that Larrea's mother, Spring's grandmother, was sick from complications from Covid. Larrea Wisdom, Spring's mother, was working for a firefighter training facility on the Navaho Nation so she could be close to her mother.

I watched the clock closely and at ten to one, I excused myself from Youngs' and started walking back to the clinic. I wanted to be there when Jenny and Spring arrived to see the puppy. The sun on my head and shoulders indicated it was going to be a fairly warm day. After two minutes in the heat, I was happy to get back in the air conditioned building.

Chapter 20

Dex said he would come over to the clinic when Spring and Jenny arrived. He could monitor the clinic parking area from the window on the second floor of his house, originally a dilapidated barn, still under renovation. I helped him with the foundation and roof when he decided to rebuild the old barn. The structure was transformed into a nice looking home with additional help from his father. They added a room to one side of the house for their bicycle and motorbike shop.

When Jenny's pickup arrived, I checked the time. The girls were sure punctual; it was several seconds before one o'clock. The office digital clock changed from 12:59 to 1:00 when the truck parked in the front parking area. I went to the front door to welcome them to the clinic. As I unlocked the door, I saw Dexter come running down the lane from his house. He had seen Jenny's pickup approaching.

"Come in ladies. I have a black Lab puppy to show you. He needs a temporary home for two months."

Jenny and Spring were dressed as twins, the same white short sleeve shirts and light-blue jeans with holes in the knees but different colored sneakers.

"Two months? It's going to take two months for his legs to heal?"

"Jenny, that's not very long. If it were a human bone it could take four to six months. I've seen that happen on the Navaho Nation. If the break is more complicated, it might take even longer."

"I didn't realize it would take that long; I thought it might be a few weeks to a month. I didn't know, I've never had any experience with animals. Well, David, show us the puppy."

"Follow me ladies."

As I started into the examination and surgery area, I heard Dexter come in the front door.

"Hey, wait for me." He hustled to get behind Spring.

I escorted my three visitors to the kennel cages where the puppy and Skimmer were being housed.

Jenny exclaimed, "Is that Skimmer?" Skimmer had reacted and moved to the front of the cage, tail wagging. He recognized all of us and started to whine.

"Yeah, that's Skimmer. He's going to have his manhood removed and get some shots that are overdue. Dex brought him in this morning for a checkup."

"Can I pet him? I think he wants out of the cage," Jen inquired.

"I guess so. We haven't done anything to him yet. Dr. Onishi and I will operate later today. But we want him to get used to the cage. He'll be a bit goofy after being anesthetized."

Spring had ignored Skimmer and was attracted to the puppy who crawled to the cage door.

"Oh, Jen, look at those lovely puppy eyes. What an adorable little dog. I'll bet he is heartbroken having to deal with two broken legs. Is he going to have to drag his hind legs around? He looks so uncomfortable wearing those casts."

"No. We have a doggy wheelchair for him. We're waiting for the anesthesia to completely wear off, maybe another day or so. Then we'll fit him with wheels so he can do zoomies."

Jenny commented, "Doesn't a young dog have to be happy or full of pent-up energy to run zoomies? When the casts are gone and he's using his hind legs again, then he'll zoom around. Don't you agree?"

I had to go along with Jen. "Yeah, you're probably right. What do you ladies think? Can you foster him?" I had a sinking feeling that the girls were going to say no. The little Lab was going to require too much of their time. They had spent six months in Arizona planning activities in the Bitterroots. Why would they give the pursuits up for a stranger's nameless puppy? Still, they showed compassion for the injured dog.

The girls stared at each other for a few seconds before Jenny said, "Let us think about it. Is that all right? We'll tell you tomorrow, okay?"

"Sure. It's not something to take lightly. You are my first choice but I'll understand if you say no. I won't think any less of you."

"We're going to see Mr. Duggar this afternoon about his sketches. We won't decide until we talk with him. I'll call you tonight, David, and tell you about our meeting with the old guy."

"Okay, Jen. Talk to you later, but don't call me after ten. That's my bedtime." I grinned, "I'll call you after dinner to see how your visit with Mr. Duggar went. Will you guys be home?"

Spring interjected, "We'll be home. Call any time; you too, Dexter."

Jen and Spring left for Duggar's after Doctor Onishi returned to the clinic. He took time to explain the procedure for Skimmer and asked if they wanted to observe. The girls rejected the offer but Dexter agreed to watch the operation, so I gave him a disposable gown and a bar stool so he could observe from a convenient location. He was most interested in the application of anesthesia. I watched Dex's concerned expressions as Skimmer went to sleep. Dr. Onishi removed the testicles and closed the incisions with stiches. Then he gave the little dog antibiotics and overdue drugs for preventing common canine diseases. I placed a plastic collar on Skimmer to prevent him from licking the wounds and put him back in his cage. I'd check on him periodically until time for shutting down the clinic. Dexter thanked us for the opportunity to observe the surgery and care we gave his buddy. He would return to get Skimmer in twenty-four hours.

"Do you know where we're going?" asked Spring.

"Uh-huh. David gave me directions. Duggar's place is on the left about ten miles from Suddenly. We can see the house from the road; it's about fifty yards from the turnoff."

"Okay, I'll be watching—but don't go too fast."

"I don't think we'll miss it. The speed limit is only twenty-five miles per hour."

"Have you been thinking about that little puppy?"

"I have, but I'm afraid it might stop us from carrying out our plans for the summer. I didn't think fostering would take at least two months. We can't take off for several days to search for cabins as art subjects if we have to nurse an injured dog."

"That's right. I'm also afraid that I might get attached emotionally and have to give him up when his legs heal. I've never had responsibility for a pet before."

We drove another mile before I had a sudden thought, slowed the pickup, pulled off on the right shoulder and shut off the engine.

"What's wrong, Jenny? Do we have a flat?"

"No, nothing's wrong with the truck. I have an idea. Remember Mrs. Sandoval?"

Spring frowned and then replied, "Oh, the lady that we met at the high school. She was applying for the art teaching job."

"That's the one. If we foster the puppy and want to go on a cabin hunt with the boys for a few days, maybe she could sub for us and take care of the pup. What do you think?"

"That would be fantastic! But do you think she would agree?"

"I don't know, but at least we can ask her. It would only be sporadic and for a few days at a time."

"That is such a good idea, Jen—an artist helping artists."

I smiled, watched a dump truck pass us and restarted the engine. We spent two more quiet minutes on the road and Spring alerted, "There's the turn—I can see the house."

I braked to slow the pickup to a crawl, made the sharp left turn and continued down the dirt lane to the main structure. As soon as

I stopped the truck, a dog appeared from the right side of the house and began to bark. I stayed in the cab but Spring got out, knelt, and snapped her fingers. The collie sat about ten feet away and stared at Spring.

"That's okay, Al. Don't get in a tizzy, it's only a young lady. She won't hurt us."

The elderly man, holding a hatchet, had followed the dog from behind the house.

"You must be Mr. Duggar. We've come to see your sketches. We're artists and have a great interest in using cabins as subjects in our artwork. We heard you have been sketching cabins."

"Who told you?"

"Our boyfriends, David Drum and Dexter Young."

Jenny joined me and said, "I'm Jenny Kincaid and this is Spring Wisdom. We'd like to take a look at your sketches, if that's all right."

"I don't understand. Why do you want to see my drawings?"

Jenny answered, "Okay. We are going to take a hike into the woods to find a cabin that we can use as a subject for some artwork. Dexter and David will go with us cause we don't know much about camping in the forest. We are afraid we might run on to a bear, a moose, or something else that is dangerous. Since you have some drawings of cabins, we thought they would give us an idea of what we want to look for, something with real character."

Mr. Duggar stood like a statue for a moment staring into space before saying, "All right, I'll show you my drawings. I'll get them for you to look at; they're in the house." He turned and disappeared around the side of the house with Al following.

Spring faced me and commented, "Mr. Duggar doesn't seem so strange. The guys gave us a different impression of the old gentleman."

"He doesn't use his front door. That seems a little strange, don't you think?"

"Yeah, why is it boarded up? We should ask him." Spring shrugged and frowned.

Mr. Duggar came back into view holding a wad of papers looking as if they had been scooped up from being scattered in disarray on the floor. I commented, "Let me put the tailgate down so we can spread them out for better viewing."

Duggar gave several sheets of paper to each of us. We smoothed them out and arranged them on the bed and tailgate of the truck. After we examined the sketches, Spring asked, "Do you know where all these cabins are located, Mr. Duggar?"

Duggar began to laugh. We were perplexed, and began to understand why the boys said Duggar was a bit strange.

I asked, "What's so funny, sir?"

"These aren't pictures of real cabins, they're what I recollect from my dreams. The only pictures that remain of a real cabin are the one my wife painted at Jean's B and B and the one in my bathroom. I haven't visited the cabin in more than a year. Come to think of it, I should go out there again before summer is gone. When the weather gets foul it's a difficult trip."

"Where is the cabin?" quizzed Spring.

Duggar waved his right arm. "Fifteen or twenty miles up north. I never kept track of the exact distance. It's a good two day hike, maybe longer. I'm not a young man anymore." He paused, nodding his head. "Say, by any chance do you young ladies know anything about that black puppy I rescued, the one with the broken legs?"

Jenny replied, "Yes, we saw it right after lunch. The veterinarian put casts on its legs and said it will take two months to heal. David Drum works there and he asked us if we could foster the puppy for that time but we haven't decided yet. Would you be able to take care of the puppy for four weeks?"

"That would keep me tied down for two months, wouldn't it? How does the little dog get around?"

"It will be using a wheelchair, an attachment so it can run around without straining its hind legs. We also want to ask if you can afford to pay for the vet bill. It will be expensive."

"A wheelchair for an animal? Never had a dog with a wheelchair. I can pay the doctor's bill. The vet only has to see Mr. Isaacs at the bank. I don't handle money out here. I don't want to take care of a little dog unless it's healthy, like Al. He's no bother. Al would help me with the little dog when he's better—teach him some things."

"What do you think of taking two girls with you to the cabin? We could help you cook and get wood for a campfire." My proposal was an attempt to go straight to the cabin without bothering David and Dexter, since they both have jobs.

Duggar scratched his shaggy gray beard for a few seconds. "No. I don't think that would work. Al and I will go alone—it's kind of a secret between Margret and me. It's a special place."

"Okay, it was just a suggestion. We'll find another cabin for our artwork."

"Well, ladies, I have to prepare firewood. It takes several cords to get me through the long winter here in the mountains. I'll sell some, too. You know your way back to town?" He started backing towards his house and tapped his leg for Al to follow. He gave us a little wave and said, "Tell Efren hello for me."

Spring and I took a few steps toward my pickup and I said, "Thanks for talking with us Mr. Duggar."

Chapter 21

On the way back to town, I commented to Spring, "I can't believe all those sketches were from him recalling dreams. How could he remember all those details from dreams? I think he was dishonest, especially after saying Margret's cabin was special to them."

"He wants to keep its location a secret. What is so significant about it? Do you think he really has fond memories of a cabin in the woods?"

"Maybe all he has are memories that he wants to preserve. But his drawings are quite good, don't you think?"

"Yes, I was surprised. That's another thing, I don't think a person can remember what he shows in those sketches. If you are dreaming and wake up, the images vanish in a few minutes, don't they? Could it be that he does the drawings so he doesn't forget—they serve as constant reminders?"

"I agree about the dreams. I think he is just imagining things. But why so many drawings? Is he trying to remember something he saw long ago?"

Spring said, "Let's visit with Mrs. Sandoval at the hardware store and then go to the B and B and find out if that's the same picture we have recorded on our phones. If there is another painting, I want to see what is so special about it. What causes Mr. Duggar to have recurring dreams about it? Is he telling us the truth?"

Fifteen minutes later, I parked in front of the Emporium. Spring and I entered the store and were greeted by smiling Mr. Sandoval.

"Well, ladies, what can I help you with today, something to decorate your house or pickup?"

"No, Mr. Sandoval, nothing like that. We would like to speak to your wife."

"Oh. Is it about the teaching job?"

We shook our heads and he said, "She's upstairs in the office. You can go up to talk with her."

I said, "Thank you," and we started up the steps. "He sure is a curious man, kind of like my grandmother." I laughed and Spring chuckled, "Mine, too."

At the top of the stairs, I called out, "Mrs. Sandoval?"

Elaine replied as she appeared from the office doorway, "Hello, girls, how may I help you?"

Spring said, "Hi. We want to talk to you about a puppy."

"Really? Please come in my office. I'm interested."

Elaine gave foldup chairs to us and we sat down in the limited office space on the store's balcony level. The office had several metal filing cabinets, a desk and chair, and a small counter occupied by a coffee maker. A computer was at the center of the desk.

"Would you like some coffee?"

I glanced at Spring and she shook her head. "No thank you. Do you know about the puppy your husband delivered to the animal clinic—the Labrador?"

"Yes. Efren and I talked about it. I want to get two puppies but Efren wants to wait until the business is more secure before we tackle more responsibilities. I reluctantly have to agree with him."

I raised my eyebrows in dismay but decided to explain. "We want to foster the puppy, but we have plans to take several days to travel into the forest to seek subjects for our artwork. When we are gone for a few days we'd like you to temporarily take over for us and be a nurse for the puppy."

Spring added, "It wouldn't require much effort. He'll have a wheelchair for mobility and wear a diaper in the house. He will just need to be fed and have a person around so he doesn't get lonely."

I had to ask, "Do you have a large house, enough space for him to be active?"

Elaine smiled, "Space is not a problem, girls." She grinned, "My husband is the problem. I'll have to talk it over with him before I can agree. I'd love to have this experience."

Efren suddenly appeared at the office door. "Did you get the teaching job?"

Elaine replied, "That's not why the girls came to see me, it's about fostering that puppy you took to the clinic."

"You know what I think about having a dog, Elaine. I haven't changed my mind."

I came to the rescue. "Spring and I want to foster the puppy, Mr. Sandoval. Your wife would only take care of it while we go on adventures with David and Dexter. At most, it would be for only a few days."

"So how much time would this require?"

"Only a couple of days twice during the summer. It wouldn't be for very long."

"Well, in that case, I'll go along with it. I can run the store by myself for a few days. How long would this fostering period extend?"

"Dr. Onishi estimates the puppy would need help for two months."

Efren nodded to us, "Okay, as long as it doesn't extend into the fall and winter. When business picks up, I'll need Elaine here."

Spring reacted, "But Mr. Sandoval, what if your wife is hired to be the art teacher?"

He smiled, "If that happens, we'll have two sources of income and we can afford to hire someone to help at the store."

We heard someone enter the Emporium. Mr. Sandoval turned away from the office and went down to the ground floor. Elaine said, "I guess I'll help with the puppy. When can I meet with him? What is his name?"

"Thank you. You can see him at the clinic. He doesn't have a name yet but Jenny and I have considered Charcoal as a name. What do you think?"

"I think that's better than Blacky. May I ask what are you going into the forest to seek as art subjects?"

"Have you seen Mr. Duggar's sketches? We want to find the cabin that he dreams of. He told us it isn't real, but his wife did an oil painting of a cabin—it's in the B and B. We think it's a real structure and we would like to sketch it and the surroundings. It's been thirty years since his wife did that picture. When we are through here, we're going to Jean's to see what Duggar's wife created. We're not sure if we already have it on our phones."

"I've seen it! It's a beautiful oil on canvas. Jean told us she had some other work of Margret's, but they have all been sold."

Spring and I thanked Mrs. Sandoval for agreeing to assist with the fostering project and left the Emporium. Five minutes later we were parked at Jean's B and B.

Spring got out of the pickup and remarked, "The parking area is completely empty. I hope Jean is not having business problems."

"Maybe it's too early in the summer. Vacationers and hunters will be visiting Suddenly before long. This is the first time I've noticed an empty parking lot here. Let's go in and take a look at that picture. I've got my camera so I can take a reference photo."

We entered the foyer and meandered to the empty front desk while we scanned the walls for paintings. Our search of the interior of the large registration area for a picture of a cabin was unsuccessful. I struck a small announcement gong at the counter and Jean approached from a distant doorway.

"I'll be right with you. One moment please."

We waited patiently for Jean to make her way down the hall to the front desk.

Jean smiled and asked, "Would you like to register for an overnight stay?"

"No, we would like to see a picture that was painted by Margret Duggar. It's of a cabin in the woods. We have pictures from here of a painting but we'd like to see if it's the same one Mr. Duggar is remembering."

"You must be artists from the high school."

Spring volunteered, "You are correct about us being artists, but we're not from high school. We graduated two years ago. We'd like to see the picture by Margret Duggar. We want to find the cabin and see what it looks like after thirty years. Could we take a picture of it?"

"I would let you photograph the painting but it isn't here any longer. I sold it to a gentleman from New Hampshire a couple of days ago."

Spring reacted, "Do you have a photo of it? A black and white one will do."

"Oh, sure. I took a picture of it before my husband took it off the wall. If you would like to wait a few minutes, I'll download and print a copy for you. It will be in black and white though; I don't have a color printer."

"That would be great. We can pay you for the trouble."

"That's not necessary. If you want, I'll email you a color photo." Jean smiled, "There isn't much color, just browns, white and a little green and blue. It's a winter scene, mostly white." Jean left the admissions desk and disappeared down the hallway. A minute later, she returned with a sheet of paper and gave it to me.

Spring and I studied the image. "That's the same one we have on our phones. If we find the structure, I wonder if we can even tell it's the same cabin."

Spring raised her eyebrows, "Perhaps Mr. Duggar will verify its identity."

Jean commented, "I've heard that Mr. Duggar is very secretive about things. I think that cabin was Margret and Samuel's private place, a sanctuary."

I grinned, "We'll try to soften him up a bit. Spring and I are going to foster one of his dogs."

"Oh, I didn't know he had any dogs. That is a big change in his behavior. He usually wants to be left alone without dependents."

"I think the Sandovals contributed to his change of heart. They're the new owners of the hardware store. It's now called Sandoval's Emporium."

"Oh, yes. They stayed here when they first came to town. I'll have to pay them a visit to get my parents' air conditioner repaired. My husband can get parts there."

"Thank you for the information and the copy of the cabin, it's a big help." I hesitantly picked up a small mallet on the counter and asked, "Can I strike your gong? Will your husband come running?"

Jean chuckled, "No. Go ahead, it's kind of fun instead of a bell."

I hit the gong, was tickled by the resounding noise and tittered. I gave the mallet to Spring. Spring handed the mallet to Jean and said, "Twice is enough," and smiled. "Come on, Jenny, let's talk to David about the puppy."

"Bye ladies."

"Bye, Mrs. Baxter." We replied in unison as we moved toward the entranceway.

The drive to the clinic was short in both time and distance. When we parked at the clinic between two other vehicles: another pickup and an older model station wagon, David stepped out of the building to greet us.

"Hi! Did you talk with Duggar?"

I was excited, rushed toward David and threw my arms around his neck, "We're going to foster the puppy! We talked to Mrs. Sandoval at the Emporium and she agreed to take care of the puppy if we want to go into the forest to find that cabin Mr. Duggar draws all the time.

Duggar told us his drawings are all recollections of dreams, but we're a little suspicious. Anyway, he doesn't want to take care of the puppy until it has recovered, so he's agreeable to let us do it." I took a deep breath and continued, "Then we went to see about the painting at the B and B, but it's no longer there. Jean sold it."

"Did she have a photo of the painting?"

"Uh-huh. Spring, show David the copy."

David unfolded the paper and studied the picture. "This is a winter scene. I don't think I've ever seen that cabin, but there are lots of cabins hidden away in the forest. Miners constructed most of them and they're run down. Did he say where it's located?"

"Not really. He said it was fifteen or twenty miles to the north, a two-day hike."

"Yeah, but he's over ninety years old. Maybe he could do it if he remembers the route. Old logging roads might be the way to go."

Spring asked, "Could we get some maps showing the trails at those distances from Suddenly?"

David was growing more enthusiastic, "Sure, Mom can get us some Forest Service maps. But that isn't in her area of responsibility. I'll find out who's in charge that far north of us. Maybe the ranger who has authority for that area knows of the cabin. Can I show the picture to my mom?"

"Not a problem. Jean is sending us an email of a color picture. She said it only has white and brown and a bit of green and blue because it's a winter scene. We have black and white photos on our phones."

"The cabin will look different in the summer, but the stream and large trees might not be too altered."

I grabbed David's hands and said excitedly, "When can we look for the cabin, David?"

"Geez, Jen, I think we'd better go on a three-day weekend. July fourth is on a Monday this year, so let's prepare for leaving early July second."

"Wow! That's more than two months from now, can't we go sooner than that?"

I watched as David conjured up an alternative. "Why don't you and Spring drive out to one of the fire watchout towers? Tower seventeen is in a good location for providing some spectacular views of the forest and mountains. Remember, we saw an eagle at that tower. You could take some belongings and stay for a weekend; get used to camping out experiences. Though it's not as primitive as living on the ground in a tent among the trees."

Chapter 22

"You know I'd like to go on an expedition into the forest with you guys and Dexter, but I have to work—so does Dexter. And you two gals have to get used to fostering the puppy. Why don't you make a list of items you will need in the woods; things you can't do without, like toilet paper, soap and deodorant. Get some deodorant that doesn't have an odor, so it won't attract bugs."

Jenny responded, "Tower seventeen is the one we worked on, isn't it?"

"That's right, but there's a lock on the door now to prevent people from destroying things like they did last time. You'll have to visit the ranger station to get the key. Rental for a weekend won't be much, especially if you don't host any parties." I grinned and added, "In the evenings, Dex and I can come out to visit and scare the bears away."

Spring added, "We'll get some bear spray and one of those air horns. Should we have a gun?"

"No guns, even for protection. You have to use your wits. Just be careful if you have food with you that will attract animals and bugs, especially if you go hiking during the day. Don't get caught in the forest at night, it's not a good situation."

Jenny commented, "Maybe we'll go looking for Duggar's cabin. We can take the pickup on those logging roads."

"I don't recommend that, Jen. There are downed trees that could block the road and you might have difficulty turning around. Those roads can be overgrown and narrow. Please go to tower seventeen for a trial run."

"Okay, we'll wait until July when we can go into the forest with you and Dexter. Since I've been to tower seventeen, we might go to a different one. How far is it to the next closest lookout?"

I thought for a moment. "Tower twelve is about seven or eight miles from tower seventeen. The last time I was there was two years ago. It's not as tall as seventeen but the view is pretty good. It has fewer steps than seventeen, so it might already be rented. Twelve is usually rented early in the spring."

We were interrupted when a man came into the clinic leading a large German shepherd that had a noticeable limp. I gave the girls a hasty goodbye and directed my attention to the newcomers.

As Jenny and Spring exited, Jenny said, "We'll come back on Saturday to get the puppy. He'll be ready, won't he?"

"Okay, I'll get him ready."

Dr. Onishi came into the lobby from the operating suite and saw the new arrivals. He noticed the dog's limp and said, "Looks like your pal has some arthritis."

"He's a retired K-9 dog. He was shot in the hind quarters and the limp has become worse in the last week. I'd like you to take a look at him. His name is Luke. I'm Jason Logan. I'm retired, too. Luke and I were partners."

After quick introductions we ushered Jason and Luke into an examination room where the doctor gave Luke a once-over. Dr. Onishi started discussing a treatment plan when I heard a familiar voice from admissions. I excused myself and went to investigate what Jenny wanted.

"I can't start my pickup. Would you please take a look?"

"Sure. What does it sound like when you turn the key?"

"Nothing. I think my truck is dead."

I chuckled and followed her out to the lifeless pickup. Spring was sitting in the passenger seat leaning back with her eyes closed. I tapped on the hood and said, "Pop the hood, Spring."

With the hood raised, I noticed the positive battery cable was off the terminal. No wonder Jen said nothing happened when she turned the key. I reattached the cable and gave it a solid bang with my fist. "Okay, Jen, try it again."

The engine started and Jen leaned out the window. "Thank you David. You can tell me about it later. We're going to the Emporium."

"Ask Mr. Sandoval to tighten your battery cables. He'll tell you what happened. See you later!"

Listening to the girls drive away, I headed back into the clinic to observe Luke's treatment.

The Emporium was pretty busy so we drifted through the aisles looking for items we were considering for our trip to a lookout tower. We noticed Mr. Sandoval was helping a customer and appeared quite busy. His wife was standing at the top of the balcony stairway and waved to us motioning for us to come up to her. She started descending the stairs and met us halfway to the ground floor.

"You look like you need some assistance. Are you after something special?"

"We're going to rent a lookout tower and need to get a few things for a weekend stay. What do you recommend?" I hoped Elaine knew what we would need, beside food and water.

"Gosh, I really don't know what is provided in those towers. Have you rented one already?"

Spring answered, "Not yet. Maybe we should do that first. The forest service might suggest things we should have."

"I'm sure they will advise you. After you rent a tower and get a list of needs, come back and we'll see what we can do for you."

I replied, "We'll do that. Thank you Mrs. Sandoval. Have you heard anything about the teaching position yet?"

Elaine shook her head, "Nothing yet, Jenny. I'd really like that teaching position. Helping run a hardware store is not a very good alternative for a creative artist—but it's good for one thing, it helps pay the bills." She smiled and motioned for us to be on our way. "Shoo, go rent a tower."

Thirty minutes later, Spring and I returned to the Emporium with a list of items suggested by the forest service to make our weekend stay more enjoyable. The store was void of customers and Mr. Sandoval greeted us at the entrance.

"Hello! Elaine told me you are renting a lookout tower for the weekend. What items are you after?"

I crossed off things we already possessed when we talked with one of the rangers. I said, "Here's what we need, Mr. Sandoval," and handed him the list.

He gave us baskets and led us around the store, asking questions as he dropped flashlights, batteries, a can opener and Swiss army knives into our containers. "You know, there's no electricity in those towers. Would you like some candles or an oil lamp for lighting? And do you have a fire extinguisher?"

We continued through the various aisles and finally finished after nearly an hour. After one last large item, we reached the end of the list. Spring remarked, "We need a small stove, don't we? We can't cook anything on an open fire like pioneers did."

"Oh, yes. I have a nice one with two burners but it's a little expensive. It uses propane and is ideal for camping but not for use inside. You could use it on the deck outside the cabin."

We looked at each other and nodded. "We'll take one of those. How much do we owe you?" I reached into my leather purse, pulled out a credit card and waved it. "I love this plastic!"

"I suppose it's better than trading with horses and turquoise." Spring tittered.

"Oh! David told us to ask you about tightening my truck's battery cables. He said you would tell us all about it."

"I'll get this transaction taken care of and then we'll take a look at your battery."

With the purchases loaded in the truck bed, I opened the hood and stared into the engine compartment. Mr. Sandoval explained the functioning of the battery that had a typical lifetime of from five to seven years with proper care. Then he pulled out a small crescent wrench from his pocket, loosened the cables and cleaned the slightly dirty positive and negative terminals. After reattaching the wires, he asked, "Any questions?"

I grinned and stated, "I'd better get one of those wrenches."

He handed his wrench to me and said, "Take this one, you've been good customers. Store it in your glove compartment. Thank you for your business."

"Thanks for the help with the battery. We shouldn't have any more trouble with it. Bye now."

"Bye ladies. Have fun at the lookout tower."

By our standards, rising at seven o'clock was early for a Saturday morning. Spring and I were loading the pickup for travelling to tower twelve for the weekend. The phone rang. Who could be calling this early? I ignored the ringing.

Spring picked up, "Hello." She pressed speaker phone so I could hear.

"Oh, I'm glad I got you at home. This is Elaine Sandoval. Would you mind if I came out to visit at your tower today? I just thought of something you girls might want to do."

"We're just getting ready to leave, so how would it be for you to visit this afternoon? We should be settled in by then."

"That's wonderful. I'll see you after lunch. Bye."

"Bye Mrs. Sandoval."

As Spring hung up, I reminded her that we were supposed to pick up the puppy today. In the excitement of going to tower twelve I had almost forgotten about fostering the puppy. It was too early to phone David so I mentioned the problem to Spring. I suggested, "Let's call the clinic. It won't open till nine o'clock but we can leave a message."

"Good idea, I'll tell David we'll get the puppy on Monday."

While Spring called the clinic, I checked on the spare tire and lug wrench in case we were faced with a flat. I once helped David change a tire and knew the procedure but had never changed one by myself. I went over the method and made a final check to make sure we had a jack in the truck bed. When Spring finished the call, we locked the house, hopped in the pickup and set off south towards tower seventeen. I helped David repair some damage and paint over graffiti at that tower almost two years ago.

When we arrived at the first tower, number seventeen, Spring wanted to stop and climb to the top. But I warned, "It's a long climb, Spring. You should save your strength for making several trips to the top of tower twelve. It's only about half as high as this one."

Spring glanced at me, "Hey, I'm part Indian, I'm pretty tough. I want to climb up there. It will only take a minute."

"Well, if you're going up, I'm going with you. I'd like to see if anything has changed inside. Also, I'll check the railing—but it should be secure. Julie Wilson usually checks it before any renters go to the top."

I pulled into one of the two parking spaces and shut off the engine. We started up the first flight of steps slowly, but Spring decided to make a race of the climb and took off darting up the stairs. I wasn't into racing and just ascended the flights as if I were climbing the Empire State Building's hundred plus floors.

I was on the fourth level when Spring yelled down to me, "There's an animal up here! I think it's a dog. I'm coming back down to get some gloves. I don't want to get bit."

When she arrived at my level, she said, "It's not very big. Maybe it's another puppy."

I replied, "I didn't hear any barking or whining. Are you sure it's a dog?"

Spring answered, "It's not very big and it went around the corner. I didn't follow it. I only got a glimpse."

"Was it black and white? If so, it's probably a skunk. Let's go, Spring. I don't want to get sprayed. That would ruin our day."

Spring looked at me realizing the animal she saw was probably a skunk, "Yeah, most likely you're right. Let's go on to our tower." We descended the stairs, got back in my little truck and continued on to our destination. The roads to the towers were well cared for and we enjoyed the trip to tower twelve, our home for the weekend.

Lookout twelve was about a dozen miles away from tower seventeen. The road was much bumpier than the road from Suddenly to tower seventeen, so I drove slowly. We had to squeeze through one place where a tree had fallen partially blocking the dirt road. Spring wanted to get out and chop some of the limbs off but I didn't stop. It took nearly half an hour to make the trip from the tall tower to the much shorter one. When we arrived, I was a bit surprised, the tower had been recently painted and looked almost new.

Chapter 23

Spring had the key to the observation cabin door. Before I got out to survey the area, she grabbed a sack of groceries from the truck bed and started up the stairs. After scanning the area for animals, I grabbed two sleeping bags, another sack of food and followed her. When I reached the top, Spring was in the cabin putting our groceries onto cabinet shelves.

She turned to me and said, "I'm putting things away about the same as we have them at home. I hope that's all right with you."

"That's fine." I dropped the sleeping bags and handed her the sack of edibles I brought up. I checked the interior and saw bunk beds along the northern wall and a collapsed cot leaning against a front corner near the door. We wouldn't need the cot.

We unrolled our sleeping bags and spread them on the bunks. For some unknown reason, Spring wanted the top bunk. Then we went down to the truck to get more supplies. After three trips up and down the nearly four dozen steps, both of us took a breather. There were a few items left in the truck, but they could wait until our legs and lungs recovered. I was glad we didn't rent tower seventeen. Spring and I decided we would rent that tower only if it had an elevator; that meant never.

The last item carried up the four flights was the two burner gas stove. I hadn't remembered to bring matches, but Spring came to the rescue with a box of stick matches. We set up the stove on the deck and had tomato soup and toasted cheese sandwiches for lunch. We didn't expect to see Mrs. Sandoval until after one o'clock, so we took a short walk along the road that continued on from the tower into the forest. We hiked until we could no longer see the tower, which wasn't very far. The trees along the winding dirt road prevented long lines of sight. More of the same, trees, nothing but trees in all directions offered nothing new to sketch or paint. A bit frustrated, we returned to climb to the observation cabin, hopefully for the last time today.

We sat on the deck sketching views to the south until we heard a car arrive far below. Spring jumped to her feet and peered over the railing.

"It's Mrs. Sandoval. I actually didn't think she would come out here. She must have left her husband in charge of the store while she went sightseeing."

I had the same thought and wondered if coming to look over the tower was her only interest. It occurred that she might have something else in mind.

"Hey, up there, anyone home?"

I yelled back, "Come on up, Mrs. Sandoval, but take your time. It's a long climb." I hoped she was fit, not suffering from any heart problems; I thought she must be around sixty years old. Maybe Spring and I should go down to talk to her. "Wait, Mrs. Sandoval, we'll come down to talk."

"No, that's all right. I'm coming up. I want to see what's inside the cabin."

I hoped we wouldn't have to drive her to the hospital in Suddenly. Spring came over to me grinning, "Do you think she'll be too tired to talk when she gets up here?"

"I don't know, but she seems very determined." I looked down the stairs and saw she was ascending the third flight at a good rate. I was a little surprised at her stamina. Maybe she is in better shape than we are, despite the age difference. We waited at the top of the fourth set of stairs ready to help her into the cabin if necessary.

When she arrived at the gallery, we ushered her into the cabin and took seats. There were only two chairs, so I sat on the lower bunk bed. Mrs. Sandoval was scanning the room and seemed particularly drawn to the little potbellied stove in the corner.

"Have you used the stove yet?"

I replied, "Not the wood stove in the cabin. We used the propane stove we bought from your husband. It worked perfectly to toast sandwiches and warm soup."

"Well, it looks like you have settled in nicely. I wanted to see the inside of one of the towers, but I have another purpose for seeing you."

Spring reacted, "Oh, have you got an art project you want help with?"

"Yes, I do. I'd like your help to locate that cabin depicted in the winter scene at Jean's B and B, the one by Margret Duggar. There is something about that structure that intrigues me."

We grinned and I said, "We've got a hike with David and Dexter planned for the Fourth of July weekend. We'll have three days to hunt for it. We want to see what it looks like now after thirty years. We plan to sketch it and the surroundings."

I watched Elaine hesitate for several seconds before she said, "Have you girls got anything planned for this afternoon? If not, I'd like you to accompany me to do some investigating of the northern logging roads. Efren is running the store this afternoon, so I have several hours to do some looking around. I don't feel confident enough traveling in the area to go alone."

I glanced at Spring and she shrugged her shoulders. I was willing, too.

"Why not? But let's take both vehicles. That way you won't have to bring us back to the tower."

We followed Elaine in her Subaru for almost an hour to get back to Suddenly, but we didn't stop in town. I had been on this road before and knew what to expect. When the road changed from asphalt to dirt after about fifteen miles, I knew we could only drive another five miles before vehicles were no longer allowed into the wooded area.

The forestry people had installed a new, larger sign on a gate warning people that no vehicular traffic could proceed any farther along the ancient logging road. Forest fires were a never ending threat and hot exhausts or careless visitors starting campfires were likely causes of dangerous fires. Julie Wilson, forest agent and wife of Sheriff Wilson, presented information about fires when I flew over this area in a helicopter piloted by the sheriff. I was hesitant about flying but David talked me into it.

We parked and got out to discuss the message. After looking around, Mrs. Sandoval remarked, "I guess to go any farther, we have to hike." She looked at the forest where the road disappeared into the tall trees.

"That's right. The trail peters out after about a hundred yards into the woods. It narrows and splits in two, one footpath goes north and the other goes northwest. It's impossible to see them from the air."

"So how do we find Mr. Duggar's cabin without some sort of vehicle?"

I answered, "You mentioned hiking. We'll have to walk into the woods from here. I won't go any farther without David and Dexter. It's just not safe. We can get some trail information from the Ranger Station though."

Elaine commented, "That's what I'll do on the way back to town. I'll return with my husband next weekend. He's been in jungles before when in the army. I'm sure nothing will surprise him."

Spring hadn't said much until now, "Has your husband ever encountered a charging moose?"

Elaine laughed, "I don't know about that, I'll have to ask him."

There wasn't much else for us to do, so I suggested, "Let's get back to Suddenly, I want to check on the puppy."

"Oh, that's right. When do you girls start fostering?"

Spring replied, "We're to pick him up on Monday. David said the pup would be ready then. I think he will be used to wearing the wheelchair and we can take care of him at home. We didn't want to have him at the tower, that would be way too difficult and dangerous."

"I'll follow you and stop at the clinic. I want to see the puppy; I've wanted a dog for a long time but conditions haven't been right. I hope I'll be able to assist you caring for the rescued dog. I'll just need a day or two warning ahead of time."

"You will be a big help if you can take over when we can't take him with us. Will you be able to foster him over the Fourth of July weekend?"

"Sure. Efren and I don't have anything planned except one of our children might visit at that time."

We started back to town with Elaine always in sight in my rear-view mirror. When we were about a mile from the edge of town, Spring unexpectedly called out, "Stop, Jenny, stop!"

I slammed on the brakes and skidded about twenty feet in the dirt. "What is it!"

"I saw a dog! It looks like Mr. Duggar's dog; Al. Pull over and let's check it out. Why would his dog be way out here?"

I did as she asked and pulled off the road in an awkward position, the rear of the truck on the shoulder, the front still on the road, but leaving enough room for cars to pass. The dust cloud had drifted away when Mrs. Sandoval pulled up next to us and lowered the passenger window.

"Why have you stopped? Are you having trouble with your truck?"

"No. go ahead to the clinic. Spring thinks she saw Mr. Duggar's dog. We're going to check it out. We'll be along in a few minutes."

"All right. Be careful. Don't get bit; it might be a coyote." She closed the window and continued toward town.

"Where did you see a dog? I didn't see anything."

"You were watching the asphalt for rough spots. Turn around and drive back where those bushes are growing next to the road."

I followed Spring's directions and drove about the length of a football field, stopped on the shoulder across from a clump of shrubs and shut off the engine. I could hear barking but couldn't see the animal. Spring was out of the truck and across the highway before I had my seatbelt off. I watched her disappear behind the scrub plants and followed. When I climbed to the other side of the ditch, Spring was running after the dog toward the trees.

"Wait! Spring, wait!" I was afraid she would get out of sight and we would get lost in the woods. What if the dog wasn't Mr. Duggar's? It might be a stray. But why would it want us to follow? I stopped at the edge of the forest and yelled, "I don't know where you are, Spring. Say something!" I waited, thinking that she must be convinced that the dog was Al. But I wasn't going any farther. About fifteen seconds passed before Spring emerged from behind a clump of trees and said, "Come with me, Jenny. It's Mr. Duggar. He's hurt." She motioned for me to follow her.

I was in disbelief. How could Mr. Duggar be this far from his home? I trailed after Spring, climbing over broken branches, around berry bushes and avoided other debris fallen from the trees. We must have traveled about thirty yards before I saw Mr. Duggar and Al sitting beside each other next to a log.

"Mr. Duggar! How did you get out here? Spring said you are injured. What happened?"

"I turned my cussed ankle and can't walk any farther. That'll teach me to step over logs not knowing what's on the other side. Can you ladies help me back to the road? I'll get a ride back to town."

I was bursting with curiosity. "How did you get way out here from your home? You must be fifteen miles from your property."

"Al and I set off this morning as the sun was rising. A couple of people gave us rides and we hoofed it the rest of the way. We had gone a short way into the trees when my ankle gave way. I told Al to get some help. I heard him barking at cars on the road but nobody stopped. I'm sure glad you did. Why were you young ladies out this way?"

I nodded to Spring and she began, "Mrs. Sandoval wanted to see what the road looked like north of town but didn't want to come alone. Jenny had been out here with David a couple of years ago so we decided to come with her. She drove her car and we came with Jenny's pickup. We'll get you back to town but I don't think we can carry you. Any ideas?"

He sat there thinking for a while and then said, "I can hop to the edge of the forest if you girls can support me so I don't fall over and bust something else. I noticed the ground is nearly flat from the road to the trees. You can drive your little truck over the level area and I can climb in."

"I can't drive over that ditch, Mr. Duggar."

Chapter 24

"I know about the ditch. There's a place that's flat about thirty yards down the road toward town. You can drive safely from there. It shouldn't be too bumpy."

I didn't like the idea. Spring and I might get stuck out here with the old man and have to stay overnight. I motioned for Spring to step aside so we could talk. I related my hesitancy and she suggested we needed more help.

The clinic was only a few miles away and David was there. "You stay with Mr. Duggar and I'll get David. It won't take more than fifteen minutes. He can carry Mr. Duggar by himself, all the way to the road. What do you think?"

"Go, Jen. I'll wait with Mr. D and the dog."

I made my way back through the ground clutter in about a minute and then ran to my pickup. Twelve minutes after leaving Spring and Mr. Duggar, I was at the clinic. Sandoval's car was parked beside David's SUV. Elaine had actually stopped to see the puppy. I didn't think she was serious. I rushed inside and called out, "David!"

No one was in the lobby, so I went behind the counter and burst into the kennel area. "David!"

David, Dr. Onishi and Mrs. Sandoval were standing in front of the puppy's cage. David turned to me and said, "What is it, Jen? Is Spring in trouble?"

"No, it's Mr. Duggar. We found him and Al in the woods not far from the road. He sprained an ankle and stopped walking. Spring and I can't carry him to the truck. Can you come and help? It's not far from here." I watched David glance at Dr. Onishi for permission to leave the clinic. The doctor nodded and David started for the entranceway.

"Come on, Jen let's get Mr. Duggar."

His words were unnecessary; I was right behind him with my key ready to start the engine. We buckled our seatbelts and I hit the gas, backed onto the road and shifted into drive. I had hardly explained why Spring and I were out this way when we arrived at the jumble of shrubs. I turned the pickup around and parked where I had been before but completely off the roadway.

We unbuckled and got out. I pointed at the tree line and we set out for the woods. I led David into the trees at what I thought was a fast pace, careful to avoid losing my balance. It seemed like it was taking forever to get to the spot where Mr. Duggar and Spring were located, but Al must have heard us coming and barked several times. His barking kept us headed in the right direction. I couldn't see any traces of previous passages.

Spring was standing in front of Mr. Duggar. She saw David and me as we came through the trees. David was calm and collected. "Mr. Duggar, I guess you need some assistance to get back to town. Do you need to visit the hospital?"

"I don't think I need a doctor, David; I just need to get back home and put my feet up. I've had sprains like this before, but it's been some time since the last one."

"Okay. I'll carry you piggyback to the truck. You can ride with the girls in the cab and I'll get in back with Al."

"Jen, you and Spring walk in front and move debris out of the way so I don't trip. We don't need another sprained ankle."

Jenny and Spring steadied Mr. Duggar and I crouched so he could get his legs around my waist. When I lifted him, I recalled training for football but he felt lighter than I remembered carrying a lineman in practice. It must have taken more than ten minutes to get clear of the trees and another five or so to reach the pickup. I had to strain to keep solid footing through the weeds, clumps of grass and twigs. I was relieved to have the extra weight off my back.

Mr. Duggar was able to climb into the truck cab without assistance and Al jumped in beside him.

Spring laughed and climbed in the truck bed with me. Jenny grinned, shrugged and said, "I guess Al gets his way."

Fortunately, Jenny drove slowly to avoid jumbling our internal organs as we traversed the bumpy part of the road leading to the smooth asphalt. Spring and I could hear each other without yelling, so I asked her, "Have you questioned why Mr. Duggar was out in the woods so close to town?"

She nodded and replied, "I asked him why he was rambling through the woods with Al. He said he was trying to get in shape for a longer trek to visit Margret's and his hideaway. He planned to make the big journey in a couple of weeks. He didn't look at me as he talked though. I have an idea he was fibbing."

"So you think he was on his way to the cabin depicted in that picture?"

"Uh-huh. Is there a stream not far from where we found him and the dog?"

"I haven't been out in this area much. Most of my time in the forest has been in the southern area. That's where my mom is responsible for the lookout towers. Have you and Jenny been to the ranger station to get maps of the northern area? Those maps show creeks and known cabin locations are marked. That's if a ranger has noticed the cabin in his or her district. Some of the waterways are known from aerial surveys but the canopy hides most of them."

"I think Jen and I will be visiting the ranger station Monday before we come to the clinic to get the puppy. The maps will give us something to study and suggest where the cabin is located."

"Good luck, but don't go traipsing off into the woods by yourselves. You've seen what happened to Mr. Duggar. Please wait until Dex and I can go with you."

"Oh, all right. But Mrs. Sandoval and her husband might be looking for the cabin, too. She wants to use it as a subject for artistic work just like we do."

We quit talking as Jen pulled into the clinic parking lot. I dropped to the ground and opened the passenger door. Duggar ordered, "Help me out, David, I want to see that little Lab."

Jenney leaned forward to get my attention, shook her head and shrugged. Mr. Duggar pushed Al and he jumped to the ground, bumping my legs. Duggar slid to the edge of the seat and swung his legs out. I backed into him so he could latch his hands around my neck and slide onto my back. Spring held the clinic door open and I carried him into the lobby.

"That's good, David. Put me down and I'll sit here in one of these chairs."

I backed to a chair and let him slide off. Jenny and Spring helped him get comfortable while I went in the kennel to retrieve the puppy.

Dr. Onishi was on his knees adjusting the puppy's wheelchair and glanced up, "Oh, I'm glad you're back. Were you able to rescue Mr. Duggar?"

"Yes. He's in the waiting room. He wants to see the puppy. He can't walk so we'll have to take the dog to see him."

"Let's put him on a leash and take him out front. He's getting used to the attachment and manages very well after only a few days using the wheels. He should recognize the man that found him."

The doctor was right, as soon as he saw Mr. Duggar, he scampered across the floor to the elderly man. Mr. Duggar was excited to see the little labrador and leaned forward to pet him. "I don't know what to call you, little man, but I'm sure glad you are feeling better."

Jenny said, "We've been considering Charcoal as a name. What do you think?"

Al stuck his nose out from under Mr. Duggar's chair and was sniffing the puppy and wheelchair.

The puppy's tail was wiggling but his legs were limp, lifeless in casts.

"His hind legs are not moving at all. Will he be like that forever?" asked Duggar.

Doctor Onishi replied, "I hope not. I think with a little time and proper care, he'll regain his leg function. The girls will be able to help him with the routine I have made for them to follow. It might take most of the summer for him to recover but he has plenty of spunk. I can tell he wants to run."

Mr. Duggar nodded and looked at the girls, "I kind of like the name Charcoal. Let's give him that name." He then glanced at Elaine and motioned for her to sit beside him.

"Come on over here, Elaine. Say hello to Charcoal. I don't think he has met you."

She was watching the rest of us but didn't seem to know how to react. It was as if she was an audience member watching the performance of a play.

I watched Jenny, Spring and Mrs. Sandoval gather around Mr. Duggar to get close enough to pet Charcoal. He began to lick Mr. Duggar's hand and Mrs. Sandoval said, "What a gorgeous little dog. I'd be proud to have a part in his rehabilitation. When you gals go for your expedition into the woods over Independence Day weekend, make sure you get in touch beforehand so I will be prepared."

Jenny answered, "We'll be sure to call you a couple of days ahead of time. We'll bring all of his things to your home."

"Oh, do that. Instructions, too."

Duggar chuckled, "Maybe they will write out directions, like caring for a baby."

Elaine sat back looking offended, "I raised two children, Samuel. A puppy in a wheelchair is a completely different experience."

Samuel grinned, "I'm sure you can handle any problems Charcoal might have. You and Efren did a very good job helping me clean up my home."

We were all startled when the phone rang. Doctor Onishi responded on the third ring.

"Onishi Animal Clinic . . . yes Mr. Sandoval. Your wife is here." There was a pause as the doctor listened and then replied, "Okay. I'll tell her. Goodbye."

We all watched Onishi put down the phone. He approached Mrs. Sandoval and said, "Your husband wants you to come and get him. There are some papers that need to be signed at the realtor's office."

"Oh, thank you. I guess I should go."

As she backed out the entrance, she waved, "You girls be sure to call me. Bye now."

Everyone waved and Mr. Duggar asked, "I think I'd better go to the hospital. My ankle is beginning to hurt bad; something's not right."

Jenny responded, "Spring and I will take you if David will carry you to my truck."

"Can Al go into the medical center with me?"

Dr. Onishi said, "I'll call ahead and find out, but if your dog is a mobility animal, they should let him go with you."

Samuel grinned, "Al sure is that kind of dog. I dropped a pencil yesterday and he got it for me. If I bend over to pick things up, I sometimes lose my balance."

As soon as Elaine came back with the car, I closed the Emporium and we walked down the street to the Realty Office. The door was locked so I tapped on the entranceway window. We heard the lock click and Arlene invited us inside.

"I'm glad you came right over. The city has some documents for you to sign. It's a new regulation for businesses in Suddenly, something the city council just devised for more income. There is a one time, one hundred dollar fee. Do you have a credit card with you?"

Elaine asked, "Why isn't the city collecting the fee?"

"The city offices aren't open today and they want the payments in by Monday. Councilman Moore asked me to handle it. He knew you would be able to get the fee paid if I arranged it, since I have all the business related documents in my files."

I had to ask, "Why is it you have all the city's official papers?"

Arlene smiled, "I have the only fireproof safe in town, Efren. The city has one on order but it won't arrive for another month. It's being shipped from Philadelphia and will be trucked in from Butte."

I chuckled, "The city should have ordered it from Amazon."

The ladies laughed and Arlene remarked, "That is probably something no one thought of. It had to be made to specifications to fit through the present doors in the courthouse so was a special order. We had to have bids . . . according to the city charter."

We signed the papers and left the realty office. Walking back to our store, Elaine said, "I've been thinking about something, Efren. Those two girls, Jenny and Spring, found Samuel and his dog not far from here in the woods. He sprained his ankle while hiking. But why was he out there without any food or water? He didn't even have a backpack. I don't understand him. It just doesn't make any sense."

Chapter 25

I offered a thought, "He must have had a destination in mind, not too far from where the girls found him."

Elaine was abnormally quiet until we reached the store. As we stood at the entrance, she said, "Let's go home. There aren't any customers and it's close to dinnertime. You just said something that I'm thinking about."

"Do you mean I said something important?" I grinned. I put the key back in my pocket and started toward our car. As we got in, she said, "Well, don't laugh at me but I think that old man was on his way to his cabin. I'll bet it isn't too far from where the girls found him. I want to find out if there's a stream nearby. Let's get a map of that area from the ranger station before we head home."

I was becoming more interested in searching for the cabin now that some clues were being suggested. I had a strong hunch the next thing Elaine was going to propose was an expedition into the woods a few miles north of Suddenly. I couldn't say more about it until we survey the area with some geologic maps. But I don't want to set her expectations too high because of my cooperation.

The ranger station was about a mile from the northern edge of town. Several pickups and a couple of cars were parked haphazardly, as if the drivers were in a hurry to get to the bathroom. I parked hear the entrance to the two story imitation log building. The state and country flags added an official appearance to the site. As we entered the structure, I commented, "Kind of impressive, huh?"

"There's a female ranger. Let's talk with her." Elaine saw the woman before I did or I would have gone directly to her to get information. She could qualify as a centerfold in a ranger calendar. I followed Elaine to the counter where we could purchase maps or other information about the forest.

She greeted us, "Hello, you are visiting Southwest Bitterroot Station Two. I'm Ranger Julie Wilson. How may I help you?"

When I realized this woman was the wife of Scott Wilson, Suddenly's Sheriff, things began to fall into place. "David Drum is your son?"

"That's right. I have two boys, David and Danny, and a daughter Gwen. Oh, you must be the Sandovals. David said he met you at Samuel Duggar's home."

"That's right. David and a friend from college helped us unload a propane tank at Duggar's."

Elaine stepped beside me and extended her hand to the ranger. "I'm Elaine and this is Efren. We came by to see if we could purchase a map of the forest from two to five miles north of Suddenly."

"Come look at the display of the southwest Bitterroots territory. The maps are numbered according to the area covered."

We followed the ranger to a counter area that showed the southern portion of the Bitterroot Mountains on the wall. She pointed out the area north of Suddenly and said, "Is this the area you want covered?"

Elaine glanced at the larger map, located Suddenly and said, "Yes, that's what we want to investigate."

"Okay, you want map number eight. Are you going hiking?"

Elaine replied after glancing at me, "Yes, I want to find a nice area to sketch and paint. Do you know if there are any streams in that area?"

Julie grinned, "Yes, there are streams everywhere in these mountains. Some water flows all year long and some have only seasonal flow—in the spring. The small creeks will dry up in the summer."

I remarked, "Runoff from snow melt."

"That's right but there are a few waterways that flow all year. Not all of the creeks are marked on our maps. Human eyes have never charted all spots in the forest."

Julie handed me a white envelope about eight by ten inches. I quickly read the sticker aloud, "**Sector 8: $3.99**." It had the American eagle on it, so I knew it was an official publication. I extracted my wallet and fished out four one dollar bills and handed them to Julie.

"Thank you. Do you want the penny change?"

Elaine giggled, "No, put it in the firefighting fund." We all laughed. Elaine took the envelope from me and tore it open. The enclosed was several pages thick and I could see that it was to be unfolded, similar to a state highway map. Elaine wanted to look at the map immediately but I suggested we look at it in the car or at home.

Elaine said, "I think we have what we came for. Thank you Ranger Wilson."

"If that doesn't give you the information you want, call me at home and I'll get you another map. I can save you a trip and bring it to your store if you like."

We thanked her for the map and left the station. When in the car, I flipped on the dome light and Elaine unfolded the map. We began scanning the area for streams. They were marked with blue dashes. There were three waterways clearly marked but without names.

"Look! They're almost parallel. We can hike into the first creek and then go north to encounter the other two." Elaine was pleased to see the relationship of the streams but I reminded her, "We might have to walk the banks of each creek for miles to find the cabin, if it is in this area. And if we find a cabin, it might not be the one you are looking for."

She remained quiet for a minute or so, then stated, "We'll just have to find out but I'm sure that cabin is in this area. And besides, if we find an old cabin it will give me a subject for some artwork."

I had to agree, "The streams might be very picturesque, also. And we might encounter some wildlife getting a drink. Deer, bears, mountain lions and moose could be in the area."

"Oh, that's right. I forgot about the animals. I've been so engrossed with finding that cabin."

"So, when do you want to set out on this expedition?"

She looked at me as if I were going to say not until fall but I knew she wanted to search for the cabin as soon as possible. "Could we leave early in the morning next Saturday and spend the weekend in the forest?"

I couldn't deny Elaine this chance to find the cabin she so wanted to sketch and paint. I replied, "Well, we won't be missing many customers at this time of year, so I guess we'll do it. During the week we'll gather equipment and supplies and pack our things. I'll scout the roads before we leave so we'll have a safe place to park the car."

"Wonderful! I'll make a sign we can post in the windshield so no one will consider our car as a derelict."

We drove home in silence. As I negotiated the familiar streets, I started a mental list of items we would have to carry in backpacks as we traipsed through the woods. I knew Elaine didn't have a pair of boots for hiking along streams. Proper footwear was essential as were several pair of comfortable socks. The main clothing store in Suddenly carried both men's and women's shoes, so Elaine should find just what she needed. Our backpacks had seen many years of use and we learned packing tricks to conserve space. I'll have to locate my handy machete and sharpen it. It might be a bit rusty.

Taking care of the Emporium by myself had worn me out, so as I pulled into our driveway, an image of a hot shower invaded my mind. I can relax while Elaine prepares dinner. I never worry what she readies for an evening meal. Whatever it is, it will be good. Tonight we'll have a great conversation as we eat. She should have a good idea of what artist's materials she wants to take on our hike, so we'll have a good discussion. I'm more interested in having enough food for five meals and several snacks—we'll be doing a lot of walking and we'll be taking numerous resting periods. As I mulled things over, I realized searching three streams might require more than one weekend. I was standing at the bathroom door. I'd better get into the shower.

Dex and David came out to tower twelve Saturday night and stayed for about three hours. We sat on the deck with our legs dangling over the edge and watched the stars appear. Much to my surprise, Spring knew most of the northern constellations and the names of brilliant stars. While living in the city all those years, I had seen only a few of the brightest stars in the night sky. One star turned out to be a planet, not a star. It was Saturn. David advised us about the celestial equator.

I had to stop him. "How do you know about this stuff?"

He smiled, "I read about it in a book. It was a textbook for an astronomy class I took at the university. That class was awesome. It showed you that the earth is such a small part of the universe and we should protect what we have."

"I agree," responded Spring. "My grandfather used to tell me stories of how the stars were placed in the heavens and the Navaho names for them. I listened to his stories for hours when I was eight years old. I miss those wonderful times."

Dex blurted, "Hey! Did you see that? It was a meteor. I read about meteors in a computer program at the library in St. Louis. There are lots of craters from meteor strikes around the world. There's a well-known one in Arizona."

Spring commented, "I've been there, Dex. It's a great place to visit. The asphalt road leading to the Barringer crater near Winslow is red. Mom, Dad and I went there a year before their divorce."

I was beginning to yawn and felt sleepy leaning against David with his arm around me. I was so comfortable. I didn't want to miss anything by falling asleep but he must have noticed I was having difficulty keeping my eyes open.

"I think Dex and I should go. You need to go to bed and get some sleep. Thanks for letting us come visit; it was fun to sit and look at the heavens."

Everyone started standing and I remembered, "Before you go, I want you to look at the map we got from your mother at the ranger station." We went into the lookout cabin.

David asked, "I didn't realize you went out there today. Did you get the one of the area where you found Duggar and his dog?"

I nodded. "Spring and I figured Mr. Duggar wasn't in that area by accident, he was on his way to the cabin. We figured he was going to visit the cabin to see if there was any damage from winter weather. We were afraid the roof might have caved in from the weight of three or more feet of snow."

Spring and Dexter were on their hands and knees spreading the map out on the floor. Jen and I joined them.

"Show me where you guys found Duggar."

Jenny located the outer edge of the city limits and traced the highway with her right index finger. "How far do you think we were from town, Spring?"

"Just a sec, I'll get my ruler."

A few seconds later, we watched Spring measure the map's distance legend. She glanced at Dexter and said, "An inch and a half equals one mile."

Jenny was wide awake now, "We were about three miles from the edge of town."

Spring added, "And about half the length of a football field from the road—to the west."

I agreed with what they suggested; it wasn't very far from the tree line. That was pretty close to where I piggybacked Mr. Duggar from the woods to the pickup.

"Okay, Dex, we'd better get back to civilization and leave these pioneer women to get some rest. I'm sure they have a big plan for Sunday."

Dexter added, "And Monday they will be picking up Charcoal from the clinic. Right?"

Jenny chuckled, "We are going to do some sketching and painting tomorrow and pack up the truck for the trip home. We'll see you guys on Monday at the clinic when we get our four legged buddy."

Dexter smiled, "You mean two legs and two wheels. He's going to be a terror with wheels."

Spring and I watched the men head for the door and stop. David beckoned to me with his right index finger and I rushed to him. I knew what he wanted, a good night kiss. Right after Spring saw us kiss, I watched her give Dexter a big smack on the lips. We heard the guys descend the stairs, car doors slam and the crunch of tires as they went off toward town. It was almost eleven o'clock. The day was over for us. Time for bed.

Chapter 26

Saturday night at the hospital was abnormally quiet. The cleaning crew had departed and I was sitting at the admissions desk reviewing patients' files. My name, Shirley Berg, RN, was chalked on the activity board for Saturday-Sunday, slated to stay overnight at the hospital. I was pleased that only three patients were admitted Saturday. Reviewing the patients' records was a normal activity: Jimmy Franks broke his left arm Saturday evening; Mrs. Parsons burned her left hand with boiling water Saturday afternoon and Mr. Duggar sprained his ankle in the forest.

Sunday morning, Dr. Rennick came in at seven and was sending all patients home. I was relieved and smiled at the reduction of my duties. I noted three more rooms could then be cleaned and ready for the next bout of accident victims. A further day and night in the hospital were unnecessary for the patients. Family members came to get the youngster and Rita Parsons, but Mr. Duggar and Al needed help returning home, so they might be kept longer. Dr. Rennick asked me to call the sheriff for assistance. The ambulance was kept stationary in case of emergencies.

I waited until eight o'clock to dial the sheriff's number.

"Hello. This is Sheriff Wilson."

"Hi Sheriff. This is Nurse Berg at the hospital. I hate to interrupt your Sunday activities but could you give Mr. Duggar a ride home?"

There was a five second pause. *"Sure, I can do that. No, wait a second."*

I could hear unintelligible voices from a background conversation.

"Would it work if my stepson drove Mr. Duggar home?"

"That would be fine, Scott. Samuel is ready to go home. His dog is with him."

"Okay. David will be right over . . . about ten minutes."

"That's great. Thank you. Goodbye."

"Bye, Shirley."

I had just finished a bowl of oatmeal with butter and syrup and was sipping a mug of coffee when Dad asked me if I would do him a favor and take Mr. Duggar home from the hospital. I was planning to help Danny start our lawn mower engine but that would have to wait.

"Okay, Dad. Can I take your cruiser?" I knew the answer but wondered if he would change his mind and let me take the city police car.

He coughed and cleared his throat. "I think you know my answer, bud. That car is only for official business."

"I know, I was just joking."

As I got up from the table, Mom tossed me the keys to the SUV. Then she handed me her credit card and said, "Please fill the tank. Gwen and I are planning on some sightseeing this week. Can you ride a bicycle to the clinic?"

"No problem. I'll check the tire pressure when I get back from Duggar's. Tell Danny I'll be back in about an hour."

When I arrived at the hospital, Al, Mr. Duggar and a nurse I didn't recognize were waiting at the curb.

The nurse forced the old man back down into a wheelchair when he tried to stand. I parked about ten feet from them and got out.

"I'm to give you a ride home, Mr. Duggar." He gave me a mediocre wave, almost as if he didn't need any help.

He looked up at me, "How's Charcoal doing?"

"He's raring to go with those girls. I think he's going to be running around without the wheels before long. The girls have been loving on him. They're going to the clinic to get him tomorrow. Let me help you into my car and get you home. I bet Al is hungry."

"That's the truth. Hospital food isn't for dogs. He needs some wild meat."

With the nurse steadying the wheelchair, I picked Samuel up and got him in the front seat. Al crawled onto his lap. I thanked the young nurse, Carlie Davis, for her help. The two Duggars and I started toward the Dillon highway.

As we turned onto the state road, I asked Mr. Duggar point blank, "Yesterday, were you and Al on the way to your cabin? You know, the subject of that painting, the one done by your wife?"

"Ha! Nope. We were just getting some real good exercise. I wanted to see if Al could follow me through the woods. He was already familiar with the region about my home, so we thumbed a ride north of town. We were doing just fine until I twisted my damn ankle. We sat there for near an hour before those girls showed up. Saved by two beautiful women. What a day."

"How far had you gone in the forest? You didn't have any provisions."

"That's correct, we didn't need anything. We were going to hike for an hour or so and then return home. A lot of people are out and about on weekends. It's easy to thumb a ride."

"I think the girls thought you were on your way to that cabin. They want to sketch and paint some canvasses of it after all these years have passed, but they don't know where to find it."

Samuel nodded and was quiet for about ten seconds. "That place is kind of sacred—Margret and I built it and lived there for about a year. I visit it in the summer to clean up the mess Mother

Nature leaves during the winter months. Margret painted that picture when we were snowed in that long winter. The snow was deep but we were visited by elk and whitetail deer. We sang to the animals at Christmas."

"I guess things are different now. You can go out to the cabin during the snow if you want to go by snowmobile."

"Oh, I couldn't run one of them things."

"If you want to go next holiday season, I'll take you Mr. Duggar. We'll rent a Ski-Doo. I'd like to see your cabin—and I can keep a secret."

"That sounds like a good idea, David. I believe you can button your lip."

"We can even take your animals with us. We'll make a dog trailer out of a sled so they don't get overexposed."

"I'll make a trailer while you are away at the university. That will keep me busy. I'll look forward to the winter journey."

"Great! Let's plan to leave a few days before Christmas and spend Christmas day at your cabin. Do you think it will be weather tight?"

"It should be. Margret and I took major steps to make it weatherproof and stout enough to withstand attack from bears. The door is three inches thick and the window is made of thick wood."

"So how far is it from Suddenly? We need to have enough gas for the two way trip."

"Well, it's a tad closer to Jackson than Suddenly, about twenty-three miles from my house. We can take a road about halfway, then use a snowmobile. I know a direct route if we have to hike. We'd have to have snowshoes, though. I don't think anyone except Margret and me has ever been there. I want to take the animals."

I slowed the car and crossed the centerline to enter the short dirt road to Duggar's. The place looked forlorn, so quiet. It's as if his house were waiting for him to return. I felt saddened to have Mr. Duggar out here with only Al for company but that's the way he liked to live and I couldn't suggest anything different. At least he had electricity for heat and light, courtesy of the Sandovals. I noticed the front door was still boarded shut, so I would have to carry him around to the back door.

Parking in foot-high grass at the far corner of his house was easy enough and I shut off the engine. Duggar opened his door and I said, "Wait until I get around to help you. Al was on the ground waiting by the passenger door when I got to Mr. Duggar. He already had his feet on the ground and looked up at me. "You gonna carry me?"

"I am. I'll put you down inside. You have a walking stick, don't you?"

"I have a staff but I can't turn it into a snake like Moses did," he grinned.

I laughed and he smiled. He should have a wheelchair.

Once in the house, he was seated in the chair where he does his artwork. I asked, "Are you going to be able to get around by yourself?"

"Oh, I'll be fine. I'm getting better and better at hobbling. Al will give me some assistance, too. Thank you for driving me home, David. I'll see you this coming winter. I'll take you and the dogs to my cabin."

"I'm looking forward to it, Mr. Duggar. Try to stay off that leg until some healing takes place. Start your normal activities slowly. Okay?"

He nodded and said, "Bye, David," and gave me a brief wave.

I returned to the car and drove home wondering how long I could live alone in the woods without human contact. Would I go nuts? I would have to have some type of project, something to keep my mind occupied—like sketching pictures of forest cabins or something else from dreams.

When I arrived home, Mom and Gwen were sitting on the porch watching neighbors up and down the street. Mom was telling Gwen each neighbor's name and occupation. I didn't think Gwen would remember much, but I later found out her little brain was like a sponge, absorbing almost everything she saw and heard.

"Where's Danny, Mom?"

"He's out back with Scott. They're trying to start the mower. Something is wrong with it. Maybe you can help."

I nodded, "I think I know what the trouble is. I'll show them the fix." I gave Mom the car keys and headed down the driveway.

When I got to the garage, Scott looked up from the mower. Danny and Scott were on their hands and knees and had pulled the gas line off. I smelled gasoline.

Scott remarked, "Well, it's not the fuel, Danny. It's something else. Any ideas, David?"

"I think I know the problem; it's the air filter. It's probably plugged with dirt and grass and needs to be cleaned. I haven't cleaned it since last season." I gave Danny a screwdriver and pointed out the location of the screw to access the filter. "When you take it off, don't get it wet or you'll spend an hour or more drying it out. Just shake it and use the shop vacuum to clean it."

I observed Danny's cleaning technique and in a few minutes, Scott got up and said, "Thanks, David. You saved us a lot of time."

"Better not thank me yet, Dad. Wait until the engine starts."

"Hey! What's going on out there?" Mom yelled from the kitchen.

I called out, "It's the filter, Mom. It's plugged with dirt." I decided Danny and Scott didn't need me and went in the house. I expected to hear the engine start in seconds. I stood beside the kitchen table to talk to Mom and Gwen. About a minute later, I heard the roar from the mower. Gwen covered her ears and I laughed. "Loud, huh? I'll shut the door."

Mom was getting the milk jug from the refrigerator and after I pushed the door closed, I set the cookie jar on the table.

Mom gave Gwen a napkin, a cookie and a small glass of milk. I took two cookies from the big ceramic jar and sat across from Mom.

She looked away from Gwen and asked, "So how is Mr. Duggar today?"

"His leg is tender but he can get around all right in his house. He's got crutches and Al retrieves anything he drops."

I expected Gwen to ask about Mr. Duggar but she was engrossed with nibbling her cookie. Scott came in and joined us at the table.

Gwen asked, "Want a cookie, Daddy?"

"Yes, please."

Gwen pointed at the cookie jar and smiled. "Did you wash your hands?"

Scott gave Julie a questioning look and said, "No, but Mom will get me a dishrag to wipe my fingers. Okay?"

So Mom wouldn't have to get up, I went to the sink and tossed Dad a wet dishrag. He wiped his hands, said "Thanks, David," and tossed it back to me. Then he glanced at Gwen and asked, "Can I have a cookie now?"

Gwen nodded, her cheeks bulging. Dad reached into the cookie jar and extracted a cookie.

I retook my seat and looking at Mom and Dad, said, "I have a problem. I'm not sure how to handle it. I'd like your opinions."

Mom said, "This sounds serious. What is it? Oh, wait. Can G hear this?"

"Not a problem, Mom."

"Okay. Let it out."

Chapter 27

"I promised Mr. Duggar to keep the location of his cabin a secret, but Jen and Spring want to look for it. I'm afraid they're going to venture into the forest by themselves. I told them to wait until the July Fourth holiday when Dex and I would go with them. But they showed me a map of the forest north of town and I think they want to go now. But Mr. Duggar told me his cabin is closer to Jackson than Suddenly. The girls would be wasting their time using the maps they have and might get hurt if alone. What should I do?"

"I helped them with the maps, David, but the area they want to search is close to town. I'm pretty sure there aren't any cabins in that section. I didn't want to dampen their spirits, so I didn't say anything."

"Have you been to the cabin?" asked Scott.

I shook my head, "No."

"Then what are you worried about? You don't know where the cabin is. If you tell them the location is closer to Jackson than Suddenly, what will that hurt?"

Dad had a point. There's no road directly from Suddenly to Jackson. They would have to drive more than sixty miles to Jackson and then hike another fifteen miles on foot into the woods. It would take them a week to get where they could start searching. I'll just tell them they'll have to wait. I'll warn them about getting lost or hurt in the forest. If one or both of them got hurt, what would they do? Besides they have to take care of Charcoal.

After our Sunday family dinner, I washed and ironed my clinic uniform and called Jen. We talked a few minutes but I didn't mention the news about the cabin. Jen and Spring had made it home from the tower without any problems and they promised to pick up Charcoal at the clinic at one o'clock tomorrow. I would have him ready, equipped with a ten pound package of food for puppies. Jen was tired from moving back home, so I cut the phone call off quickly. Tomorrow I'll tell the girls what I had found out from Mr. Duggar about the location of the cabin. Then I went to bed.

In the morning before breakfast, I made sure I had a road map in the car to show the girls how difficult the cabin search was going to be. After eating, I dressed in my clinic outfit, talked with Mom and Gwen for a few minutes and went to work. Mom was going to work half-days this week, in the afternoons. Gwen would be with a sitter. Dad had already eaten and gone to his office by the time I got up and Danny was still in bed when I left for the clinic. He had always been a slow riser. I love my brother, but that sun of a gun is lazy unless he has his sights on making money.

I saw Dr. Onishi's car arriving at the clinic a few seconds before I braked and slid off Danny's bike where I usually parked my car. As I set the kickstand, the chilly air shocked my system. When pedaling, I hadn't noticed the cold. Before I could get in the building, I had goose bumps but was wide awake for the morning's activities. I hoped we were going to have a busy day so time would pass fast.

"Good morning, David. How was your weekend?"

"It was a little unusual. I took Mr. Duggar home from the hospital. We made an agreement to visit his secret cabin during my winter vacation. We're going to rent a snowmobile to travel through deep snow."

"Sounds like you are planning a big adventure. Have you done something like that before?"

I had to laugh. "No, I normally stay at home and keep warm beside the fireplace and read a book, but this time I'll have input from my parents. They have experience in foul weather, especially my mother. She's been a ranger for more than fifteen years. Dad has flown over the area in a chopper several times. I might be able to get my brother to go along, or maybe Dexter. But that depends on Mr. Duggar. He has sworn me to secrecy about his cabin's location."

"So, you don't know where this cabin is?"

"Nope, just a general idea. Dexter and I are going to take our girlfriends on a journey during the Fourth of July weekend and try to find it. They want to investigate the woods and sketch the cabin. They're interested to see how it has changed in the thirty years since it was built."

Our conversation was interrupted when a flatbed truck pulled into the parking area. Our attention was directed to watching two men unload a wire animal cage from the truck bed and start toward the clinic front door. I rushed to open the door; the cage looked heavy. The two men introduced themselves as Jake and Luke Branson and set the cage on the floor. It was nearly covered with a blanket so we couldn't see what was in the container. I suspected it was a small bear but it might be a large wolf because the cage appeared heavy.

Jake said, "We found this bird off the road to our rental. We think one of its wings is broken; it doesn't seem to be able to fly."

Luke raised one side of the covering and surprise! I recognized the bird as a young eagle. How could it have gotten injured?

Dr. Onishi asked the men to carry the cage into the investigation room where the new x-ray unit was housed. The doctor motioned for me to turn off the overhead lights. He wrapped the large bird with a blanket and carried it to the x-ray unit. The monitor showed the damage done to the bird's right wing. I could see a small solid object and pointed, "What is that spot?"

"That is a bullet, David. This bird was shot. We need to call the ranger station to make a report."

Luke Branson stated, "We have to go, Doctor. Can we have our cage?"

"Where are you gentlemen staying?"

"We're renting fire lookout tower seventeen. It's not far . . . "

I interrupted, "I know where it is. I helped renovate the cabin. An adult eagle flew off the roof when I took some people out to show them the tower. This bird could be one of the American eagles living in that area."

Onishi asked, "Did you men hear gunfire?"

They glanced at each other and shook their heads. Luke commented, "No, we were driving back to town and saw the bird flapping along the road. We covered it and put it in our cage and drove directly here."

"What do you guys use the cage for? It's extremely well built."

Both men became a bit uneasy and fidgeted for a moment. Jake replied, "We're scouting for a movie company and once in a while we encounter wolverines or small bears. We lure them into the cage, take them out in the forest and release them—away from our camp."

Something in the manner Jake answered didn't strike me as the truth. It wasn't what he said but the way he said it. He didn't look at me or Onishi. I decided to change the subject. I'll talk with Dad and Mom tonight. "How long will you be at tower seventeen?"

"Another week. We paid for two weeks. Then we'll return to LA."

Dr. Onishi said, "Well, thanks for bringing in the young bird. Good luck with your search for movie locations."

Jake responded, "Thanks. I guess we'll shove off. Hope you can fix the bird."

I held the door open so the men could carry the cage out with ease. I followed and waved as they drove away. When they were out of sight, I went back in the clinic to phone Mom. I figured she should know about the eagle and the two men. I doubted their story. I think they shot the eagle, probably thinking it was a hawk. I hoped it was only a mistake. Mom will be able to check the men to see if they have rifles. They had to have visited the ranger station recently when renting.

After making the phone call, I checked with Dr. Onishi to see what we could do for the eagle. He had placed it in one of the portable dog crates lined with a soft blanket and moved it outside the building to a quiet area away from barking dogs. When I asked about the bird, he said, "I'm going to take it to my wife. I don't know much about the care and rehabilitation of raptors. She has experience with large bird rehabilitation. I'll leave you in charge. I'll be gone for about an hour."

I helped the doctor load the crate into his car. When Dr. Onishi headed for home, I went into the kennel and got Charcoal out of his temporary container. I attached his wheels and placed him on the floor. He scrambled toward the front entrance. I think he wanted to go outside, but I wasn't worried, he wore a diaper. The active puppy didn't realize he was going to be cared for by two pretty young women and would be leaving the clinic before long. I expected Jen and Spring would spoil him rotten. I hoped the girls would arrive on time at one o'clock to pick him up. As the little dog scooted around the lobby, I gathered everything I could think of for his foster care. If Mr. Duggar couldn't afford the expenses, I would use some of my salary.

The hour passed quickly with no new clients appearing, human or furry friends. I refilled Charcoal's water bowl and put him back in his crate a few minutes before Dr. Onishi returned. It was eleven thirty. We'd break for lunch at noon. I was curious about the eagle.

"Did you and your wife remove the bullet?"

"Yes. Fumiko and I performed the surgery. It was quick and we got the bird sequestered in our small aviary. We'll feed it and start exercises in a short time. As soon as it can fly, we'll release it."

The doctor saw my little pile of materials by the front door and commented, "I see you have things ready for the girls to foster Charcoal."

I nodded and asked, "Can you think of anything else they should have?"

"I imagine they'll need plenty of diapers. Do you anticipate that being a problem?"

"I don't think so. Since her grandmother passed, Jenny has used her old clothes for rags. Diapers will be made from clothes and burned. Jenny already mentioned it."

"That's good. Let's go for lunch and get back before the girls show up to take Charcoal home."

I chuckled, "Good idea. Jenny will undoubtedly show up a little early."

We locked the clinic and the doctor motioned for me to join him in his car. I got in, buckled up and wondered where we were going for lunch. A little nervous, I assumed he was going to buy; I didn't have enough cash in my wallet to pay for the cheapest burger. I didn't possess a credit card either. Then it occurred to me that we were going to his home where I would meet his wife. I wouldn't need any money. That idea was soon dismissed when I realized we were going to the Dairy Queen restaurant.

We were on Main Street passing by the Emporium. It looked like the Sandovals were dealing with a number of customers, I could see figures through the front windows and people were entering the store. What could the Sandovals be offering to attract such interest?

The doctor and I ordered and waited for less than five minutes before our number was called. The girl that waited on us was several years younger than me, but I didn't remember her from high school. She gave me a big smile and said, "You're Danny Drum's brother aren't you?"

I nodded and before I could say anything, she added, "Tell Danny Pam asked about him."

"I'll do that, Pam. This gentleman is Dr. Onishi. He's the veterinarian at the new animal clinic. He'll pay you. I don't have any money."

She looked at the doctor and said, "I have two young kittens. I'll bring them in for shots after payday."

Pam was obviously underage. How could she be working? She couldn't be sixteen yet, so I asked, "Aren't you too young to work here?"

She started laughing. "It's all right, my parents own the business. They even pay for my social security and insurance. My parents are Pat and Dick Albert."

Pam accepted payment from Dr. Onishi. We sat in a cushioned red vinyl booth and talked about our recent patients as we ate. I asked the doctor how his wife developed an interest in raptors. He explained meeting her in a research symposium in Japan. She was a research assistant at a bird rescue group. They were at the meeting to explain their work to veterinarians who were not trained to work with raptors. We then discussed the fostering of Charcoal. I was to give tips to Jenny and Spring about the care of young canines. At 12:45 we left the restaurant and headed back to the clinic.

Chapter 28

As we drove by the Emporium, I saw a sign in the store's window: **One day only: Free doughnut and coffee for any purchase.** I laughed and remarked to Dr. Onishi, "We should offer free dog food to anyone bringing their animal in for shots. When people see the word free, they react."

He didn't respond for a moment and then said, "What about cats?"

I laughed and replied, "We should trap mice so cats would have something to play with. That would be free of any expense to the clinic."

"That would be a difficult project. Most mouse traps are not made to preserve the little buggers."

"Yeah. I remember one time when our refrigerator wasn't working. Mom called a repairman from the forest service and he found a shriveled up mouse body keeping the fan from turning. He tossed the carcass in our garbage. The refrigerator worked fine after that."

"Huh. I'll keep it in mind; that could save me from paying for a house call."

As we approached the veterinary building, I saw Jenny and Spring standing beside Jen's pickup, waiting for the clinic to open.

Danny's bicycle was in the parking area and Jen had undoubtedly tried the entrance with no result. I waved to the girls as Onishi parked in his usual space at the left of the lot. Jen and Spring walked toward the front entrance as the doctor and I exited his car.

The girls wore shorts and sweatshirts with the arms cut off near the shoulders. I would have bet they had trimmed each other's hair, short for countering summer heat. Jen came up to me and placed her left arm around my waist.

"We've come for the puppy, David. Is he ready for us to take him home?"

"Do you have a box in your truck?"

"We'll carry him in the cab with us. We don't need a box."

"Not for the dog, sweetie, it's for the supplies. We have food, medicine, diapers and a couple of toys for the pup. There's a small pile inside the door."

"Oh, I thought Spring and I would buy everything he needed."

"What we have will get you off to a good start. I told the doctor you would probably have plenty of old clothes that can be used for diapers. When they're dirty, you can burn them."

The doctor opened the clinic and went inside with Spring following closely. Jen started in and I grabbed her hand to keep her close and whispered, "I have some info about the cabin."

Startled, she frowned and called out, "Spring! Come here!"

It took about five seconds before Spring reappeared from inside the clinic.

"What is it, Jen?"

"David has something to tell us about the cabin."

I glanced at their expectant faces and said, "It's not in the area where you guys found Mr. Duggar the other day. He told me his cabin is closer to Jackson than Suddenly. It's going to be about a seventy mile trip by vehicle, followed by at least a sixteen mile hike, maybe longer."

Spring was confused. "I don't get it, David. Why would it be seventy miles from here? Mr. Duggar couldn't hike that far without assistance."

"Okay. By car, we'd have to drive almost to Dillon and then take route 278 to Jackson. It's forty-four miles from Dillon to Jackson. Then we'd have to hike into the forest back toward Suddenly, nearly fourteen or fifteen miles and not knowing where to look. If you guys and Dexter still want to go for it in July, I think we should drive as far as we can on logging roads and then hike toward Jackson. We could stay out of the timber until we get closer to Jackson than Suddenly." I raised my eyebrows and said, "What do you think?" I waited about a minute while the girls considered the options.

Jenny moved closer to me and looked into my eyes. "We're going to get maps of the area that you told us about—north of Suddenly and closer to Jackson. After we look over the terrain, we'll make our decision. Is that all right?"

"That sounds like you guys are thinking right. I'll ask Scott if he can somehow arrange a chopper to take us to the area we want to search. Mom might have some ideas, too."

"That would be awesome!" Then she kissed me.

I grinned and responded, "*That* was awesome."

When Spring quit giggling, she pulled on Jenny's right arm and said, "Come on, Jen, let's get Charcoal. Then we'll go to the ranger station for more maps."

I gave Jenny a little shove and followed the girls into the clinic. Dr. Onishi had Charcoal on a leash.

He stated, "I know you have chosen the name Charcoal for the puppy, but I think a one syllable name would be better. How about shortening the name to Coal? If he were a female, Char would be a great name. It's all right to call him Charcoal but dogs react better to simple names. It's something I've learned over the years."

Jenny looked at Spring and asked, "What do you think? I'm willing to call him Coal."

Spring smiled and replied, "Charcoal and coal are the same color. Coal is fine with me and it's easier to say."

Jenny turned to Dr. Onishi, "Okay, it's Coal for his name. I hope Mr. Duggar likes it."

I laughed, "Well, I think Coal is better than Al." Everyone laughed in agreement.

I could hear Spring whisper to Jenny, "Let's spell it C-o-l-e; make it a regular male name."

Jenny responded, "Good idea. If someone asks, we can tell them it's because of his color. They'll assume it's spelled c-o-a-l. That gives us something to talk about."

Dr. Onishi's arms were loaded with the puppy and the boxed wheelchair. "David, have the ladies practice attaching the wheelchair so there is no confusion." He handed me the wheelchair and gave Cole to Jenny.

I started with a caution, "Don't attach the chair on a counter, keep Cole and the wheels on the ground. If he gets excited with the wheels on, he might jump to the ground and get injured, just like a person tipping over in a human's wheelchair."

I dropped to the floor and had Jenny place the puppy in front of me. After attaching the apparatus, I let him run around the reception area for a minute and then took the wheelchair off. Spring and Jenny worked together and reattached the two-wheel unit as I watched closely. I didn't have to comment, they had done a perfect job. They were ready to take Cole home.

I pointed at the small pile of supplies being donated and said, "A box?"

Spring had picked up Cole and exited the clinic. Jenny shook her head. "We don't have a box." She stood there a few seconds, a bit frustrated and then smiled, "I know, I'll get something."

She dashed to the truck and returned with a small plaid blanket. I helped her place the materials in the center of the blanket and gather the corners together. She swung the bundle over her shoulder and as she went toward her truck, she quipped, "I feel like a hobo," and laughed.

As my smile faded, I asked, "Is it okay if I come over tonight to check on Cole?" I expected a witty reply but she just grinned and said, "We should have time for you but don't make it too late. Cole has to get to bed before ten o'clock." I watched as the girls climbed into the pickup, adjusted their seat belts and pulled onto the highway. As they drove away, I heard two beeps from their horn.

The remainder of the afternoon was spent in the surgical suite neutering two dogs and spaying a cat. We would keep them for at least a day, probably two, before having their owners return to get their animals. After cleaning up the operating area and making sure the animals were recovering well, I started pedaling home.

I had ridden a few blocks when I decided to stop at the Emporium for a free doughnut and coffee. I had to pass by the store anyway on my way home. Dr. Onishi and I hadn't taken a coffee break all afternoon and I wanted to purchase a new set of screwdrivers for Danny to use for the lawncare business. His birthday was coming up in two weeks. When I arrived at the store, Mrs. Sandoval was putting up a sign on the front door. Before entering I stopped momentarily to see what was being advertised; I assumed it was something special. Her note was distinct; it was a notice that the store would be closed on the coming weekend but would reopen the following Monday.

As I entered, I asked, "Are you and your husband taking a trip to Butte this weekend?"

"Oh, hi David. No, we're going on a hike. The summer weather is beckoning. We've both been sitting too much. We need to get some wholesome exercise."

"I can understand the sedentary life. Going to classes and studying is a lot of sitting. Jenny, Spring, Dexter and I are planning a trip into the forest over the July Fourth weekend. The girls want to rough it for a weekend. They just experienced being alone by renting a fire tower for a couple of days . . . I guess you knew about that."

She nodded. "We sold them a camping stove and a few other things. I hope they had fun."

"I guess so. They came to the clinic today and picked up the puppy to foster. They should enjoy the experience. They gave the puppy a name. It's Cole."

I knew where the screwdrivers were located and started toward them with Mrs. Sandoval following me. I expected to see Mr. Sandoval. Where was her husband?

She asked, "What can I help you with today?"

"I'd like to buy a set of screwdrivers as a birthday present for my brother. He took over my lawncare business and needs some tools. Also, I'd like some coffee and a doughnut."

She smiled, "I can get you only two of those things, screwdrivers and coffee. We're completely out of doughnuts, sorry. We gave away three dozen of them today."

"I laughed, "That's all right, I'm on my way home. Mom will have some cookies for her starving son. Could I have the coffee to go?"

"Sure, we have plenty of cups with lids. Meet me at the register."

While Mrs. Sandoval disappeared down the adjacent aisle, I moved toward the register near the front door. I heard Mr. Sandoval's voice from the rear of the store.

"Elaine, I hope those dirty napkins don't attract any bears. You know, those animals have a sweet tooth."

"I'm waiting on a customer, Ef," she yelled.

"Well, we're out of doughnuts!"

"He already knows that, dear. I'm getting him some coffee and a set of screwdrivers."

Within a second or two, we all arrived at the main register.

"Hi, David. I didn't hear you come in. I was taking out some trash. We're about ready to go home. How's work at the clinic going?"

"Fine. Dr. Onishi and I were busy all afternoon and I wanted to get some free coffee and a doughnut but your wife told me you are out of pastry. I'll pay you for the set of screwdrivers; they're for my brother's birthday."

Mrs. Sandoval stated, "That's seventeen ninety-nine, David. Two dollars off for a birthday present. Tell Danny Happy Birthday from Elaine and Efren Sandoval."

Mr. Sandoval grinned, "Actually, she's taking two dollars off because we ran out of doughnuts. I should have ordered three and a half dozen so I could take five of them home."

"Efren! Always joking."

I had to laugh at their banter. I gave her a twenty dollar bill and she handed me a receipt and change. I was the last customer for the day and they were ready to close and go home. They thanked me for my business and as I started to toward the door with the screwdrivers and a cup of coffee, I heard Mrs. Sandoval say, "Let's lock up, I'll do today's books at home on the computer."

Efren replied, "I'm ready. Let's get out of here."

When outside the store with both hands occupied, I realized I had a problem. I looked at the bike and knew riding without at least one hand steering was going to be impossible. I started to dump the coffee in the gutter but when I glanced down at my feet, I got an idea: I could tie the screwdrivers to the handlebars with one of my shoestrings and steer with one hand, still able to drink the coffee.

On the way home I thought about the Sandovals and how much they seemed to be like my parents. When I rode in the driveway, I could hear noises coming from the garage. I concluded Danny was at work on the mower engine. I'll go in the house and put the screwdrivers under my mattress and wrap the present later.

Dad wasn't home yet but I announced my presence to Mom and Gwen. "I'm going to my bedroom and change clothes. Do we have any antacid tablets? I had some coffee at the Emporium and it's eating at my stomach walls."

"There are some pills in the medicine cabinet. Take a couple and drink some water. We'll have dinner when Scott gets home. He called a few minutes ago and said he'd be home in about thirty minutes."

Chapter 29

While we were eating dinner the phone rang. Mom, nearest the phone, answered.

"Hello." She handed me the phone. "It's Dexter."

"Hi Dex. What's up?"

"You gonna see Jenny tonight?"

"I thought I would. You want a ride?"

"Not tonight. I figured I'd ride a bike out to see Spring."

"Not a good idea around here, Dex. Have you got a bright headlight?"

"No, that's why I wanted to know if you're going out there. I'll need a ride back. My bike folds up. It'll fit in your car."

"Not a problem. See you at Jenny's."

"O.K. Thanks David. Later."

"Bye, Dex."

After we finished dinner, Dad went in the living room, sat in his overstuffed chair to relax and read a mystery novel. Gwen was playing with a doll house on the floor in the den next to the dining room. I don't know what Danny was up to. I asked Mom if she needed me to do anything.

Mom answered, "Nothing I can think of. Are you going over to Jenny's?"

"Yeah. I want to see how the girls are doing with the puppy." I laughed, "I want to make sure they don't give the dog any chocolate. See you later." I started out the door.

"Tell the girls hi for me."

"Okay."

The drive to Jenny's took about five minutes. On arrival, the dashboard clock registered 7:18. There was no sign of Dexter, but he had much farther to travel and at a slower rate than me by car.

Jenny and Spring were sitting on the porch swing with Cole between them. He was asleep on a big pillow.

Jenny pointed at Cole, "He's tuckered out. We gave him a lot of activity today. After we had dinner he whined at us until we removed his wheels. Then he curled up and fell asleep on the living room rug underneath the coffee table. We put him on the pillow. He didn't even wake up when we moved him. Poor little guy."

Before I could join the girls on the porch, Dexter rode up and hopped off a bicycle. He was out of breath but guided the bike to the edge of the porch and parked. He grinned at me and asked, "How long have you been here?"

"About an hour."

"No way!"

"I got here about thirty seconds ago, Dex. You haven't missed a thing."

The girls were smiling. Spring quipped, "You guys haven't even brought anything—like flowers."

Dexter replied, "We brought our bodies, especially our lips. Local residents call us the kissing devils of Suddenly."

We all laughed and Jenny said, "Would you like something to wet your lips, like coffee or pop?"

I said, "No coffee for me, thanks, but a can of pop would be great."

Dexter agreed, "Pop for me, too. Coffee will keep me up all night."

Jenny looked at Spring and she nodded. Jen went in the house and returned two minutes later with four cans of ice-cold Pepsi. We left the sleeping puppy in the porch swing and sat on the grass to watch the stars begin to appear in the night sky. Apparently, Spring hadn't noticed changes in position of the northern constellations until tonight.

"Where's the North Star, Dex?"

"Polaris?" Dex glanced away from Spring and pointed. "There it is. I thought you knew the northern constellations."

Spring grinned. "I do. I was just testing you. I wanted to know if you could navigate at night. When we take our July trip I don't want to go if you can't navigate at all hours."

I looked at Spring and smiled, "Dexter and I will have compasses. We won't get lost, but it's nice to know that you can travel using the stars as beacons."

Dexter laughed, "I'll bet Spring can climb trees to see the stars if the canopy is too dense to see them from the ground."

"Oh! Did you see that . . . a meteor."

I saw it flash across the sky and said, "Good eyes, Jen. That was probably some space junk from all the crap we've put in orbit. By the way, have you ever been lost?"

"Uh-huh, in St. Louis. I was about twelve and was running away from home. A cop found me and took me back home. I can't remember why I was on the run. Probably about something my parents wouldn't let me have. I was pretty spoiled back then."

I heard the buzz of a mosquito and suggested, "Let's call it a night before the mosquitoes eat us alive."

Jen commented, "I haven't noticed any yet. It's so dry here, where they are coming from?"

"Streams and puddles from all the melted snow?" Spring questioned. "Let's go inside and put Cole in his bed. How are you going to ride home in the dark, Dex?"

"My bike can be folded up and put in David's car. He'll drive me home. I guess we should say good night." I watched him take the last remaining sip of pop and crumple up the thin-walled aluminum can.

When we were in the house, Jenny gathered the empty cans and dumped them somewhere in the kitchen. We could hear the crashing of the cans. I had picked up the sleeping puppy and took him in the house. Spring pointed to his bed on the floor under the TV table. I carefully laid him down and grinned. He must have been really tired. The girls showed me a diary for him so they could comment on his journey recovering the use of his hind legs. The vet and I hadn't thought of keeping a record of Cole's progress. The girls followed us out on the porch, kissed us good night and we loaded Dex's bike. I gave one beep on the horn as we hit the road.

The rest of the week was full of work—Dex and I had little time for relaxation. Each evening when I phoned the girls, Cole was already sawing logs, dead to the world. Jen and I discussed going out and decided it would work if we alternated with Spring and Dex so one couple was always with Cole. Spring and Dex claimed Thursdays. Jen and I gladly accepted Friday nights and went to a movie at the downtown theater. There was talk about opening up the outdoor theater, but it turned out to be wishful thinking.

Elaine and I packed our car for the weekend sojourn into the forest and went to bed early Friday evening. Elaine was so eager to find that cabin, we decided to get up, eat, and set out at dawn Saturday morning.

It was still fairly dark and when we went through the downtown business district, I almost expected the streetlights and the stoplight to be turned off. That wasn't the case, but we didn't see any movement from man or animal as we drove down Main Street, not even a police car. In my rearview mirror, I saw the stoplight turn red. It reminded me of a sci-fi movie, the street vacant.

As we passed the animal clinic at the northern edge of town, I asked, "Where do you want to stop to leave the road?"

"It's still about three more miles, Efren. I think it will be light enough for me to see where to exit. Then we'll have to park the car where it will be out of sight. I don't want anyone messing with our stuff while we hike."

I nodded, "Good idea."

We proceeded for about five minutes at forty miles per hour . . . a little over three miles. Elaine watched the left side of the road and when we both saw a large clump of bushes, she said, "Stop, Efren. This is the place."

"So you want to enter the forest over there?" I pointed at the trees to the west.

"Yes. Turn the car around and pull off the road."

As requested, I turned the car around and parked on the shoulder next to the bushes. I wasn't going to pull off the road until I could clearly see the terrain. There wasn't any traffic, so I wasn't worried about other vehicles hitting our car but I didn't want to get stuck or puncture a tire. The sky was turning a light gray-blue and I could make out a shallow ditch off the shoulder south of the shrubs. I wasn't going to drive out to the trees from this location without inspecting the area first. I shut off the engine, got out, and began to walk toward town. About fifty yards from the shrubs, I noticed tire tracks. I assumed it was where David left the road when he took Mr. Duggar into town. I decided to take the same route.

I went back to the car where Elaine was waiting and told her what I was going to do. She didn't comment. When I entered about two car lengths into the shelter of the trees, I looked back to see if I could see the road. Nothing but trees, a good place to leave the car. I wished someone would drive by so I could see headlights. No one was on the road, so Elaine and I got out, put on our packs and started making our way farther into the forest. I went first with a small flashlight to illuminate our path through the timber. I was following my compass direction northwest.

We had trekked about a quarter of a mile when Elaine, a little winded, said, "Stop, Efren. I want to look at our map." She unfolded the forest service map for the area and I illuminated the paper with my flashlight. She asked, "Where do you think we are?"

I pointed to a place on the map and said, "We're about half a mile from that no named creek to the northwest. Should we proceed to it?"

"Uh-huh. I've got my wind back. Let's go. It's almost light enough to see without the flashlight."

We encountered a few places that required some chopping with my machete, but each time I cut into the wild bushes to allow us passage, Elaine caught her breath. I think she was slightly overconfident about her physical stamina. Going up and down to her balcony office at the store a few times a day had not prepared her for trudging through overgrown wooded areas with downed trees and out of control growth of vines and bushes. I assumed the search for that cabin was the force impelling her forward. If we continue for the remainer of the day, Elaine's legs will be sore tomorrow. In my case, I go running about three times a week, early in the morning. I try to run and walk two miles each time out.

After half an hour, we arrived at the waterway marked with a dotted line on the survey map. It was a dry creek bed. Without doubt, the reason we hadn't seen any animals was the lack of water. Only approximately eight feet wide, this remnant was probably active for only a short period carrying off snow melt. I doubt if this was the creek pictured in the painting of the cabin. That depiction had a stream that was only partially frozen over and looked to be carrying a reasonably large amount of water, probably year around.

A bit frustrated at the lack of water, evidence that there might be a cabin nearby, Elaine sat down on a large rock and surveyed the area. She didn't even try to take a picture. Nothing drew her attention for doing any artwork. I expressed my conclusions about the dry bed, and by the few exposed rocks indicating the shallow depth of water when it drained the area.

"I don't think this is anything resembling the creek in that picture, Elaine. I think we should move on to stream number two on the map, the next one to the north. It's about half a mile farther. Maybe it will be larger and have some flowing water."

She gave me a wry smile, slowly stood up and adjusted her backpack. "Let's go. When we get there, we'll have some lunch. I hope there's some water so I can cool my feet. I think I'm going to have some blisters."

"Do you want to take off your boots and have me massage your feet?"

"No thanks, dear, not now. You can do that at the next creek, wet or dry."

I doused my light and set off north, stopping momentarily after moving through a rough area of broken fallen trees. We had to climb over some logs resting on top of other fallen timber and I gave Elaine a boost after she temporarily removed her backpack. When I stopped, I raided some huckleberry bushes while waiting for her to catch up. Only a few berries were ripe, it was too early for a full crop. It was like having a tiny bite of dessert before lunch. I gave Elaine a few berries and carried both packs until she finished with the snack. It didn't take long.

In the proximity of the stream, we could hear the water. Although only faint, the sound of water running over rocks was quite distinctive. Elaine was encouraged and we hurried ahead. The water was only about twenty feet wide but cascaded over large rocks creating the sounds we heard. It looked like someone had tried to dam the flow.

Chapter 30

The rocks didn't exhibit any scaring from mechanical manipulation but I couldn't do a thorough examination; signs of scraping might be underwater. The position of the near boulders didn't look random. Could someone, maybe loggers, have placed them there for some unknown reason? While I checked the rocks, Elaine sat on a nearby outcrop and removed her hiking boots.

"Where do you feel pain when you walk?"

"Just on my right heel."

"Remove your right sock and let me take a look."

As she took off her stocking, I got our mobile medical kit from my pack and opened a small tin of petroleum jelly and unwrapped a gauze pad. I applied the jelly to the red area, covered it with gauze and taped it in place. Then I smeared a light layer of petroleum on the inside heel of her boot. "Okay, put on clean socks and replace your boots."

She looked at me and said, "That's it? Aren't you going to massage my foot?"

"Not now. Let's have something to eat and then we'll start walking along the bank moving upstream. I think we'll make good time hiking along the far bank. I'll tend to your feet when we set up camp. You know, you have sexy feet."

Between chuckles, Elaine replied, "I'll bet you say that to all the girls."

We finished eating In thirty minutes and resumed our cabin search. We could have started a small fire to warm some soup, but we wanted to save time and cover as much territory as possible before camping. I hoped to find that cabin or at least some type of shelter before nightfall. I'd like to have a roof over our heads out here in the forest. I didn't know what to expect from marauding wildlife foraging at night. However, I was prepared to have a sleepless night with one eye open.

We explored the gradual uphill slope for almost an hour with little hindering our passage. I estimated the distance covered was two miles when we came to a rocky projection about eight feet high. The stream fell about half that height to a pond before continuing its downhill path, the waterway we had followed. Elaine found the spot a good subject for some artwork, so we rested about ten minutes while she took several pictures.

We found an easy assent to higher ground and continued another hundred yards before the stream lost its soil bank as the water swept around a hill. A wall of rocks intersected the water at an angle I estimated to be seventy degrees, too steep and rough to scale. We were at an impasse and could go no farther without crossing the stream. Unfortunately, the water was at least four feet deep. We were left with one choice; we had to backtrack to find a fording spot.

Elaine didn't require an explanation. She had eyes and realized we had no other choice if we were to continue following the stream. I asked, "Do you want to lead?"

"How far do we have to go?"

"Watch the depth of the water. When it doesn't flow over the tops of our boots, we'll cross."

During our short descent, we stopped twice. Each time, she gave me a questioning look. I glanced at the water and shook my head, no need for words. It was still too deep, even though the bottom was obvious, the water was crystal clear but the depth was deceptive where the stream was narrow. I could see where the water broadened about fifty yards farther downstream so I pointed.

Elaine led the way and after walking about ten yards, she stopped, picked up an old branch about three feet long and knelt on the bank.

"Efren, could you give me a piece of tape about six inches long?"

As I opened the medical kit, I realized what she was up to. I watched as she made a depth stick using the height of her boots as a ruler, marking off the branch with the adhesive tape. When we arrived at the wide spot, Elaine probed the depth with her device and started across. I was happy to see that she was making some good decisions. Being careful not to slip on algae covered rocks, we successfully crossed and started back upstream to the sharp bend. Elaine led the way and when we rounded the bend, she yelled, "Efren! A cabin!"

The structure resembled a lean-to more than a cabin and it was on the opposite side of the stream. I had seen the picture of the Duggar cabin before and this wasn't it, not even close. I was positive Elaine wanted to investigate, but I wanted to move on. We marked the position on our map to investigate at some future time. Several more hours of hiking were ahead before camping for the night. Hoping for more huckleberries and another mini-snack, I convinced Elaine to continue moving. She reluctantly agreed after looking more closely at the dwelling. It could probably shelter only two people, more like a large outhouse with a steeply canted roof. There was no sign of life. Someone in the past must have spent some winter days in the area.

Expecting to see large quadrupeds and a bit worried as we moved upstream, we only encountered a small flock of birds. We must have interrupted them, they weren't singing. The birds were probably there for water and feeding on insects. We continued our hike for another hour and stopped at the apparent source of the water, a small kidney-shaped lake perhaps a half-acre in size. We decided to camp overnight and move out in the morning to seek the last tracing on our map that indicated water. Walking the circumference of the pond didn't divulge the water's source. It must be coming from underground, being fed from higher elevations some distance away. I estimated we were at sixty-five hundred feet, slightly higher than Suddenly.

Two stout trees about twenty yards from the edge of the pond, separated by about eight feet would support our lean-to tarpaulin roof. I whittled several wooden spikes to attach the edges of the tarp to the trees and the ground while Elaine assembled our cooking stove. We'd have a hot meal for dinner; the shelter being readied for comfortable sleeping conditions. Elaine went to the pond for water to be boiled. We didn't want to attract animals so we kept food odors to a minimum by heating items in water. We'd have bacon and eggs for breakfast, generating odors from food cooking in hot grease, and then leave the area after burying greasy materials.

We talked about our journey while we ate and Elaine stated, "Where do you think the water comes from? It's so clear and quite cold."

"There must be an underground source. One of the higher peaks is contributing snow melt. I'll bet this little lake will disappear by the end of summer, then fill up again when rain and snow come to higher elevations. Any remaining water will probably freeze over by the time winter arrives and the stream will vanish."

It was still light when we went to bed but trees concealed direct rays from the horizon.

"Efren?"

"Yes?"

"I have to go."

"There's a roll of paper in my backpack. You can go anywhere, no one will see you but stay away from the water."

"What if I lose my way in the dark?"

"Don't go that far from here. Make it quick before sunlight completely disappears. I'll leave a flashlight on for you."

She laughed as she stood there looking for a good place. Then we heard an owl. She commented, "I feel like I'm being watched."

"You probably are. Owls have great eyesight. Don't worry about Mr. Owl, he won't gossip. Just hurry up and come back to bed. I'll massage your feet. We want to get an early start tomorrow. We'll have to scout the last creek and get back home. It will be a long arduous day. We have to be back at the store on Monday."

I was sleeping soundly when Elaine woke me, "Efren, I can't go to sleep." With no moon, it was impossible to see anything in front of my face. I turned toward the voice, "Count trees, sheep or money. Don't think of anything, you'll fall asleep. One more day and we'll have our soft beds. You can sleep in on Monday and come to the store at noon, or if you want, take the whole day off. Your legs are going to be sore."

"Okay. You can go back to sleep. I'll be all right."

I woke up at five o'clock. Some rustling about was coming from nearby trees, but it wasn't Elaine. There was barely enough light to see. Elaine was still asleep. I'm glad she finally got some rest. Today should be a reasonably productive day even if we don't find that cabin. I'm sure we'll find some subjects for photography if we lower our expectations.

I slipped into my pants and sweatshirt, pulled on my boots and got out of the shelter to investigate the sounds. With my machete in hand, I stepped toward the pond, locked my legs in place and listened. In the dim light, I moved slowly and carefully toward the noise, avoiding the creation of sounds from stepping on debris. The scraping was coming from trees about twenty feet from the edge of the clearing. Squinting to see into the timber, no movement was detected.

There it was again, that same scraping sound. Then it repeated, and again. Sneaking closer to identify the animal, I kept large trees between me and the critter, whatever it was. Wishing I possessed a firearm, not just for protection. A discharge would scare it away; I moved closer. The bushes moved and the dark brown, almost black hide stood nearly five feet high. It wasn't moving away, just standing there among the shrubs and trees. I was close enough to hear its breathing. If it was a bear, I couldn't outrun it; I would have to climb a tree.

The nearest large tree, fifteen to twenty feet from the critter, had a limb I could reach to start the climb. With the machete in my belt, I struggled up about ten feet to a sturdy branch that would hold my weight and give me a better look. When I saw it, I began to laugh. It was a bull, scratching its neck against the bark of a tree. I yelled at it and it lumbered away, apparently satisfied with scratching.

I dropped to the ground and slowly walked back to camp to tell Elaine of my brush with death.

"Where did you go, Efren? I heard you yell." Elaine was fully clothed and setting up our small camp stove.

"I heard a noise I couldn't identify and went to investigate. It was a bull."

"Really?"

"Really. It must be from a nearby farm. Probably got out of a corral. We'll report seeing it when we get back to town. Some farmer is undoubtedly looking for it."

"What is a farm animal doing out here in the forest?"

"Scratching himself."

"Oh. I shouldn't have asked."

"He was rubbing his neck against a tree, that's all."

"How many eggs do you want? We have three."

"One and one half."

"Okay. You get two. I'll cook all the bacon and make sandwiches for lunch."

"I'm going to relieve myself. I'll be right back."

"I put the paper roll in your backpack."

"Don't need it, thanks. I'm going to pretend to be a dog and hose down a tree."

Elaine laughed. "Don't splash on your boots."

We had a quick breakfast and cleaned up our mess. We'd haul out any waste materials. By eight o'clock we were on our way to stream or creek number three. We left little evidence of our visit at the little lake. The contours on the map indicated a straight north passage would be quickest, so we expected to encounter the waterway within an hour. However, the valleys we took were covered with dense vegetation and it took nearly two hours to make the slightly over one mile journey.

We stopped for a ten minute break at nine-thirty. A strip of bacon, a drink of water and we were back on the compass setting. Elaine was being a real trooper. I felt sure her feet were sore and walking was painful but she didn't utter a disheartening word. We stopped to take a couple of pictures at a beautiful meadow that was filled with colorful wildflowers.

A short time after taking pictures we arrived at the stream, or what a sane person would be kidding themselves to call a stream. It was more like the water flowing along a city street gutter during a half-inch rainfall. We were both disgusted and started downstream on the southern bank. We made good time and if we hadn't stopped for lunch, we would have started back to our car before two in the afternoon. After eating, however, we discovered a small sod hut, probably used as a blind for hunters in the past. It wasn't in good shape, having probably suffered through ravages of the weather for several years without attention. We reached the edge of the forest at two forty-five. We hoped to get back home in time for a shower or bath and a wholesome dinner.

Chapter 31

e arrived in Suddenly at half past five, checked the store and were home twenty minutes later. The house had been closed since early Saturday morning and smelled a bit stale. I opened the front door and turned on the furnace fan to circulate the air. Elaine went in the bathroom and I started unloading our things from the car.

Most of the contents of our backpacks had locations for them in the house, so I began returning items to their normal places. A short time after emptying our packs on the sofa, I heard Elaine's muffled cry, "Efren! I need help."

What had happened, was she stuck on the toilet? I tapped on the door and heard, "Come in!"

Elaine was sitting on top of the toilet lid with her right boot removed. She had taken off her stocking which was soaked in blood. I grabbed a washcloth, immersed it in warm water at the sink and dropped to my knees to get a better look at her wound. As I carefully washed her foot, I could see a large blister had broken open and was bleeding but not profusely. I didn't want her blister to become infected so I said, "I think we need to go to the hospital. You need some medical attention so your foot doesn't get infected. Our meds here aren't very strong."

"What about dinner?"

"Let's take care of your foot first. Dinner can wait."

I taped two gauze pads over the blister, smeared it with petroleum jelly to cut the friction and helped her put on a clean white sock. We skipped putting the boot back on and I helped Elaine hop out to the car. I wanted to carry her out but she refused. She said I would hurt my back and then we'd both need medical aid. Reluctantly, I agreed. It was ten minutes to the hospital and nurse Berg was on duty at the front desk. When I told her what was going on, she grabbed a wheelchair and followed me to the car.

Sandie Reeves, the newest and youngest nurse in Suddenly, took over for Mrs. Berg and we went to ER2. Nurse Berg reappeared and removed Elaine's sock. Then she peeled off the dressing I had applied.

"Well, you really hiked beyond your pain threshold, didn't you? This is a nasty blister but I can take care of it without the doctor's assistance." She smiled, "We'll let him stay at home this evening. The doctor deserves a break."

After nurse Berg treated Elaine's blister and applied a bandage, she joined me in the hallway and inquired, "How did your wife get such a terrible blister?"

"We just got back from a two day hike. I knew she had a blister and applied some first aid, but she didn't comment again until we got back home. We must have walked nearly ten miles, so she walked halfway with that blister. She didn't say anything . . . not wanting me to have to go for aid. I think she was frightened about being in the forest alone, so she didn't say anything."

"I'll give you a week's quantity of antibiotics for her. If it doesn't begin to heal, come back and see Dr. Rennick, okay? Watch the damaged area closely. She doesn't need an infection."

"Thank you for your help."

"You are welcome. Please see nurse Reeves at the front desk before you leave. I'll get you a chair to take Elaine back to your car."

There was a wheelchair outside the ER, so Nurse Berg didn't have far to go. Elaine wanted to walk and asked for crutches, but nurse Berg wouldn't have it. She added, "If your wife is going to work, have her wear padded flipflops to avoid friction on her heel. Have a good evening."

With Elaine in the mobile chair, I rolled her to the front desk where we arranged for payment. After a quick swipe of my credit card, we headed for the main entrance where a man in uniform was entering.

It was Sheriff Wilson, a concerned look on his face. He glanced at Elaine and then me. "Oh! I've been looking for you. I went to your home but no one was there. I decided to come here . . . just in case. Did you have an accident?"

"No, we went hiking and a blister developed on Elaine's foot. Nurse Berg just treated her. We're on our way home. Were you looking for us? Something about the store?"

"No, nothing like that. Mr. Isaacs called me to see if I had seen Mr. Duggar. He didn't show up for his normal visit to the bank yesterday. Have you seen Samuel?"

"Afraid not, Sheriff. We haven't seen anyone except nurses since Friday. I'll call your office if we see him."

"Where were you hiking?"

"About three to five miles north of town. We were looking for that cabin Margret Duggar depicted in the painting that was exhibited at the B and B. Elaine wants to use the cabin as the subject of some artwork, so we went looking for it. We didn't find it but we found a bull." I chuckled, "Do you know of a farmer that has a bull that's AWOL?"

"I'll ask my wife to check with the forest service. That's more her area of expertise than mine. I'm more responsible for people and pets in Suddenly than in the outlying areas, unless a death occurs. I have a personal interest in Mr. Duggar because of my stepson's relationship with him and his pets. Please call my office if you hear of anything involving Mr. Duggar."

"Okay, we'll do that. Good evening, Sheriff."

He looked at Elaine, "Take care of that blister. Good night."

Dad got home in the evening as the sun was sneaking toward the horizon. It was getting difficult to see the football in the air, so Danny and I stopped playing catch and were sitting on the porch with Mom and Gwen.

Dad sat with us and asked, "David, do you have any idea where Margret Duggar is buried?"

"Isn't she buried in the cemetery?"

"I checked the city records and didn't find anything about her burial. Could she have been cremated?"

"Mr. Duggar never speaks of her except to talk about her painting. I'm thinking she passed away at their cabin and he buried her there. Why?"

"I just came back from Duggar's house. There was no sign of him but I found a note on his back door. It said he and Al were going to talk to Margret. He didn't know when he would return. Have you found out any more about the location of the cabin?"

"Sorry, Dad. Nothing more than what I told you before; it's closer to Jackson than Suddenly. Do you need to speak to him about something?"

"No. Bruce Isaacs needs to talk to him about some payments."

I laughed and Dad said, "What are you thinking?"

"I'll bet Mr. Isaacs wants to borrow some of Duggar's money to pay for Megan's Stanford tuition."

Dad grinned, "I don't think so. Bruce has plenty of investments and cash. Megan doesn't lack tuition money."

We sat there in silence for about a minute before Dad said, "I'm a bit concerned about that old man. If I don't find him by Tuesday, I'm going to ride out north and carry out a search."

"Ride?"

"In a chopper. I'll borrow one from the forest service. Do you want to go? I could use a spotter to watch the infrared screen. Your Mom doesn't want to go, do you, dear?"

Mom gave Gwen a hug. "I don't think I can be of assistance in searching for Mr. Duggar. You men go ahead. I'll call the service number and reserve an aircraft for you if they aren't out on fire duty."

"I'll go, Dad. Can Jenny go along? She and Spring are dying to get a glimpse of Duggar's cabin. They want it as a subject for their art." I knew I'd be a dead man if I didn't ask Jenny to come with us.

Dad was contemplating, "Well, if it's the small chopper I expect, I can't take more than two passengers, you and Jenny. Duggar and his dog will put us over our weight limit. That chopper has a lift restriction and needs some work. If Samuel is hurt, we'll be tight on space and weight. I might have to leave you and Jenny at the cabin and bring Duggar and his dog back, then return for you and Jenny."

"That's all right. I'll take provisions in case we have to stay overnight. Okay?"

Dad nodded and said, "That's a good idea. Be sure to tell Dr. Onishi what you're going to do on Tuesday."

"Oh yeah, I won't forget. I don't want to keep anything from him. He'll be writing a recommendation for me at the end of the summer. Working at the clinic is a two credit hour class and part of the pre-vet curriculum."

It was slightly after nine-thirty when I called Jen. Spring answered the phone.

"Hello David. I'll call Jenny for you."

"Thanks, Spring."

"What's up, David?"

"Do you have anything going on for Tuesday?"

"You have something planned, don't you? No, I don't have anything to do but stay home and work with Cole. I want to do some sketches of him. He is so cute."

"Well, Mr. Duggar has disappeared and left a cryptic note about taking Al to talk with Margret. Dad's going to borrow a chopper and look for him. I'm going with him. Want to go with us?"

"I sure do! Wait! Didn't Margret die about thirty years ago?"

"Exactly. That's the problem. We believe he has gone to his cabin, but Dad thinks the hike is going to be too much for him. Duggar is too frail, mind over matter at his age won't dictate. Mr. Isaacs wants to talk with Duggar about his finances. That's what prompted the search for the old guy. I expect his funds are running low."

"David, what about Spring? Can't she go, too? She wants to see the cabin as much as I do. We can leave Cole alone for a few hours."

"There's a weight limit, Jen. The chopper Dad thinks we'll be getting is small and there's a weight limit. If we find the old guy, you and I might have to stay overnight at the cabin while Dad takes Mr. Duggar to the hospital."

There was a several second pause before Jen said, *"That might be exciting, an overnight date out in the woods without a chaperone."*

"Could you make some sandwiches? I'll bring some drinks, a couple of blankets and some cookies. That should hold us over for an evening."

"You'd better bring a Swiss army knife. No telling what we'll encounter."

"Don't worry, I'll be prepared. But if Dad finds Mr. Duggar tomorrow, we won't be going on Tuesday."

"Tell your Dad to not look too hard. I really want to see that cabin. Oh! When do we leave on Tuesday?"

"Not too early but I expect Dad will want to leave by eight o'clock. You'd better drive here for breakfast and we'll go to the chopper in his police cruiser."

"Awesome! I've never ridden in a squad car."

"Dad will probably have you ride in the cage in back. That's for dangerous criminals."

"Funny, David. You can ride in back—in the trunk."

"As long as we're in the same car, I'm happy. Good night Jen."

"Night. See you Tuesday morning. Call me if we're not going."

"I'll do that, bye."

I spent all Monday's hours at the clinic expecting a call from Dad telling me he found Mr. Duggar but it never came. Jen's interest in viewing Duggar's cabin had stimulated my curiosity, so I found it difficult to concentrate on activities with the animals at the infirmary. Although not an artist, I was beginning to be sensitive to the girls' desire to find the cabin. The passage of time since Margret originally used the cabin as a subject for her art would have at least added some character to the structure. In my moments of spare time, I made notes of items to take on our search. I'd call Jen after talking with Dad when he's home from work to inform her of any last-minute change of plans.

When Dad got home, I could tell it had been a frustrating eight hours trying to discover leads on the whereabouts of Mr. Duggar and his dog. No one had seen the elderly man since the previous Friday.

"Why do you think no one from Suddenly has seen Mr. Duggar?"

"I think he thumbed a ride to Dillon from a tourist and hitched another ride to Jackson. Then he set off on foot to his cabin."

"Yeah, Dad, but he would still have to hike ten, maybe twelve or more miles. He's not too steady on his feet."

"True, David, but he has a tremendous desire to return to his cabin."

"I hope when I'm in my nineties, I have as much stamina as he has."

Dad chuckled, "Well, if we don't get some rest, none of us will live that long. Make that call to Jenny and hit the sack. We'll be leaving early tomorrow."

Chapter 32

Up and dressed a few minutes after seven o'clock, I started the coffee maker and dropped two pieces of bread in the toaster. I heard a knock on the kitchen door; Jenny had arrived. She was never late for an outing and especially this one that promised to be a glimpse of Duggar's cabin.

I opened the door and said, "Hi, babe. Come in."

Jenny wore jeans, a red sweatshirt and hiking boots. I hoped she had something under the long sleeved pullover; it was going to be a warm day. If we had to do much hiking, the long sleeves would have to be divested, she would get overheated.

She stepped inside, and looked around, "Are you the only one up?

"Uh-huh. Dad will be up in a few. He usually only has coffee and toast. I'm the big eater in the morning, oatmeal, a scrambled egg and orange juice. I've backed off my football diet."

Dad appeared in his sheriff's uniform. "Good morning, guys. How are you doing, Jenny? Ready for a chopper ride?"

"Hi Mr. Wilson. I'm fine and ready to go flying. I want to find Mr. Duggar and see that cabin."

"That's the plan for today. I hope we find him. He's got some pressing business at the bank. Do you want some breakfast?"

"I guess I could eat some toast, but no coffee. You have barf bags, right?"

Dad grinned, "Not a problem. David has some with your name on them."

Jenny frowned and replied, "All right Sheriff, it's too early to start picking on me."

I took a swig of OJ and chuckled. I almost had orange juice go up my nose. I gave Jen a piece of toast and she buttered it. I buttered the other piece. She glanced at the strawberry jam and shook her head.

I skipped oatmeal but nuked an egg. The three of us ate quickly and were out the door in about ten minutes. We didn't see Gwen, Danny or Mom. Jenny got in the passenger seat of the cruiser with her container of sandwiches. I slid into the cage carrying my stuffed backpack and pulled the door shut. Dad backed out onto the street and accelerated toward the Ranger Station.

We pulled into the facility parking area ten minutes later. Dad was right, we had the small chopper that was used for spotting fires but wasn't meant to carry water. A pilot was waiting for us. When he saw Dad, he motioned for a talk. They spoke for less than a minute and he went in the building; the pilot wasn't needed. We got in the cockpit, fastened our seatbelts, donned helmets and took off. Jenny latched onto my right arm, took a deep breath and closed her eyes when we lifted off. This was only her second ride in a helicopter. I gave her a big smile and patted her hands.

I watched the compass as Dad flew us west-northwest a few hundred feet from the ground. As soon as we were over the forest, we climbed to five hundred feet and veered north. Dad switched on the infrared scanner and I began to watch for small spots of movement. I noticed three blotches slowly moving together and said, "I think those are deer."

He nodded in agreement. We couldn't make a visual identification. The animals creating the elongated spots were hidden by the trees. We would have the same problem finding Mr. Duggar and Al but we had to find only two spots, one nearly stationary, the other smaller and moving erratically. We began a serpentine search pattern slowly penetrating farther into the forest. Rare were open spaces where we could observe the ground. We couldn't see any places to land the small helicopter without great danger.

Dad spoke into his microphone, "If we see them, I'll have to drop you guys at a high spot. I can't set the craft down out here. There's no room for the blades to clear the trees. You'll have to do some hiking."

"We expected that, Dad. If we find them, we'll hike in." I grinned, "Try to keep it about a quarter mile." I was confident Jenny and I could hike four hundred yards without any problems. We had food, equipment and were in good shape. The next movement we saw on the screen occurred about five minutes later. Dad glanced at the spot and said, "A bear, too big for a man."

We searched for a distance of a mile before reversing direction. After slowly scanning for a minute or so, we reversed again, moving deeper into the forest and at a slightly higher elevation but still no luck finding Mr. Duggar and Al. I was starting to wonder if we were going to find them. Perhaps they had not made it this far or already were at the cabin and out of detection with the infrared camera. But Dad was determined to continue the search. Without comment, Dad scanned another swath of timber.

Jen poked me in the shoulder to get my attention. I glanced sideways to see her expression of frustration, no greater than my own. But then, she suddenly pointed at the screen, "Look, David!"

Two spots appeared: a smaller one coalesced with the larger. "Is that them?" She yelled over the sounds of the rotor. Our frustration had changed to excitement.

"I think so," I smiled, "Good eyes!"

Dad hovered the ship over the ground signal and started slowly dropping in altitude. I watched the spots closely and detected movement. It was Mr. Duggar; he was waving to us. He might be in trouble and needs attention. How close is he to his cabin?

Dad spoke through his headset, "There's a small clearing not too far from here but it's at a steep angle. I can't land but I'll put you and Jenny on the ground. Do you think you can hike back here?"

"Yeah. We can make it back. We might need some help with directions. When you drop us off, give us a compass reading, we'll follow it."

"Right. I'll set down as close as possible and meet you. Take the onboard axe. It's under your seat."

Jenny and I prepared to drop to the ground with our belongings. When we reached the small area devoid of tall trees, I tossed the axe out. Dad lowered the chopper to about six feet off the ground and gave me a compass reading. I didn't have to say anything to Jenny, she hung her feet out of the cabin and vaulted away from the landing struts and huddled on the slope six feet below. I followed, landing a few feet from her. I asked, "Are you all right?" She nodded and I started looking for the axe.

The chopper rose above us and zoomed off to the east, leaving us in the quiet of the forest. Standing upright was difficult but we moved slowly and got off the steep hillside to level ground. The red paint stripes on the axe made it easy to find. I checked my compass and we set off to find the old man and his dog.

"How far do you think we have to hike?"

"Maybe a quarter mile — hopefully less. I'm gonna be tired of avoiding trees. I hope we don't have to ford a stream. Soggy shoes make hiking a little unpleasant."

"Oh, I don't know. I kind of like that squishy sound," Jen chuckled and I had to laugh. She was in a good frame of mind and I was enjoying her companionship.

I estimated we had gone about a hundred yards when I asked Jenny to sing. She surprised me with her answer.

"I don't do a cappella, David. You'll think less of me if I sing." She grinned, "I can whistle."

I laughed and suggested, "Okay. Whistle our high school fight song."

"You sing and I'll whistle. How would that be?"

"Okay, Al will hear us and start barking. Maybe we'll find them quicker that way. At least Mr. Duggar will have hope that someone is on the way. I hope he isn't hurt, just tired."

"I'm getting tired, too. I want him to take us to his cabin. Spring and I want a panoramic view."

"What about the inside?"

"That, too, the works."

We continued walking, avoiding tree trunks, low branches and bushes. Few of the huckleberries were ripe; it was too early in the summer. As I sang and Jen whistled, I hoped we would hear barking. After hiking about ten yards, we would stop and listen, then resume the procedure. After the third time through the fight song, I wished I knew another tune. After another ten yards, Old McDonald came to mind and Jen followed, adding a few new verses.

We regretted forgetting many of the words, so for the next several refrains, we made up more of our own lyrics. I don't remember McDonald having elephants or goldfish on his farm. Jenny decided to sing and she actually has a good voice. She was self-conscious about singing until she heard my less than mellow tones. We made it through another fifty yards when we heard a loud bark. It was coming from the compass direction, so we knew we were almost ready to meet with Mr. Duggar and Al.

We came upon a sunny spot and Al met us with a growl. Jen and I crouched down, spoke to him and he came to us hesitantly, tail wagging but still a little unsure of who we were.

"Where is Mr. Duggar, Al? Take us to him."

Al reacted immediately, turned and bounded off. We followed, trying to keep the dog in sight, but he was too fast for us. We continued, following our compass and in a couple of minutes, Al reappeared. He didn't bark but reversed course moving more slowly than before, walking a few feet and looking back at us. He must have figured out that we couldn't follow if he was out of view.

About five to seven minutes later, I wasn't keeping accurate track of time, a very loud bark penetrated through the trees. Jen said, "We must be getting close, David." Nodding to each other, we surged ahead, maybe twenty feet and there was Mr. Duggar, petting Al. Duggar was sitting on a large diameter rotting log, drawing in the dirt with a dead branch large enough to be a cane.

He looked up and smiled, "Well, it's about time. You're David but I forget the pretty girl's name."

"We didn't know exactly where to look, Mr. Duggar. Jenny is her name. You only saw her once before."

"You were in that helicopter? Who was flying it?"

"My stepfather, Sheriff Wilson. Your banker asked him to find you. Mr. Isaacs needs to talk to you about your bank holdings."

Duggar frowned and closed his eyes, apparently thinking. "I guess my account needs some fortification." He sat there thinking for a few seconds. "I suppose you two youngsters want to see my forest abode."

"We'd like to see your cabin, Mr. Duggar. Jenny and her friend are both artists and they think your cabin would be a great subject for their artwork. They really admire the picture your wife painted years ago but they don't want to go where they aren't wanted."

Mr. Duggar stared at us for what seemed a long time but was for less than a minute, long enough for us to become uneasy. "I don't mind if you see the cabin. It probably needs work, I haven't been here in . . . about a year, I guess. Follow me. Come on, Al, let's see what's for lunch."

Jenny whispered, "What does that mean? Is someone at the cabin?"

Duggar staggered a bit as he got to his feet, steadied himself with that dried branch and started walking towards the nearest trees. We followed him easily, Al acting like a guide dog for a blind man.

After five minutes, Jen was getting impatient, "Are we ever going to get there?"

Smiling, I replied, "Be patient, Jen. We'd better be ready for a big surprise."

There was a growth of young trees with a four foot wide stream winding through the woods. Duggar waded through the shallow water and Al jumped from one bank to the other. Jen and I waded across where Duggar had gone, avoided several mature trees and stepped out into an open area in front of a log cabin.

"We're here." Mr. Duggar spread his arms out, presenting the structure like a TV game show model. "This is Margret's cabin. Margret and I built it thirty years ago. It's a beauty, don't you think? Let me see what she has for us to eat."

Jen whispered, "I think he sees it as it was when newly built. There's fallen branches on the roof and moss is growing everywhere. He's going to need some help to clean up."

We watched him at the entrance. He removed two wooden pegs, one on top and one on the side of the door and swung it open. The cabin was larger than I had estimated from Margret's painting. Duggar had undoubtedly worked on the structure over the years, probably increasing the pitch of the roof. He and Al disappeared inside and in seconds the single wooden front window swung up, propped open by a foot-long small diameter stick.

Duggar leaned out the doorway and said, "I'm cleaning up and getting oil lamps lit. You can come in shortly." The door slammed shut and the window was closed. Curiously, we were prevented from entering. Was Duggar embarrassed by the cabin's interior disarray?

"Jen, there's work to do on the roof, but I don't know whether I should get up there. The shingles look fragile. I might cause damage. I'll wait to see what work he wants me to help him with."

"Give me your knife, David. While we wait to go inside, let's cut down some of the plant growth on the outside walls."

Jen took my knife to cut vines and I used my hatchet to make short work of the larger vegetation. There were several small trees beginning to grow within two or three feet of the cabin. Removal was easy. A quarter of an hour later, the cabin looked like someone currently resided there.

We were surprised when the door swung open. "All right, you can come in now. I've done some badly needed housework."

Jen glanced at me and grinned. I smiled and we stepped into the cabin. The interior of the roughhewed building was unexpectedly nice. A small potbellied stove sat slightly off center on the left defining the kitchen area. Shelves along the wall behind the stove were stocked with canned goods and large to small metal containers labeled flour, sugar, salt and baking soda. A shallow partitioned box contained knives, forks and spoons of all shapes and sizes sat on top of a crude shelf. Jutting out from the back wall was a table that could seat four if guests were not too plump.

Connected to the wall, the table looked as if it could be folded up to give more floor space. Dried leaves, a few tree cones and dirt from shoes still needed to be removed from the unfinished floorboards. Jen got busy with a straw broom sweeping dust and debris out the door, rubble that Duggar had missed.

There didn't appear to be any wood for a fire, so I asked, "Should I get some dry wood for a fire, Mr. Duggar?"

"That is a good idea. Margret is out picking berries for dessert. She'll be back soon."

Jen stopped sweeping and gave me a puzzled look. I realized Mr. Duggar was out of tune with the present, or was he just kidding us? Maybe the trip had worn him out so much he was deprived of reality. Perhaps senility had begun to take over his mind and body. We would have to be careful with what we said, his reactions unpredictable.

Jen finished sweeping and went outside with me.

"Is he suffering from Alzheimer's, David? Does he really believe Margret is still alive?"

"I don't know but it is alarming. It's the first time I've ever questioned his mentality. I hope Dad gets here before long. He'll know how to handle the situation. In the meantime, lets humor Mr. Duggar. Don't say anything about Margret."

"Okay, that sounds like the right thing to do. Where would Margret be buried?"

"Why don't you scout around while I gather some wood for the stove."

Chapter 33

Jen disappeared around the corner of the cabin and I began picking up small dried branches, old cones and a couple of larger dead limbs that had fallen from nearby trees. I'd have to break them up with my hatchet. With a large load, I started back to the cabin. Barking suggested Dad was approaching. Al was definitely a good alert dog. Dad must have found a landing area within a half-hour walk from us.

Mr. Duggar emerged to help me unload my arms. He took the larger diameter, longer limbs and piled them next to the door. He looked at me and said, "Someone else is coming to eat, Margret will have to know. Where's the girl?"

"She's looking for the outhouse, Mr. Duggar. She'll be back in a minute."

"It's out back a ways," he pointed over his shoulder with his right thumb. I handed him some of the smaller twigs and dried cones and leaves. "Why don't you start a fire so we can warm up something. I'm getting hungry. We only brought sandwiches."

"You youngsters should be better prepared when you go on a hike from Jackson. I'll start some beans and biscuits as soon as I get the fire going."

Duggar went back inside and Jen appeared from the other side of the cabin. "I heard Al bark. Is your Dad coming?"

"I think so. What did you discover?"

"A grave and an outhouse. The grave is marked 'Margret 1929-1994.' I didn't go in the outhouse, but it doesn't stink. I doubt if it has any toilet paper; we'll have to use our own. I guess the only water comes from the stream we just crossed."

"Good job, Jen. That answers some of my questions. I noticed Duggar has a sink with a faucet inside. I'm thinking it dispenses rainwater. Let's ask about it."

Jenny snickered, "So you think he has a barrel of water in the attic?"

"Just a guess. Maybe the faucet is just for show and isn't hooked up to anything." I heard footsteps coming from the edge of the clearing.

Dad moved gingerly from the timber. He waved to us as he dusted off debris from his shirt and pants and walked toward the cabin. Jen and I gave him a hug and he asked, "Is Duggar in the cabin?"

"Yeah. The old guy made several comments about Margret, as if she's still alive."

Dad looked at the cabin for a moment and then inquired, "Have you two had anything to eat?"

"Nothing since breakfast. Duggar is warming up some beans and making some biscuits."

"Let's go inside and see what he's prepared." Dad grinned, "Does he have any catsup or jam?"

Salt and pepper were available, but no condiments. Not surprising, Duggar had no refrigeration at the cabin. Dad and I loaded on the pepper but Jen and Duggar just added pinches of salt. I expected to have a vicious attack of heartburn. Dad's stomach was made of steel or Teflon, generated during his FBI days.

While we ate, Dad told us about a site not too far from the cabin where he could land the chopper, provided some trees were removed. Duggar told us two axes and a two-man saw were stored in the outhouse. Jenny volunteered to help Mr. Duggar wash dishes, a collection of slightly chipped porcelain plates of different colors, but still serviceable. Dad and I stepped out into the bright early afternoon sunlight to retrieve the tools and found the outhouse. We used the little building for its intended purpose and recovered the implements.

The axes and saw had been coated with bear grease to prevent cutting edges from rusting. Duggar knew what he was doing, care of his tools might be an action that life in the forest might depend on. Dad stated that three trees had to be removed to create clearance for the rotor blades.

"Should we tell Jen and Mr. Duggar where we're going?"

"You do that. I'll take the saw and start to the area. I'll whistle so you can follow me with the axes."

It was about fifteen minutes later when I came into the area we had to clear. Dad had started sawing the largest of the three trees but hadn't made much progress, just getting the saw teeth through the thick bark. I dropped the axes and grabbed the handle on the other end of the saw. After cutting halfway through the tree, Dad signaled to stop and we removed the saw. Thinking we were just taking a breather; I sat on the ground and checked out the other two much smaller trees. Dad took a drink of water and handed me his canteen. "Don't get too comfortable, David."

That was a warning. The lull from sawing didn't last long. Dad gave me one of the axes and pointed at the big tree. "Remove lower limbs you can reach opposite the saw cut, then start cutting into the trunk on that side, a little below the cut. I'll fashion a wedge."

I understood what he wanted me to do, so I got after it. Scott sharpened a foot-long piece of a large, dried branch. As I cut a big notch, I worried that the tree would come down any minute but surprisingly it stayed upright. Scott had me step behind him as he drove the wedge into the cut we had made with the saw. The treetop began to shudder and with a loud snapping sound, the tree fell toward the growth surrounding the clearing. But now there was another problem, the downed tree trunk and limbs were too high and would prevent the chopper from landing. What was the solution?

Dad said, "Let's knock the other trees down and maybe something will come to mind."

The smaller trees were not a problem and in about thirty minutes, both were down and moved out of the way. Back to the big problem. Dad had come up with a tentative answer.

"David, do you know if Mr. Duggar has some rope, at least a hundred feet?"

"Yeah. I remember seeing a large coil, but I can't remember where it is. Want me to get it?"

"Yes. While you're gone, I'll lighten the load a bit."

I took off at a run, following the path we had made in the grass and weeds. As I made my way, I realized what Dad was going to do. At first I thought we were going to use the rope for a mechanical advantage to apply muscle to move the heavy tree, but then it came to me. He was going to use the chopper and tow the tree to the edge of the clearing. I hoped the rope was in good condition.

Out of breath when I reached the cabin, it was difficult to answer Jenny's questions. All I was able to blurt out was, "I need a rope." I looked around for Mr. Duggar, but he wasn't in sight.

Jenny realized what I was looking for. "Mr. Duggar is lying down. He hurt his back."

"I've got to talk with him about some rope."

"He might be asleep, David. Don't wake him."

"I might have to. Have you seen a big coil of rope?"

"Yes. There's a curled up rope underneath the bunk Mr. Duggar is on. Let me get it."

I waited by the door while Jenny tiptoed into the cabin. I heard muted voices but couldn't make out the words. Jenny soon appeared at the door carrying just what Dad and I needed, a large coil of rope.

"He called me Margret and said the rope was almost 100 feet long, except for a few feet he had cut off to make a belt, then he drifted off. I've never been around anyone that old before. I'm worried that he has only a short time remaining."

"Dad and I almost have a clearing ready for the chopper to land. We have to move a downed tree out of the way. Dad's going to tow the trunk to the edge of the clearing so he can land. As soon as he's got the chopper on the ground, we'll come for Mr. Duggar."

"Do you have an idea when you'll be back?"

"I'm sorry, Jen. You're stuck out here with nothing to do. I expect it should be about an hour before we can return for Mr. Duggar. Dad and I will have to carry him to the chopper but it's not too far. You can come with us and after Dad leaves with Duggar and Al, you and I will stay the night in the cabin. Dad thinks there might be a big storm coming. It should be fun, thunder and lightning in the wild."

"Great, David. I can hardly wait. Maybe we'll have a forest fire to keep us warm." She scrunched up her face, gave me an air kiss and waved as I disappeared into the woods.

Dad had removed most of the lower limbs from the trunk and started sawing off about eight feet of the big trunk.

"Grab the other end of the saw and let's get this thing cut off. I'll use the chopper and drag the upper part out of the way. I just hope the chopper has enough power to move it."

Ten minutes later, we had the heaviest part of the trunk loose on the ground. Dad slung the rope over his shoulder and said, "I'll be back with the rope dangling. You'll have to tie it to the big end of the top section, then get into the trees for safety. If the rope snaps, I don't want you struck."

I remembered when Rick Hadley's logging accident occurred and he had to learn to walk again after being a star athlete. I had to get behind some trees when Dad started pulling the rope with the chopper.

Dad left swiftly with the rope over one shoulder. I moved the saw and the axes away from the tree trunk. It still had two large lower limbs attached but was only about four feet high. I hoped the limbs on the upper section would act as skids. I sat down on the ground next to the trunk. I thought about our trip to find Mr. Duggar's cabin. If Jenny and I had been looking without the aid of the chopper, we'd still be searching. I was sorry that Spring couldn't come with us, but the small chopper wasn't in good enough shape to exert maximum lift. We were weight limited, so we couldn't all ride home together in the aircraft. I must have dozed off for a few minutes, because I suddenly heard the rotors. It was getting close.

At first I didn't see the rope dangling. What looked like a bird fluttering to stay aloft was a rag attached to the dangling rope. When the craft appeared directly overhead, I could clearly see the hanging cord. I got to the swaying rope quickly, secured it to the tree section and waved. Dad waited for me to take cover before the line tightened and the upper portion started moving, initially slowly and then at a steady pace, swinging out of the clearing towards the surrounding trees. I moved into the open and waved, giving our prearranged signal. The job was complete.

As soon as the chopper landed, we removed the rope from the tree and the landing skid, recoiled it and started back through the forest to the cabin carrying the saw, rope and axes. Al met us, sniffing our pant legs when we were about a hundred feet from Duggar's prized structure. It had been close to an hour when I left with the coiled line, so Jen wasn't disappointed when we reappeared from the woods.

Jenny welcomed us back with some details. "I told Mr. Duggar you would be coming for him and Al to fly them back to Suddenly to see Mr. Isaacs at the bank. He had me leave the cabin when he packed up things he wanted to have at home. I think he desired privacy because some things were Margret's. He must have loved her very much."

"Has he called you Margret again?"

"Nope. I think he was just play acting. He has been calling me Jenny since I got the rope for you."

Dad was talking to Mr. Duggar, explaining what we were going to do.

Mr. Duggar motioned for Jenny and me to come closer. In great detail, he explained how to lock up the cabin before we leave for

Suddenly. He understood Jen and I would be staying overnight. Then he said, "Are you going to carry me piggyback to the helicopter?"

"Yes sir, at least halfway. Have you gained weight since the last time?"

He smiled, knowing I was joking. "Not more than a few pounds."

Dad wanted to get going, he had seen clouds beginning to develop to the north. "Mr. Duggar, do you have everything you want to take back to town?"

"I'm ready. I want the young lady to carry my backpack. Let's go." He handed his pack to Jenny and after evaluating the weight, she accepted it without complaint.

I shut the cabin door and had Mr. Duggar climb aboard from the cabin porch. Dad led the way, Jenny followed and I was next in line supporting Mr. Duggar's thighs. Al dashed ahead and then returned to trail the safari. I think he wanted to be close to his master.

We were about halfway to the chopper when Jenny stopped, waiting for me and Mr. Duggar to catch up. Dad and Jen had gotten about forty yards ahead.

"You're getting tired, aren't you?" Jenny's face showed concern.

"A little bit. Dad and I should trade places, I know the way." Failure was not something I wanted to admit, but the earlier sawing and swinging an axe had worn me down. Plus, I wasn't in football playing condition. Before I asked Jenny to whistle, she did just that. Ten seconds later, Dad came crashing through the trees. "Is there a problem?"

"Yeah. I'm running out of gas. We need to switch."

"Not a problem, David. Put Mr. Duggar down. He could probably use a rest, too. Being carried is not fun due to jostling around."

Following the transfer of Mr. Duggar to Dad's back, I set off leading the pack. We arrived at the chopper about ten minutes later. Loading the old man into the helicopter was an easy task and Al vaulted in beside him. Dad tightened seat belts and Jenny transferred Duggar's belongings. He grabbed at the backpack and held onto it with both hands. He had no intention of losing his memorabilia. Mr. Duggar gave Jen and me a confident look and said, "Take care of my cabin. On the way back, get some fuel for the stove. If it storms tonight, it will be chilly without a fire."

Dad was waiting for us to back away from the chopper but started the engine. Mr. Duggar motioned for me to come closer. "David, that girl, Jenny, she's a keeper."

"Thanks Mr. Duggar, I think so. Have a nice ride back to Suddenly."

The clinic jolted my mind and I yelled at Dad, "Please tell Doctor Onishi that I'll be a day late." He waved that he understood. I joined Jen at the edge of the clearing and we watched as the craft lifted straight up and vanished beyond the treetops.

When the rotor noise had subsided, Jenny grabbed my arm and asked, "What did that old man say to you?"

"I don't think I should tell you; it's kind of personal."

"David! I should hit you." She gave a heavy sigh and then groaned.

I laughed, "He told me you were a keeper but I already knew that."

She smiled back and latched onto my right hand. "Come on, Romeo, let's start getting firewood ready for tonight. I sure wish we had some marshmallows."

By the time we reached the cabin, we had arm loads of dried branches. I had found a large dry branch about three inches in diameter and eight feet long. Foot long sections would burn for the best part of an hour. Of course, I'd have to chop it into short pieces.

Jen remembered I had commented about the cabin's roof when we first arrived and she asked me, "Do you think you should check the roof before it rains?"

I gave it a long look and replied, "I might cause damage. I think we should leave it alone and find out if it needs repair. We can collect rainwater with pots and pans if necessary. We might hear a symphony of water dripping from the ceiling."

"I've got to make a trip to the potty. Go ahead and start chopping up the log you found."

Chapter 34

Although the thick branch wasn't accurately described as a log, I retrieved an axe from the cabin and started cutting the dead limb into one foot lengths, about the right size for the potbellied stove. I heard a rumble of far off thunder and felt a cool breeze causing tree limbs to flutter.

Jen reappeared carrying a section of a tree trunk about eighteen inches long. It must have required a good deal of strength for her to pick up such a heavy load. "Look what I found, David. There's more behind the outhouse. Can you cut them up?" She dropped her unwieldy load and brushed herself off.

"Sure can. What a find! You earned your supper today. How did you happen to find chunks of logs like this?"

"I started wandering around looking for more firewood and saw these things in a jumbled pile. They must be leftovers from when Duggars built the cabin. Do you think they're too big?"

"We can cut them up, but only the ones that are off the ground. They should be dry and mostly free of bugs. Take me to your treasures."

Jen led me past the outhouse to a half dozen chunks of logs about three feet long, most on the ground. I figured only two of them were usable. It was easy to rearrange two of the ground pieces as a support for a dry log to be sawed in half. I retrieved the saw and we cut the two useful logs into smaller pieces. We carried them to the front of the cabin where I split them into manageable sizes for the stove. The thunder was getting louder as we carried our firewood into the cabin. I commented, "Sounds like a herd of buffalo is approaching."

Jen laughed, "When did you ever hear a herd of buffalo?"

"In a western movie on TV."

"Oh, I heard that it was a farmer dumping a load of potatoes from his wheelbarrow."

"I'll bet your grandmother told you that. The storm is going to be on us in less than an hour, so put on your sweatshirt and get ready for a temperature drop. Let's go inside and get a fire going. It will take a while to warm up the cabin. I believe it's going to be a cold and noisy night."

Jen grinned, "We need to watch a scary movie."

"Maybe the thunder will be loud enough to scare you."

Jen found a small package in the kitchen area and said, "David, what's this?" My attention was fixed on lighting the stove and her words didn't immediately register. As I struck a match, I looked at Jen. "What?"

She was unwrapping a small package and exclaimed, "Look! Butter, cheese and honey. Your Dad must have left them for us. Cheese with the beans, butter and honey for the biscuits. We're going to have a feast."

I laughed, "After the beans we're going to have thunder inside the cabin."

"I hope that won't be immediate. You can save the sound effects until we're sleeping."

The fire was beginning to snap and pop and we could feel the heat starting to warm us and the inside air. It wouldn't surprise me if the temperature dropped to nearly freezing at this altitude. The firewood Jen found was going to keep us warm and provide heat to prepare our dinner. The biscuits Duggar had prepared were all gone, so Jen was going to make us some from what she remembered of her grandmother's recipe. My only contribution would be from what I knew of pancakes and we didn't have any eggs. No syrup either.

Jen made biscuits that were tasty with butter and honey added. The main course was primarily beans but we added cheese and tossed in our leftovers from lunch. Kind of a bean stew. We sat on the floor next to the stove, ate dinner and listened to the noises from the approaching storm.

At one point, we heard an abrupt increase in noise coming from the roof. It was intense. Jen gave me a strange look, put down her plate and ran to the window to take a look. "It's hail, David! Lots of it! The ground is almost white."

Curious, I joined her at the window and peered out into the gray surroundings. The ground was being covered with marble sized hail, but the clamor on the roof was short lived. We watched the last of it and returned to our places next to the stove. As Jen sat down, she leaned back, almost hitting her noggin on the floor and made a strange observation.

"Did you know Mr. Duggar had a ladder in the kitchen?"

"What? What are you talking about?"

"Lean back, David. Look under the table."

Although I was skeptical, I relented and followed her directions. Sure enough there were four braces across the bottom of Duggar's crudely constructed dining counter. "You think that's a ladder?"

"Look closely, the boards are worn on one edge. If the counter-top is folded against the wall it becomes a ladder."

I was beginning to believe what she was saying. I noticed a hook that might be used to hold the raised countertop against the wall. But that would mean the ladder is for assisting access to the attic. I looked closely at the ceiling boards, maybe Jen was onto something. I had to ask, "What made you look under the table?"

"I was looking at the ceiling for leaks and just happened to spot those boards on the bottom of the counter. They don't seem to be there for any structural reason but reminded me of a ladder."

A loud boom of thunder caused us to embrace. "That was a close one!" Jen cried out.

Something seemed to be sifting through cracks in the ceiling but it wasn't water. I assumed it was just dust that accumulated over the years, like in any old attic. But Jen's artistic eyes noticed something. She held her right palm out to collect some of the particles. A second boom rattled the cabin and more specks fell from overhead.

Jen moved over to the closest oil lamp and said, "Look, David. The bits of dust are yellow."

"Let me see what you are looking at." I was thinking Jen had salt crystals on her fingers from making the biscuits but just in case, I had to look closely at what she had in her palm.

When I looked at her hand with my face no more than six inches from what she had collected, I realized the particles were gold. Duggar had gold dust hidden in the cabin's attic! Now I was a real believer of the ladder idea. I had to see what was above our heads. Should we wait until morning when the storm has passed or should I climb into the attic and investigate now?

"Jen, Mr. Duggar has gold hidden away in the attic. Should we check it out?" I wanted her to say we should investigate immediately but I'd go with her decision.

"Are you kidding me? Let's climb that ladder and see what's up there. But you go first. I'll hand you one of the lamps."

The last time Jen and I investigated an attic, Jen went up the ladder first and nearly fell when she thought she saw rats looking back at her. So, I understood why I was to go first. We flipped the tabletop against the wall and hooked it in place. From the first step, I reached the ceiling and pushed on two of the boards. With little effort, they gave way, but I was unable to see anything in the darkness.

"Pass me an oil lamp. I can't see anything but shadows. As I waited for the lamp, I heard a scurrying. There was something alive waiting for me, probably a rat. It would avoid the light and me. I didn't feel a weapon was necessary. The base of the lamp was cool but it was awkward getting into the attic. There wasn't enough space to stand, so I crawled to the origin of the yellow specks.

What I found was two flour sacks, one tied shut with a leather strip, the other leaking gold from what looked like a hole a rat had chewed through the sack.

Jen's head appeared above the ceiling boards where I had entered the attic. "What have you found?"

"Two sock size cloth bags, one tied shut, the other tied shut but leaking. I'm sure there's a rat up here. It chewed a hole in one of the bags."

"You're sure there's a rat? You know I hate rats. Are you trying to scare me?"

"No. I heard something scamper away when I looked above the ceiling. I'm pretty sure it's a rat. Something ate a hole in one of the bags."

"Why would a rat do that? It can't eat gold."

"It was a flour sack. What container do we have that has the cheapest contents—that we can throw away?"

Jen replied immediately, "That's easy, the one with salt in it."

"Get it for me. I'll pour the gold dust in it and hand it to you. I'll put the other bag under my shirt and come down. It's getting cold up here."

The heat from the lamp warmed my fingers and in less than a minute, Jen reappeared with the former salt container. She tossed it to me and the gold was transferred, including the cloth bag. I gave Jen the half-filled container, waited for her return for the oil lamp, and started down the odd ladder. I could have almost dropped to the floor but I didn't want anything to happen to the bag of gold under my shirt. Now we can inspect the treasure we found.

We lowered the tabletop to its original position and set both oil lamps on it for the best illumination available. I fished the bag from under my shirt and handed it to Jen. She poured the contents on one of the dinner plates so we could see clearly what we had.

"A bunch of rocks?" Jen said in disappointment.

"I think it's quartz—gold ore. The gold has to be extracted from the quartz."

"What do you think the value of this stuff is?"

I had to think for a short time before I could answer. I guesstimated two pounds of gold and maybe a half pound of quartz with gold veins. I came up with about a hundred thousand dollars, so I told her my estimate.

"A hundred thousand?" she exclaimed.

"It could be more; it's just a guess."

"What are we going to do with it, it's not ours."

"We'll give it to Mr. Isaacs. He's in charge of Mr. Duggar's affairs. He'll know what to do with it."

"Did you hear that? The thunder is moving away. I'm gonna look outside."

I laughed, "You heard my stomach sending bean signals. It won't be long until . . ."

"Until you'll have to take a blanket and sleep in the outhouse."

Jen had moved to the door, opened it and peeked outside. "It's raining but not very hard. Thank God it's not snowing. Your Dad won't have any trouble coming to get us, will he?"

"Nah. It will be clear by noon tomorrow. Let's try to get comfortable for sleeping. We'll clean the cabin in the morning."

The rain lasted for about thirty minutes during which time we arranged for sleeping next to the little stove. With our clothes on and one blanket each, we chose to lie on the floor instead of using the bunk beds far from the heat of the stove. I made sure we had plenty of wood for an all-night fire. Jen wanted to have a light on while we slept, so we adjusted one of the oil lamps to be a night light.

"Can you put a wedge under the door so no one can enter at night?"

I didn't understand why she was worried about someone coming to the cabin during the storm or even showing up from out in the forest but I did what she asked. It was something we should talk about when we get back to civilization, about twelve hours away. First, I'll talk to Mom about Jenny's peculiar request.

It was a little bit after midnight when we were awakened by a crashing noise at the cabin door. Jen was totally unhinged and I was at first concerned that a bear was trying to get into the cabin. But with the wedge firmly in place, no animal, man or beast could enter. As I considered various possibilities, I decided wind following the rain must have dislodged a branch from a surrounding tree and blown it against our door. Surely, that's what happened.

I sat with my arms around Jenny, trying to calm her fears. "Relax, Jen, the wind has blown a limb against the door. We'll check it out when it gets light. We're safe in here—and warm." I tried to make light of the situation. "Jen, you're safe in here with me. Nothing but a tank can get through that door. Curl up next to the stove and we'll share blankets."

Her trembling ceased in a few minutes and we fell asleep, spooned together. Neither of us slept well, tossing and turning while the storm diminished and passed. At five o'clock, unable to sleep any longer, we got up and talked about the storm and our return home. Jen had enough of the forest for her first overnight venture with me. We wanted to see what had struck the door, but had to wait until daylight. We were anticipating my dad's return to take us back to Suddenly. He would be surprised that we found Mr. Duggar's stash of gold.

Jen made some dry biscuits for breakfast, nothing else was available. After eating there was light enough to look outside through the cabin window. Jen took the first look and reported, "There's a limb leaning against the door. If we're pinned in here, we might have to wait for your dad to free us."

"Let me take a look." The broken off limb was surprisingly large, but I thought I could push the door open and squeeze out. I'd move it away from the cabin and make more firewood from it.

Jen said, "Can you please hurry up? I need to use the facilities."

Her urgency spurred me into service. I removed the wedge and gave the door a shove. The opening was only about two inches wide.

I got down on the floor on my back and used my legs to push the door open far enough for Jen to squeak through. She was in such a hurry the limb stayed in place. Now, I was trapped, temporarily. I waited for about ten minutes before I heard noises at the door.

The door swung open and Jen was standing there exhibiting a big grin. "Did you think I wasn't coming back?"

"No, that hadn't crossed my mind. A visit to the outhouse shouldn't take too long. Thanks for releasing me from cabin confinement. Let's take a look at the stream. I want to see what the rain has done."

"I saw a deer. I think it was getting a drink."

I quipped, "Nonalcoholic."

The stream was twice as wide and twice as deep as it had been when we crossed it about twenty four hours earlier. As we walked along the bank, Jen commented, "I love the smell of the forest after the rain. Everything smells so clean and fresh. Where do you think the water's origin is?"

"I like the smell, too. It's great to not have car exhaust and fireplace odors to inhale everywhere you go. Mr. Duggar has the right idea, live outside of town in solitude. Well, with his dogs."

"So, you don't think about being married?"

"That's not what I mean. After raising a family, responsibilities change. The Duggar's had a wonderful life, each excelling at what they did best, but lived together, celebrating the rich environment. They built this cabin and Margret painted beautiful pictures. And Duggar must have enjoyed accumulating his gold, undoubtably preparing for retirement."

Jen grabbed my hand, smiled and looked back at the cabin. "Are you going to build a cabin while I paint beautiful pictures?"

I grinned and gave her a kiss, "Something like that. I'm wondering who owns this cabin."

"Gosh, I was thinking it was Mr. Duggar's but It must belong to the government. Who can we ask about that?"

"I'll grill Mom. She should know how to proceed. Maybe Mr. Duggar knows, he built the cabin."

Jen added, "Or Mr. Isaacs. I'll bet he knows all about property rights."

As I watched the water rush by, I thought I noticed a few tiny yellow specks in the muddy bottom, but nothing on the surface. "I wish we had some direct sunlight."

Within a couple of seconds, the sun's rays appeared from behind malingering clouds. The colored spots were definitely coming from the bottom of the stream. Had this been the source of Mr. Duggar's gold? Had precious metal appeared in his front yard?

Jen chuckled, "Are you in touch with the man upstairs? Someone must be listening to you."

"That was pure luck, nothing more. I haven't spoken to Him lately."

"Jen, take a look at the stream bed. See those tiny yellow spots? Let's take a sample and check for the metal. If that is gold and not pyrite, Mr. Duggar didn't have to go mining. His stash came from the stream in his front yard."

"I'll get a coffee cup so we can scoop up some of that stuff. Would that be enough to do a check?"

"That'll do. Bring Duggar's fry pan, too."

She ran to the cabin leaving me talking to the atmosphere.

"We don't need much. I'll wade in and get a sample."

While I waited for her return, I looked for the most intense color and found it where the water changed direction, bending around the roots of a large tree. I considered, what if I was looking at was iron sulfide, fool's gold. But the metal is very dense. So that should tell me what the yellow material is.

Our test confirmed my suspicion; the yellow specks were the real deal. The little stream was transporting gold right before our eyes. Now Jen and I had a problem, we couldn't tell anyone. It had to be a secret or the place would be overrun with riffraff, and the cabin would be ruined.

"Can I tell Spring?"

"We can't tell anyone, Jen, except my dad."

Chapter 35

"But if I want to say something to you about specks of gold in the water, what can I say?"

Jen had forced me to think; we needed a code word. Sand came to mind. "Let's have a code word for the gold. How about sand?"

"Ah, intrigue. Sand is our code word. That's easy to remember, and it's so common, no one would suspect anything."

"Exactly. Let's get the cabin in order, lock it up and head for the clearing. You can do some sketching or take some pictures while we wait for Dad."

"What will you do?"

"I'll watch over you, keep you safe from flying tree limbs. I'll have memories of being out in the forest, spending the night in a log cabin with my girlfriend."

Half an hour later, we were ready to make our way to the clearing. Jen had the canister of gold dust and I had the sack of quartz with gold inclusions. I had taken only a few steps away from the cabin when Jen said, "Stop!"

I turned around and asked, "Do you need to use the outhouse?"

She giggled, "No, I want to carry all the sand."

"What?"

She grinned and explained, "I just want to be able to say I once was in possession of a hundred thousand dollars of sand."

"You can say gold, Jen, there's no one else around."

"I know, but doesn't it sound stupid?"

"Yeah, but we won't be talking about it that way. We'll only say sand if a peculiar instance arises."

"I know, but I still want to carry all the gold. Humor me."

I gave her the sack I was carrying and we continued into the trees toward the clearing. The forest seemed quieter than normal. Maybe stillness was an after effect of the storm. The only thing beside the quiet was the wet grass we had to tramp through. Our feet were going to be wet before we reached the landing area. We'd ride back to Suddenly barefooted.

We hadn't spent more than five minutes at the open area before we heard the chopper. I hoped Dad brought us something to eat. I was starving. Jen hadn't said anything but I bet she was hungry too. We stepped behind some trees and watched the helicopter settle to the ground. Dad saw us and didn't bother to shut down the engine. Jen and I hustled to the chopper, got in and tightened our seatbelts.

Dad yelled over the engine noise, "Got everything?"

"Yeah, and something extra."

That was the extent of our conversation. Jen and I would elaborate when we got back home.

It was a short ride of about ten minutes to the Ranger Station. I ushered Jen into the building because I knew where doughnuts and coffee were available. She looked over the large, icing covered pastry and shook her head. Then she said, "Give me a bite of yours, David."

I held out my chocolate covered doughnut and let her take a bite. She poured a cup of coffee, added creamer and a little pouch of artificial sweetener, and sipped while we waited for Dad to turn in the logbook from the chopper flight. The doughnut was enough for me, coffee would alienate my stomach and I would suffer until I could get some antacid tablets.

Dad joined us and said, "Are you guys ready to go home? I'll bet you'd like to take a shower and change your clothes."

Jen replied, "We have something to show you. It was in the attic of Mr. Duggar's cabin."

Too many people were milling around in the station to show Dad the gold, so I suggested, "Let's get in the squad car before we show him what we found."

Jen agreed, "Another good idea, David."

We followed Dad to the car and got in the front seat. It was a bit tight, but I didn't want to be isolated in the back cage.

Dad asked, "OK. What did you find?"

Jen grinned and opened her backpack. "We found about a hundred thousand dollars of gold." She pulled out the canister and the bag of quartz pebbles.

After Dad inspected the loot, he said, "I leave you two for a short overnight stay in a mountain cabin and what happens? You find three pounds of gold. I think it's more than you estimate; closer to a hundred and fifty thousand. We'll have to get this to Bruce Isaacs."

"What about Mr. Duggar? Should we tell him how we found the gold?"

"I don't think that would make any difference, he's in the hospital. He's not expected to live much longer. He's on life support and can't communicate."

I couldn't understand. "What happened? Did he fall and strike his head?"

"First, he had me call Mr. Isaacs and tell him to come to the hospital. Samuel knew he wasn't going to live much longer, that's why he had to go to the cabin—one last time for memories and to get enough gold for his expenses. He wanted to arrange to pay for his funeral and finalize his will. Bruce Isaacs has power of attorney and has taken care of Duggar's finances for the last ten years."

Dad took a deep breath and continued, "Samuel requested that you and Jenny and the Sandovals see Mr. Isaacs about his last wishes. Samuel said he knew he had a fatal bone disease and wouldn't be around much longer."

Jen's face showed sadness, "That poor man. What could he want to tell us?"

"Maybe something about the cabin or his wife's grave. Let's get cleaned up and have something to eat. I'll call Mr. Isaacs and make an appointment. I guess you'll want to see Spring and tell her about the cabin and see how Cole is doing. I'd like to know, too."

Jen reacted, "Oh! What about Al? Where will he go?"

Dad answered, "He's with Samuel. We can't get him to leave. Maybe you guys can get him out of the hospital."

"We'll get some food and clean up, Dad. Then we'll tackle the problem."

Jenny commented, "Spring might have an idea, she's really good with animals."

I added, "Do you think Cole might help with Al?"

"Maybe. Let's go to your place so I can get my truck."

Gwen was at the sitter's across the street, Mom was working and Danny was cutting someone's lawn, so I ate breakfast and took a shower. Dad had business downtown at his office, so after he dropped Jen and me off, he went to work. It was a few minutes after nine o'clock when I answered the phone on the second ring.

"Hello."

It was Dr. Onishi. *"Hi David. Can you come to work this afternoon? I have some errands to run."*

I had some things to do, also, but I had responsibilities at the clinic. "Sure, I'll be there at one."

"Okay, thank you. See you then."

That took care of the rest of my day. Spring and Jen would have to handle the problem with Al. Maybe they would take Cole to the hospital as an assistant. Another dog just might help them coax Al away from Mr. Duggar's bedside. But Al's attachment to Samuel had grown extremely strong.

Not more than a minute after speaking with Dr. Onishi, the phone rang again. It had to be Jen.

"Hello, Jen."

"David! Have you called Mr. Isaacs?"

"Dad was going to do that. I just got off the phone with Dr. Onishi. I have to go to work at one o'clock. Let's make an appointment with Mr. Isaacs for tomorrow morning at ten, that's when the bank opens. Can you get in touch with the Sandovals and have them meet us at the bank?"

"Sure, I'll do that. What are you going to do until you have to go to work?"

"I thought I'd drop by the hospital and see if I can get Al to come with me. That might save you and Spring a trip. You guys don't need to be stressed out seeing Mr. Duggar hooked up to machines."

"I've talked with Spring and she said she can handle it. We're going to the medical center in about half an hour. I guess we'll see you there."

"Okay, bye Jen."

"Bye, David."

Another more immediate problem arose. How to get to the hospital without a vehicle. Danny had the SUV, Dad had taken Mom to the Ranger Station when he borrowed the chopper this morning, so I had no wheels. I couldn't ask Dad to run a taxi service. I had no choice; it was Danny's bicycle. I hoped the tires hadn't lost pressure since I last used the bike. I locked up the house and went to the garage. The bike was leaning against the interior wall, just inside the door. I squeezed the tires, finding them firm, took the bike outside, hopped on and set off to the hospital. I should get there in about ten minutes, much better than a half hour walk.

The bike rack was nearly empty, only two other bikes were parked where there was room for at least ten two-wheelers. Sandie was at the front desk and asked, "How may I help you?"

"I've come to see Mr. Duggar. Is it possible?"

"Yes, David, but he is unable to speak. He might not even recognize you. He's fighting to stay alive."

"I wanted to try to get his dog to leave him. I heard Al won't leave Samuel's side."

"Mr. Duggar is in room seventeen-w."

"Okay. Thanks."

Nurse Berg accompanied me to room 17W. Al was lying at the foot of the hospital bed and looked up at me when I entered the room, then dropped his head back to the bedding. Samuel was not breathing without assistance; the machine noises gave me an uncomfortable feeling. Samuel's eyes were closed as if he were sleeping. I didn't make a noise.

Nurse Berg commented, "Samuel left you a note, David." She handed me a folded paper napkin. "He asked me for a pen and wrote something on it before he lost consciousness. He said it was confidential."

I unfolded the napkin and found a printed message: WHAT'S IN THE CABIN ATTIC IS YOURS FOR SCHOOL. FIND A GOOD HOME FOR AL. THANK YOU FOR ALL THE HELP.

I couldn't keep tears from flowing. Mr. Duggar had guaranteed the rest of my education. I just stood there holding that paper napkin. I had forgotten the reason I was in Mr. Duggar's hospital room.

A woman's voice jogged me back to clarity; I was there to get Al away from Mr. Duggar.

"David, I have Cole with me. Jen has his wheels. Shall I place him on the bed with Al?"

I slowly turned around to see Spring and Jen standing at the doorway. "Uh, yeah, let's see what happens."

Spring placed Cole next to Al. The puppy scooted up to Samuel's right hand, licked his fingers and waited for a petting. When there was no reaction, Cole whined and looked at Spring and Jenny. Al must have been watching, because after he followed Cole's action, Al rose to all fours and jumped off the bed.

Spring hurriedly grabbed Cole and whispered, "Quick, let's get out of here."

Al followed me as I left Mr. Duggar and caught up with the girls. When we got outside, Jenny inquired, "What are you doing with that napkin, David?"

"Duggar wrote me a message. Here, take a look."

I knelt, petted Al and asked the dog, "Are you hungry, Al?" Al wagged his tail; he knew the word hungry.

Jenny reacted to the note excitedly, "David! Now you can finish school without working your butt off. What a wonderful thing Mr. Duggar has done."

"I didn't expect any reward for helping him. I kind of felt sorry for the old guy."

Spring was putting wheels on Cole and reacted, "What are you talking about?"

I requested, "Can you please take me home so I can feed Al, two girls and a puppy?"

Jenny laughed, "Put your bike and Al in back and climb in. We'll drive you home."

I snapped my fingers and Al came to me. I picked him up, put him in the truck bed with Danny's bicycle and sat down with my arms around the collie ready to enjoy a short ride with Duggar's sidekick. Jenny yelled back to me, "Are you ready?"

I rapped my knuckles on the truck cab and we began rolling away from the hospital. That's when I realized I would never see Mr. Duggar again but Al would stimulate fond memories, especially of the trip to Samuel Duggar's cabin.

Chapter 36

Back at home we assembled in the living room. I asked Jenny, "Were you able to contact the Sandovals to arrange tomorrow's meeting with Mr. Isaacs?"

"Yes and no. I talked with Mr. Sandoval. He told me he would have to confer with his wife. They would have to close their business for an hour."

"Did you mention the cabin?"

"No, I didn't think of that, but I told him Mr. Duggar was in the hospital."

"That's fine but please call the Emporium and tell Mrs. Sandoval you have been to the cabin and have pictures you can show her tomorrow at the meeting with Mr. Isaacs. You hope she can attend. Oh, do you still have that napkin?"

"I sure do. It's probably a legal document. Maybe you should have it, in case something comes up about the gold."

I gave Jen a frown, realizing she must have told Spring about the gold even though we weren't going to tell anyone.

Spring said, "She couldn't help telling me about happenings at the cabin, David. Sand was a good idea though, still is. I promise to keep quiet."

"I guess it's all right. You two are just like sisters."

"I'm sorry, David. I was telling Spring about the cabin and I didn't think about saying sand, gold just slipped out. But I didn't make a big deal of it."

"Don't worry, Jen. When we visit the cabin during the Fourth of July weekend, she'll learn everything we know. It will only be news to Dexter."

As we talked, Danny drove up in the SUV and stumbled into the house dragging his feet and pulling off a sweaty T-shirt. He ignored the girls and asked, "Who does the dog belong to?"

"This is Al. He was Mr. Duggar's. Duggar is on life support and won't live much longer. I'm going to find Al a new home. He's coming with me to the clinic this afternoon."

"I'm gonna take a shower. You can have the car. I don't have any lawncare appointments this afternoon."

"Thanks, Danny. You're such a gem."

Danny disappeared down the hallway and the girls started laughing. Smiling, I said, "I won't admit to being his brother. He's still growing up. I hope he gets better."

Jen and Spring started toward the door. "We have some projects going, David, and it's too soon for lunch. I'll call the Emporium and talk with Mrs. Sandoval. If they can't make the meeting, I'll call you. We'll make other arrangements. Okay?"

"All right. If the meeting is a go, make sure you bring the sand." I grinned, "Bye."

I watched the pickup pull away from the curb and vanish behind the corner house. "Come on, Al, time for you to eat." We always had dog food in the house for rescued animals Dad brought home, so I opened a bag of dry food, poured about a cup into a bowl and filled another bowl with water. While Al ate, I made a sandwich and found a piece of apple pie in the fridge.

When I was dressed in my clinic outfit, I took Al into the back-yard and tossed a ball for him to chase. I lost interest before Al did. Danny rarely filled the SUV's gas tank, so I checked it. Surprisingly, the tank was three quarters full. The time was half past twelve. I decided to go to the clinic a little early.

I was curious to see if Al had ever ridden in a car, so it was time to find out. After the house was locked, I opened the SUV's passenger side door and called Al. He came running and hopped right in. He had been in a car before. Once the engine started, Al sat on the seat looking out the side window. When we started moving, I lowered his window and he put his nose into the breeze. I had to smile.

The clinic was locked with a sign in the front window reading: Out to Lunch. Back at 1:00 p.m. After parking in my normal space, I unlocked the front entrance and took the sign down. I was ready for business. Al sniffed around the lobby, apparently not finding anything of interest and curled up in front of the counter. I got him a blanket to lie on but he ignored it.

I busied myself looking over records of clinic visitors in the last two days. Two small dog Immunizations, a dog's broken foreleg and a cat that had a burr removed from its mouth were all I had missed. An order of dog and cat food had arrived from Butte. Dr. Onishi hadn't been very busy.

The traffic in the afternoon was mostly for purchasing special dietary food for pets but nothing requiring Dr. Onishi's experience. Each time a customer arrived, Al would rise, sniff the patron's legs and their pets, walk to the door, look outside and return to his spot. He used the soft blanket only once to lie down. I reasoned he was watching for Samuel to come to the clinic.

Dr. Onishi returned at four o'clock, asked if I had any problems and after a brief conversation during which I told him about tomorrow's potential meeting with Mr. Isaacs, we shut the clinic. When I got home, I called Jenny and she said everything was all set, the Sandovals would be there.

The evening and night passed quickly. Al stayed at my bedside during the night and showed interest in little Gwen in the morning.

Gwen didn't have much interest in breakfast, she wanted to play with Al. She loved the name Al for the dog.

I didn't have use of the car so Al and I left the house at nine forty and walked to the bank, arriving at nine fifty seven. We were met by one of the bank secretaries and escorted to Mr. Isaac's office. The Sandovals and Jenny were already present and seated. Coffee and doughnuts were available on a serving table. Al lay down close to Jenny. I sat beside her.

Mr. Isaacs stood and stated, "It looks like everyone is here. I will read Samuel Miles Duggar's will. If you are unaware, Samuel passed during the night. I have power of attorney."

No one commented and the room was deathly quiet except for the soft hum of a ceiling fan.

Mr. Isaacs began, "My home between Suddenly and Dillon is now owned by Efren and Elaine Sandoval. They were very kind to me. The taxes have been paid for five years. They may do with it as they see fit."

Mr. Isaacs shook hands with Efren and Elaine and said, "If you have any questions about the property, please come see me. There is a legal transfer of property rights necessary; some signatures are required."

He took a sip from his coffee mug and continued, "The cabin is gifted equally to three people, David Drum, Jenny Kincaid and Spring Wisdom. They have all mineral rights on the two acres but are never allowed to use gasoline or battery powered machinery, including chainsaws, on the property. They must abide by all government requirements for maintenance of a dwelling in the forest."

Jenny and I gave each other a big hug and I whispered in her left ear, "Have you given Mr. Isaacs what we found in the attic?"

"Not yet. I thought you should give him the napkin first."

I had it in my shirt pocket, extracted it and handed it to Mr. Isaacs, "Samuel wrote this the day he entered the hospital. He gave it to one of the nurses."

After reading the note he enquired, "Where is this material?"

Jenny spoke up, "I have it. Should I put it on your desk?"

"Yes, please. An excellent idea."

Jenny's backpack was under her chair. She unzipped it and put the metal container and the bag of quartz on the desk. "That's what we found in the cabin's attic."

Mr. Isaac investigated, sat down and wrote out a receipt. "David, I'll have these things evaluated and send you a certificate of deposit."

"Thank you, Mr. Isaacs."

The banker asked, "What are you going to do with Al?"

"I'd like to keep him but I can't take care of him when in school, so I'll have to find a temporary home for him."

Elaine stood up and announced, "I'd like to foster him until David finishes school. I've always wanted a puppy, but Al might be a better choice. My husband will agree." She glanced at Efren and smiled.

I shook hands with Mr. Isaacs, thanked him for reading the will and we left the bank with the Sandovals. Jen and I watched Efren and Elaine get in their car, wave and drive away. Jen looked around and asked, "Where's your car?"

"Al and I walked here from the clinic. It's not that far." I put my arm around her waist and said, "I'm making reservations for dinner at Timber Inn. I'm buying. You and Spring, Dexter and his dad, my mom and dad and Danny and Gwen are all invited."

"Really? What about Al?"

I grinned, "I'll ask the restaurant to prepare him a takeout steak."

Acknowledgement

Thanks goes to Efren Sifuentes for proofreading the manuscript.